D0500277

FIND ME

FIND ME

A NOVEL

ALAFAIR BURKE

HARPER

An Imprint of HarperCollins*Publishers*

FIND ME. Copyright © 2022 by Alafair Burke. All rights reserved. Printed in the United States of America. No part of this book may be used or reproduced in any manner whatsoever without written permission except in the case of brief quotations embodied in critical articles and reviews. For information, address HarperCollins Publishers, 195 Broadway, New York, NY 10007.

HarperCollins books may be purchased for educational, business, or sales promotional use. For information, please email the Special Markets Department at SPsales@harpercollins.com.

FIRST EDITION

Art by Yeti Studio/Shutterstock, Inc.

Library of Congress Cataloging-in-Publication Data has been applied for.

ISBN 978-0-06-285336-3

33614082513424

22 23 24 25 26   LSC   10 9 8 7 6 5 4 3 2 1

For Danielle Holley-Walker

"Louise, no matter what happens, I'm glad I came with you."

—Thelma

From PATCH
Hopewell-Pennington, NJ

POLICE SEEK WITNESSES
TO ROLLOVER CRASH

A woman was found on Tuesday night with critical injuries, not far from an overturned 1999 Toyota 4Runner. Emergency crews responded at 11:20 PM to a report of a single-car accident on East Mountain Road in the Sourland Mountain Preserve.

The survivor, described as a young woman estimated to be in her late teens or early twenties, was transported to Capital Health Medical Center, where she remains in critical condition. Law enforcement is asking any witnesses who may have information about the cause of the accident or the identity of the vehicle's occupant to contact Hopewell Police.

1

Fifteen Years Later

Saturday, June 12, 6:32 p.m.

Hope Miller shifted her gaze from the gas nozzle to the pump. When the gallon counter hit twelve, she scolded herself for not filling up before her trip into the city. She couldn't risk an empty tank.

The nearest customer leaned against his green Jeep, sharing her same awkward wait, watching the digital numbers tick by. She noticed him looking at her. When he noticed her noticing, he flashed a practiced grin. She didn't smile back.

That phrase, "It takes more muscles to frown than smile"? She had googled it once. Turns out, facial descriptions are subjective. Smiles, sneers, frowns, and smirks are all in the eye of the beholder. And the so-called facial nerve controls forty-something muscles, but some people have all of them, while others are missing almost half.

But scientists did agree on one thing—that smiles are innate. Reflexive. And viewed across cultures as a sign of friendliness.

A single man smiling at a single woman alone at a gas station at night?

He could be flirting. Hope didn't think of herself as pretty, per se, but how many times had Lindsay called her a magnet for male attention?

Or he could be suggesting that she smile back, the nonverbal version of those comments men let fly so freely around total strangers—"Smile, honey. It's a beautiful night"—as if it's their business how a woman holds her face.

Or, she wondered as she risked another glance in his direction, this particular man might know her. Was this simply random eye contact from a stranger, or the reflexive smile of a person who thought he recognized her from his past? She imagined him saying, *Hey, aren't you . . .*

She pushed the thought away. He didn't seem especially curious. He was simply one of those guys who smiled at strangers for no reason at all.

One of the many downsides of using cash at a gas station was having to guess how much to prepay. She had a credit card from Lindsay for emergencies but tried not to use it. She squeezed the pump handle—one, two, three—to top off the tank at the forty bucks she had already given the cashier inside, patting herself mentally on the back for being so close. Returning the nozzle to the pump, she forced a polite smile in the man's direction.

As she climbed into the front seat of her Honda Civic—Lindsay's car, technically, like her credit card—she noticed Jeep Guy finishing up as well, sparking her anxieties again. He seemed to move too fast, both in terms of how long it had taken to fill the tank of an SUV and how quickly he maneuvered himself behind the wheel. She started the ignition, not bothering with her seat belt until she was out of the station and onto the service road. In the rearview mirror she saw the Jeep follow, making the turn from the station without slowing.

She merged onto the LIE. So did the Jeep. She tried to tell herself that most of the cars in the area were on the same route. She stayed in the right lane, waiting for him to pass, but two miles later, he remained directly behind her. He wasn't exactly tailgating, but not even an attempt to pass on the left? Maybe the types of friendly people who smile at strangers for no reason are the same oddballs who, like her, obey the speed limit at all times.

Her grip tightened around the steering wheel when the Jeep's headlights followed her off Exit 70 onto Route 111. She scolded herself: Stop. Wigging. Out. It's the weekend, and you're on the main road to the Hamptons in the summer. He's just one car.

A different set of headlights suddenly appeared in the left lane, maybe a quarter mile back, closing the distance. As the new arrival cruised beneath a streetlamp, she could see that the vehicle was a police car—white with lights on the roof. Her foot immediately moved from the gas pedal to the brake, her eyes drifting involuntarily to the speedometer. She was now ten miles an hour beneath the speed limit. Going too slow, like going too fast, was good cause for a traffic stop.

She gave the engine more gas, and then shifted her gaze to the rearview mirror again. The Jeep was still on her. Maybe if she were a different person, she would tail the cop in the white car, or even barrel past him on the right, triggering a stop. She could explain it was all because of Jeep Guy, with the worrisome smile, still following her after nine miles.

But Hope didn't have the luxury of that option. Her explanation for not having a license (at all) or a registration (in her name, at least) could lead to worse allegations—intoxication, insanity, a stolen car, something. So Hope maintained a perfect forty-five miles per hour through Manorville, waiting for the cop to pass.

The police car was two lengths behind her before she realized that what she had assumed were overhead lights was actually a luggage rack, mounted on a regular old Chevy sedan. "Jerk," she whispered to herself. There should be a law against strapping stuff to white cars.

Jeep Guy finally turned off the main road once they hit Westhampton. All that worry for nothing. How many times had her imagination gotten carried away during the last fifteen years? She was so relieved that she didn't give a thought to the white pickup truck that replaced the Jeep in her rearview mirror.

HOPE HAD BEEN TO THE house only once previously, and that was when Evan had been pitching himself to get the broker gig. He only brought her along to make his one-man outfit appear bigger than it was, but she promised when he gave her the job that she was willing to take on any assignment he'd entrust to her—even today's last-minute drive to Manhattan and back because one of his renters ran off with a set of keys.

The listing was a five-bedroom, four-bath in Sagaponack, on the south side (aka, the good side) of the Montauk Highway. Asking price: $2,999,900, to keep it from hitting the $3 million mark. It would never sell for that, but Evan dangled a high number to lure the owners into hiring him. Hope knew from the math the realtor had scribbled on the back of an envelope after the initial visit that he planned to push the couple to accept any all-cash offer over two-point-five. With an all-cash offer, Evan would write up the deal on paper as $2 million, and then put five hundred grand in the owners' hands tax-free, using a point of his commission as necessary to sweeten the deal. The Stansfields—Stan and Robin, the couple that owned the house—had struck Hope as much too nice and normal to accept that kind of arrangement, but according to Evan, everyone out here did it. *Sure, Evan*—just like every legit realtor is willing to hire a former waitress who doesn't have a social security number and needs to get paid in cash.

Evan was shady, no doubt, but he'd proven himself to be a good coach since she moved to town the month before. She had watched him set up open houses before, and he had taught her exactly how a property should look and feel and even smell to reel in a buyer right away.

Besides, this kind of task was right up her alley. How many times had she been told she had an obsessive eye for detail?

Three hours after her initial arrival at the house, she ran through her mental checklist. Decluttering was the fun part. Evan had the owner's permission to tuck away distracting personal items such as family photos and knickknacks. The flowers she had purchased—at a deli in the city instead of a florist in East Hampton so she could pocket the extra cash she'd been given—were split between two vases in the living and dining rooms. The area rug she had brought as instructed from Evan's office was in place in the front hallway to conceal the wear and tear on the floorboards. She even had the cinnamon rolls ready to go in a pie pan in the refrigerator. Evan could arrive tomorrow at noon and do nothing but turn on the oven. A hint of Barefoot Contessa, courtesy of Pillsbury.

Of course, none of these superficial touches should actually matter. This house, by $3 million South Fork standards, was a dump. Terracotta kitchen tiles, laminate countertops, dingy, dated wallpaper. The real draw of the house was the lot—two full acres on a dead-end road. Whoever bought this place would tear the house down and start all over. But in the Hamptons, even a teardown was supposed to be staged.

She had nearly completed her inspection when she spotted the problem. The windows!

"Hamptons buyers want a light, bright, airy home, not a man cave," Evan had told her.

She quickened her pace with each additional shade pulled. All she could see outside was darkness. Standing alone in the isolated living room, backlit in front of all those windows, was giving her the heebie-jeebies.

She took one final look around the house. It was perfect. She sent a quick message to her boss: The place is all set. I did it tonight to make sure I didn't run into a time crunch tomorrow morning. Thanks again for trusting me, Evan. Hope you and the kids are having the best time!

She returned the key to the lock box hidden on the back deck and locked the sliding glass kitchen door. The front door would lock automatically behind her. As she made her way to leave, Hope felt a surge of pride. She had found this job entirely on her own—no help from Lindsay or anyone else from Hopewell. And she was actually good at it. Maybe if people got to know her as Evan's assistant—instead of "poor Hope"—she could eventually find work as an interior decorator, or maybe one of those professional organizers who streamlines a house from top to bottom. She could find clients through Yelp and Instagram and get paid in cash. Lord knew there was plenty of money to be had in the Hamptons.

She smiled reflexively when she saw his face at the front door. It wasn't like her response to the man at the gas station. She smiled at a neurological level, straight from some primal, emotional part of the brain.

It was the way a human face responds on instinct when a person sees someone from their past in an unexpected place.

It took her brain a few seconds to catch up to her facial muscles. *He shouldn't be here*.

She turned to run, but he grabbed her arm. The feeling of his fingers digging into her skin burned hot with a distant memory. It had been fifteen years.

He leaned close toward her and smiled, nothing friendly about it.

"What kind of game are you playing, *Hope*? Isn't that what you call yourself now?"

2

Saturday, June 12, 10:45 p.m.

Lindsay Kelly reread the text she had drafted: Haven't heard from you for a few days. Is everything still okay?

Too anxious. She erased and tried again. I was thinking about coming out to see you next week. Too soon?

Six weeks before, when Hope suddenly declared that she was moving to East Hampton, Lindsay had played devil's advocate, reminding her friend that she had a life in Hopewell. She had a community and security.

"But I don't have privacy," Hope had said. "Or anonymity. I just want to go someplace where I can blend in. I want to be normal."

Lindsay could still recall the hurt expression on Hope's face when she had responded, "You have no idea what you're saying. I mean, it's not like you even know whether you ever *were* normal."

She regretted the words the second they escaped her lips. Even now, she didn't really understand why she had allowed herself to say something so cruel. In that moment, Lindsay immediately vowed that she had to support her friend, no matter what she decided. And so, two weeks later, with a sinking feeling in the pit of her stomach, Lindsay had helped

Hope move to the eastern end of Long Island's South Fork, riding the train from Penn Station to Princeton, where Hope had picked her up to go to U-Haul, where Lindsay rented the moving van she would drive while Hope followed in her own Honda Civic. Of course, in Hope's case, "her" Honda Civic was also in Lindsay's name—title, registration, insurance, all of it—but explaining a borrowed car from a friend was easier than an unauthorized driver on a rental in the event that they ran into a problem.

They had managed to pack all of Hope's belongings from her garage apartment except for one piece of furniture—a solid oak armoire. Lindsay smiled to herself, recalling the ridiculousness of their failed attempt.

"All right. We're taking this armoire," Hope had announced, "and that's all there is to it." It was a reference to both a classic Seinfeld episode and the fact that Lindsay had, in fact, taken the armoire after finding it abandoned on the curb with a "Free" sign taped to it. She discovered later that a visiting professor at Princeton had bought the armoire from one of the vendors at the Antique Center and then ditched it in the front yard at the end of the semester when he decided that schlepping it back to his permanent residence in New York City wasn't worth the effort.

They managed only to tip the clunky wardrobe onto the floor horizontally before Hope burst out in laughter, wiping her palms on the baggy denim cutoffs she had worn for the move. "Oh my god, it seems even bigger now that it's empty." She had tugged her sandy blond hair from the long ponytail at the nape of her neck, shaken it loose, and then pulled it into a sloppy topknot instead. "Gross, I'm super sweaty. How did we even get this thing up here in the first place?"

"You don't remember?" Lindsay had done her best to impersonate Hope trying to wrangle the thing down the street by herself, one scoot at a time. "Tony made Max and Bobby carry it for you once they all stopped laughing." Tony and Grace Beckett were Hope's landlords, and Max and Bobby were their now-grown sons.

A look of recognition had washed over Hope's face. That's when Lindsay said the armoire might be trying to send a message that it wasn't too late to unload the van and stay put. Before Hope could respond, Lindsay had jumped in to clarify. "I just want to make sure you're a hundred thousand percent certain before we break our backs getting this lead-filled coffin down the stairs."

It wasn't that Lindsay was unsympathetic to Hope's complaints about Hopewell. Lindsay loved her hometown, but there was a reason she had opted to stay in Manhattan after graduating from law school. In a borough of fewer than two thousand people, not too many of them were strangers, and Hope had it worse than the usual resident. When she first arrived, everyone was curious about her. She was a walking, talking, living, breathing real-life mystery. But over the last decade and a half, Hope had woven herself into the fabric of the community, and it was precisely because of the incestuousness of their small town that Lindsay knew Hope would always be safe in Hopewell. The doctors still took care of her pro bono, even for things that had nothing to do with her original trauma. She had a rent-free garage apartment, thanks to Tony and Grace, the couple who organized the first prayer circle after word got around town about the stranger who turned up at the hospital with life-threatening injuries but no identification. All they asked in return was that she watch the house when they left for their frequent camping trips. The police understood why she couldn't have a driver's license, and also knew that their beloved ex-chief—Lindsay's father—considered Hope a second daughter, so they pretended not to see her on those occasions when they spotted her behind the wheel.

She had worked her way up to manager at Rex's Diner, all the while getting paid under the table. Lindsay supposed she could take credit for that one. The owner wasn't a Rex, as the name would suggest; she was a Miriam and had practically raised Lindsay from the time she was seven years old, thanks to the eight years she had been married to Lindsay's father.

When Hope was in Hopewell, Lindsay knew that she was being looked after—by her father, by the Becketts, by Miriam, by that tight-knit community that had apparently come to feel like an anchor around Hope's waist.

In a way, Lindsay blamed herself for Hope's decision to leave. She had been the one to invite Hope to tag along two months before to look at a Hamptons rental she was considering for the summer. No surprise, given the price, that the place turned out to be a dump, but Lindsay and Hope had spent the weekend checking out the shops and restaurants that would soon be too crowded when summer rolled around. They even took a fishing trip as an excuse to get out on the open water. After a third man made some not-too-subtle moves in their (meaning, Hope's) direction, Hope had announced a new life plan: she'd meet a rich man and spend the rest of her life at a beach house. By the close of the weekend, Hope was saying she was serious about not wanting to leave.

Nine days after returning to Jersey, without telling Lindsay, Hope took the train back to Long Island, renting a backyard Winnebago off Craigslist for $70 a night so she could determine if the Hamptons really might be the right place for her to "start over." She later explained that, the way she figured, the area was bustling enough to provide the ano-nymity she yearned for, without the big-city chaos that—to her knowl-edge, at least—she had never experienced. Due to its popularity as a vacation spot, it drew plenty of short-timers and newcomers, so she'd blend in from the outset. And in her words, it was "the right amount of shady." Rich people who bought beach houses under LLCs, perhaps tossing some unreported cash around in the wash along the way, would have no qualms about paying her for work under the table if it meant they didn't have to cover the payroll taxes. She was confident she could find a landlord and an employer who were willing to deal in cash, at least for the right kind of person.

Hope's gut instincts must have been right, because when she called Lindsay at the end of her trip, she had found both a house and a job. The owner of Hope's tiny cottage was an older woman who needed to go to

Indiana for six months to take care of her even older mother. She wanted someone responsible to cover the costs of keeping the house running and to watch over the place in her absence. Lindsay was mortified when Hope confessed that she'd "borrowed a few details" from Miriam's biography to explain her need to live "off the grid." Hope justified it by pointing out that, unfortunately, Miriam's harrowing move to Hopewell to flee an abusive boyfriend wasn't especially unique. It turned out Miriam hadn't minded one bit, assuring Hope that if what she went through could help another woman in even a tiny way, she was all for it. Once Lindsay and Miriam provided glowing personal references, the owner was willing to accept cash as rent. Done.

Lindsay was more concerned about Hope's job. She had started with the big property management companies and realtors, thinking they would need seasonal help to turn over the short-term rentals. She got a few nibbles, but even with her Miriam-inspired cover story, they all balked at the idea of paying her in cash. But then she'd found an "independent" realtor named Evan Hunter. Lindsay had googled him, of course. He looked slick. Like, literally slick. Dewy skin. Lips that looked freshly licked. Blond hair swept back with plenty of product. At best, he'd pawn all his work off on Hope without cutting her in on his lucrative commissions, knowing she had few options. Or worse, he'd try to use his power over her in other ways. He wouldn't be the first to try to take advantage.

Hope had eventually decided to leave the armoire as her gift to the Becketts' apartment, but the rest of the move went forward as planned. According to Hope, everything was going well. The cottage was comfortable and homey. Evan dumped a lot on her plate, but she was enthusiastic about doing something new and thought she could leverage the knowledge she was gaining for bigger opportunities down the line. She had even become a semiregular at one of the local restaurants, where her favorite meal was something she called a "bottomless sandwich."

Lindsay tried to remind herself that Hope could have chosen worse locations than East Hampton. It was a little farther from New York City than Hopewell, but at least she was still relatively close. Lindsay had even thought about taking a rental—maybe they could find a way to share it. But Hope had asked for space as she got adjusted to her new surroundings. At first, she was at least texting regularly. But for the last two weeks, it had been Lindsay doing most of the reaching out, and Hope's responses had gotten slower and shorter.

She erased her latest draft message. It was nearly eleven o'clock on a Saturday night. No matter what she typed, Hope would know that Lindsay was worried about her ability to navigate through life anywhere outside of Hopewell. And she'd resent her for it.

Her phone was still in her hands when a new text message arrived. It was from Scott. How was girl day? Wish you were here.

Here would be about a mile away from Lindsay's Greenwich Village one-bedroom, where Scott owned an apartment overlooking Gramercy Park—the apartment that in theory could be hers by now, too.

Was only girl brunch. Many bloody marys were involved. Surfed Netflix the rest of the day.

She saw three dots appear on the screen, indicating that Scott was typing. She expected a lengthy message based on the delay but received only one word in response. Alone?

Yup.

Oof. Those three letters looked snippier on the screen than she had meant them in her head. And maybe his one-word question wasn't as clingy as she first read it. She tapped a quick addition. How'd the weekend go?

One little rough spot when I declined an invitation to go to American Girl, but otherwise, it was great.

Rock Center on a weekend? You're a wise man.

This was Scott's weekend with his seven-year-old daughter, Nora. He had raised the possibility of Lindsay meeting her with increasing frequency over the past two months, and Lindsay kept finding reasons to defer until another time.

I told her we'd save that trip for you. JK.

Lindsay hoped that he was also kidding about mentioning her to his daughter. Her own father had remarried when she was the same age as Nora. When he and Miriam split eight years later, Lindsay was almost as devastated as that day in kindergarten when her mother finally explained why she had lost so much weight and seemed tired all the time. She and Scott had been dating for almost two years, but on the spectrum between having designated drawer space at each other's apartments (check) and picking out a china pattern (nope), meeting Nora felt like nailing things down for good.

Her father, on the other hand, liked to remind her that she was "already" thirty-six years old. In his world, that meant she should be married by now and working on getting pregnant, and with Scott being forty-five, he might not be interested in a second kid for long. Her father, like everyone else who met Scott, declared him to be "perfect." Only Hope knew Lindsay's reason for not jumping all in.

As if reading her thoughts, he texted again. Did you make a plan to see Hope?

She had told him yesterday that she wanted to drive out east and make sure everything was okay there. No. Like you said, she asked for space, and I need to give it to her.

Maybe when you do visit, we can make a weekend out of it. Beer and Jenga reunion.

It was a reference to where they had first met, on the patio at Montauk Brewery, on opposite teams of a game of Giant Jenga, stacking blocks the size of shoe boxes into an increasingly precarious tower until the entire structure came tumbling down.

You can't throw the game if you're on my team, though. The first time they spent the night together, Scott had admitted to tipping the blocks intentionally so he and Lindsay could continue their conversation without interruption. Miss you.

You up for a guest tomorrow night?

Would love that. She knew he'd be dropping Nora off to his ex's apartment on the Upper East Side after an early dinner. When she had asked recently if they could spend more time at her place, she had expected another push for her to move in with him, but instead, he had been staying more nights with her than not.

Can't wait. Then more dots. Don't worry about Hope. She's a survivor. More dots. Honestly, I think it'll be good for both of you if she gets on her own two feet.

Lindsay tried not to let the last comment get beneath her skin. In her experience, prefacing a statement with "To be honest" or "To tell you the truth" is a sure sign you're telling someone else what to believe—such as what was "good" for her, in this instance. *Honestly*, Lindsay wondered why Scott could never seem to understand that she and Hope were more like family than friends. The doctors said Hope probably would have died if Lindsay hadn't happened to take the scenic route through the preserve as she was heading home from NYU that rainy night. Lindsay assumed that the taillights off the side of the road belonged to a driver who had pulled over to wait for the storm to pass. When her own car began to hydroplane, she swerved into the opposite lane to avoid crashing into the parked vehicle. Only when she regained control of the wheel did she realize she was looking at an overturned SUV.

Running toward the scene in the pouring rain, she was certain the person splayed on the road in that awkward position had to be dead. She checked for signs of breathing and found none, but the emergency first aid training her father insisted on in high school kicked in. If a person's unconscious, you check the ABCs—airway, breathing, circulation. She tried a jaw thrust, tilting the head back and pulling the sides of the jaw forward to clear the airway. When she suddenly felt the warmth of shallow breathing, she quickly called her father, who sent out the alert to police and paramedics. As the EMTs loaded the young woman onto the gurney, her arm moved, as if reaching for Lindsay. On impulse, Lindsay jumped into the ambulance, holding the woman's hand until they got to the hospital.

When her father offered to drive her back to the preserve to get her car, Lindsay decided to wait until the next day. She needed to know if the woman was going to survive. At three in the morning, the doctors told her that the car's occupant was alert and able to communicate but had no recollection of the events preceding the accident and was unable to tell them her name, date of birth, or address. Lindsay would learn the next afternoon when she returned to the hospital that memory loss was relatively routine after a head injury, and that patients typically recovered nearly all of their memories over days and weeks. Lindsay's visits continued. With the summer off at home until law school began in the fall, she had enough time to spend nearly all of it with the girl whose life she had saved. And when the memories didn't return after days, weeks, or even months, Lindsay was still there for her.

So, no, Scott would never convince her that they'd both be better off if they leaned on each other less. But she had made a promise to Hope, and she needed to keep it. She'd wait a few days before checking in with her to plan a visit. Until then, Hope would be fine. Like Scott said, she was a survivor.

3

Saturday, June 12, 10:45 p.m.

Nearly seventeen hundred miles away, NYPD detective Ellie Hatcher felt the weight of a warm, bare arm wrapped across her chest. Her skin felt clammy. She couldn't move. She was pinned against the bed.

A scream jarred her awake. It took her a few seconds to realize that it had come from her own throat. The arm moved, and a hand stroked her shoulder soothingly. "Sssh," a voice whispered, "it's just a dream."

Ellie opened her eyes and blinked several times before she remembered where she was. She registered the faint sounds of the ceiling fan—*click, click, click*—and crickets outside the window. Frogs? Some sort of tiny creature.

It was so damn quiet. Too quiet. At home, she was used to a constant symphony of sirens, car horns, and garbage trucks on Third Avenue, Ellie's version of white noise, allowing her to disappear until she re-emerged into the world the next morning.

She had no idea whether she'd been muttering, sweating, or kicking, but somehow she had managed to awaken Max, who could sleep through anything. She rolled over to face him. This was their first trip beyond the tristate area together. Hell, it was her first real vacation since making detective with the NYPD five years earlier.

"Are you okay?" His voice was sleepy. Even though they had showered before dinner, he smelled like sun, salt water, and coconut.

"I'm fine." She nestled her head in the crook of his arm and placed one hand across his stomach until his breath became deep and rhythmic. He was already snoozing again. The fan continued to click as Ellie alternated between blanket-off and blanket-on, trying to find the right temperature.

It had been Max's idea to come to St. Barts. He thought she was kidding when she asked where it was. Ellie had been outside the United States exactly three times: once in high school, when she and two of her friends decided one Friday night that it would be fun to drive to Mexico; once two years before, when she'd flown to Toronto to interview a witness in a shooting connected to the Russian mafia; and once to London with the only other man she had ever tried to live with.

At least Max had chosen a warm place with beautiful white-sand beaches instead of a rainy version of New York City. The original plan had been to come in March, but Max's trial schedule had veto power.

She knew plenty of people would cut off a limb to enjoy a week looking out over turquoise-blue water with the best man they'd ever known. But the very fact that Max had chosen a place she still wasn't sure how to pronounce—Was it Saint or Sahn? Bart or Barts or Barth or Barths?—was another reminder of how different they were. Max made a government salary as an assistant district attorney, but had friends who were partners at major law firms, with second homes in East Hampton and the Berkshires. He'd been to Paris multiple times and seemed perfectly at ease ordering foie gras and escargot on this trip. As far as Ellie was concerned, a beach vacation should mean tacos, barbecue, and margaritas.

She kicked off the covers once again. How in the world could the most expensive hotel she'd ever stayed in not have better air-conditioning? Say what you will about Kansas, but at least the Midwest understood the importance of climate control.

And there it was. The reason she was tossing and turning in the middle of the night—Wichita, Kansas. It was a good enough place to grow up, the kind of little city where a cop dad and a bookkeeper mom could afford a three-bedroom ranch house, complete with a finished basement and a picket fence. The public schools were better than average and, at least back then, provided a haven where kids were all treated the same, regardless of zip codes. It had been a middle-school PE teacher who convinced a skeptical Ellie to enter a junior-miss beauty pageant to start squirreling away some college money, a few hundred dollars at a time. Kansas had turned her into the kind of person who could move to New York City at the age of twenty-one and sign up for criminal justice classes at John Jay.

But Kansas was also the state she never left—not once, not even to Kansas City, Missouri—until she was in the tenth grade for that impromptu trip to Mexico. It was the home that had never taught her about delicacies such as foie gras and escargot. And it was the place where her father died when she was only fourteen years old.

She shifted from her comfortable spot in the crook of Max's arm and fumbled around on the nightstand until she found her phone. The glow of the screen lit the room in a yellowish haze, but Max seemed undisturbed.

She suddenly remembered she was in a foreign country and would have to pay data fees. Fuck it. A few texts would cost less than dessert at tonight's overpriced restaurant.

Are you up?

Dots immediately appeared in a text box on the screen, suggesting that her brother was indeed awake.

I am now. You know I leave my phone on in case of last-minute cancellations.

She felt a pang of guilt. Jess was a barely-working musician. Here she was, feeling sorry for herself for being a fish out of water in St. Barts, but she was a detective with a salary, benefits, overtime, and a pension waiting for her down the road. Jess had to keep his cell phone on max volume next to his pillow in case some dive bar needed an over-the-hill punk band on short notice.

Sorry, she typed. I had a dream about Dad.

No dots. No response. Jess never wanted to talk about Dad or Wichita or anything else that brought up old feelings. But he was her only person when it came to this particular subject.

Finally the dots reappeared. His reply was brief.

What about him?

Some kids, they remember their parents pushing them on swings or coaching their teams or hugging them at graduation. But Jess would know those weren't the kinds of dreams Ellie would have about their father. When she thought about her dad, it was almost always about either his death or the deaths that obsessed him while he was still alive.

When we went to the hospital, she typed.

More dots. Yeah, that sucked.

You were right, you know. About the hospital. You knew before anyone.

She pictured her brother fully awake now, in bed at the Murray Hill rent-controlled one-bedroom that had been hers before she moved in with Max. Maybe he was alone. Maybe not. Jess was Jess.

I don't think they give trophies for that particular skill. Long pause. Seriously, R U OK?

She stared at her screen as she listened to the fan click. She adjusted the blankets again. One leg under, one leg out.

I don't know.

Jess's response took so long that she wondered if he had decided to go back to sleep. Dad killed himself, but we're over that, remember? Get your groove on at that fancy island.

She shut her eyes, rolled over on her side, and tried to find a spoon position beside Max before another message popped up again.

Do you need me to call you?

She typed no and regretted it as soon as she hit send.

She sifted through the events of the day, wondering what had led her subconscious into the past. Then she heard her brother's voice in her head, speaking the words he had just texted: *Dad killed himself.* They had finally learned the truth about her father's death almost four years before, when the Wichita Police arrested the man she had always assumed was her father's killer. *We're over that, remember?*

She turned off her phone and laid it next to the lamp on the nightstand.

By the time Ellie fell asleep, the five-bedroom, four-bath house in Sagaponack, on the south side of Montauk Highway, listed for not quite $3 million, was spotless and staged, ready for the next day's open house.

Ellie would not learn the name Hope Miller for another nine days. She had no way of knowing that what had happened nearly seventeen hundred miles away on Long Island at the exact moment she had dreamed about her father would force the past to collide with the present once again.

4

Two Days Later

Monday, June 14, 7:20 p.m.

Robin Stansfield stood in the middle of the living room, her quilted Vera Bradley tote still in hand. It was a favorite among her collection—black with yellow-and-white sunflowers. Everything about it made her happy.

But she wasn't thinking about her cheerful bag. Her focus was entirely on her surroundings as her eyes darted from one area of the room to another. Sofa. Media cabinet. Coffee table. Something wasn't right. Something.

She didn't even notice her husband, Stan—his parents had actually named him Stanley Stansfield—make his way into the room. His left hand pulled her giant Tumi roller case. His right managed to juggle both of their carry-ons.

"Thanks anyway, Robin." His voice momentarily interrupted her meditation. "Really, I've got this all under control."

She muttered an apology and made a kissing sound in his direction, which he returned. "I'll leave a nice tip for you on checkout."

She had known Stan since they were in the ninth grade. He was the sort-of-cute band geek who sat next to her, a junior varsity cheerleader, in algebra. He became her harmless, reliable friend when he got a provisional driver's license and began offering her rides from school. She never thought of him as anything more until he and his friends formed a band the summer after sophomore year. The sight of him and his bass guitar playing "Hungry Like the Wolf" at yard parties had locked her down.

Now she was fifty-five years old, but they'd just celebrated their thirty-fifth anniversary with a week at the Four Seasons in Maui. Her gift to him was all the golf he'd played this week. Stan loved golf almost as much as he loved Robin.

Stan disappeared into the kitchen, then walked through the living room again, eating a piece of string cheese on his way to the garage to grab the next round of bags from the car.

By the time he returned, she was rotating slowly and methodically in a circle.

"You look like the top of a music box with a bum battery. Are you going to keep doing that?"

Yes, she was. At least until he returned a second time to the living room, plopped himself onto the sofa, and pointed the remote at the plasma screen TV on the wall. He had just landed on ESPN when she turned to face him.

"You know those days where you think you're losing your mind?"

"A lesser man would say something slightly misogynist around now."

Now he was just pushing her buttons. "You're gaslighting me, aren't you? Did you do this while I was dillydallying in the driveway?"

"Don't you remember? I was getting my golf bag ready so I can take it to the club tomorrow. How am I gaslighting you now?"

He had a point. Robin did have a tendency to accuse him of mischief every time she couldn't find her keys. He called her the girl who cried wolf. She told him that's what he got for being such a practical joker.

She did another slow, circular turn. She didn't want to accuse Stan again, but she was certain that the house wasn't as she left it. Little things were different. The Marimekko throw pillow was in the center of the sofa, not stacked in front of the larger, solid green one in the corner. When Stan reached for the remote control, it had been on the coffee table, not on the porcelain tray on the media console beneath the TV, the way she liked it. The blinds over the sliding glass door to the deck were flipped up, not down.

She asked Stan if he had arranged for the housekeeper to come while they were out of town.

"You give me far too much credit if you think I know how to call . . . huh, I don't even know her name."

"Gina."

"Whatever," Stan said. "Stop obsessing. I'm sure it was probably Evan not putting things back after the open house."

Robin felt stupid the second her husband mentioned Evan. Right, of course: the realtor. After living in New York City for nearly a quarter century, using this house as their weekend respite, Stan had declared two months earlier that he was tired of what he had taken to calling "this garbage city." Now that their daughter was out of college and working in Phoenix, he wanted to accept his company's offer of a transfer to Irvine. How could she say no?

She knew that plenty of people would kill to be in her position. She was in love with a husband who loved her back and asked little in return. And the new place would be closer to Hannah.

But, man, she was going to miss this house. They were only going to be here for three days before they headed down to Palm Beach for another vacation. Stan was taking full advantage of the downtime he had negotiated before he needed to start work in California.

"Is it awful that I keep forgetting we're selling this place?"

Stan's face softened as he looked up at her from the sofa. "We've got a lot of good memories here, sweetie. We've still got half a lifetime left to make some more. Now turn off your OCD and keep me company on the sofa over here."

But as she took her usual spot at his side, she couldn't shake a nagging feeling that something wasn't quite right.

5

Two Days Later

Wednesday, June 16, 10:40 a.m.

Thanks to summer traffic, even on a Wednesday morning, Lindsay was nearly three hours into a 107-mile drive when the GPS began to guide her through a network of back roads. In a stop-and-go line of vehicles stretching from Southampton through Sag Harbor, she watched the sunlight glisten blue on Noyack Bay and tried to still her thoughts. What had begun as lingering anxiety about Hope's new life had evolved into full-blown panic after four days. Until Hope moved to East Hampton, they had never gone more than a day without talking. It had now been a week, even after Lindsay broke her vow to give her friend space and began calling and texting frantically.

Her cell phone announced that she was approaching her destination. As Lindsay came to a stop, she pictured Hope arriving at this exact spot a month earlier. She had given a quick *beep-beep* with her car horn and then gestured out the window for Lindsay to pull the moving van into the driveway. Hope nearly tripped as she tumbled from the driver's seat, beaming as she spun in circles on the lawn.

When she finally stopped spinning, her almond-shaped green eyes squinted against the sun. "It's cute, right?"

The cottage was tiny and the siding weathered, but the front door was painted bright orange, and white-and-purple hydrangea blossomed across the yard. Lindsay assured her that it was adorable.

"This is my very first time having a whole house all to myself." That she knew of, of course. That was always an unspoken truth with Hope.

Lindsay had hugged her friend and told her she'd never seen her so happy. "It's like rainbows are bouncing off you right now. That's how happy you look."

Hope had opened her mouth as if to say something, but then stopped and shook her head. "Just excited is all," she had said. "I think I might actually have my life back soon."

Lindsay had been replaying that moment in her mind over and over again for days. *What life, Hope? What life did you have before I found you?*

She banged on the front door and peered through the windows. Through a part in the bedroom curtains, she could see that the bed was made. Nothing seemed out of place. But no Hope, and no Honda Civic in the driveway or on the street. She'd need to track down the landlady's contact information to see about getting a key, but she had an appointment in a few minutes that she fully intended to miss.

LINDSAY LOVED TO LINGER AT the real estate offices along Main Street in East Hampton, browsing the listings in the windows of Corcoran and Sotheby's. Six-bedroom, nine-bath houses on two oceanfront acres. Old farmhouses brought up to pristine standards. Even a mid-century ranch slapped with some white paint could garner more than a million if it had room for a pool. Primo real estate porn.

But Evan Hunter, Hope's under-the-table employer, was definitely not that caliber of listing agent. His office address didn't even appear in his sponsored ads on Facebook and Instagram. Evan's flinch when Lindsay stepped through the door made it clear he wasn't used to walk-ins. He scrambled to his feet to welcome her with a handshake.

In person, he looked older and more bloated than in his online photographs, with thinner and more disheveled hair. Even so, if she were searching for someone to trust with a major real estate transaction, she actually preferred the real-life version to the slickster featured in his official headshots.

"What brings you in this afternoon?" he asked with a chipper smile.

Three unreturned calls brought me in. "My name's Lindsay Kelly. I left you a couple of messages?"

He turned his focus to arranging the loose papers on his desk into tidy piles, avoiding her gaze. "Sorry, I was about to get back to you. It's a nonstop crush out here in the summer. I drove to Amagansett just now only to have a client stand me up. Not even a phone call."

"That's so rude." After Lindsay's voice-mail messages went unreturned, she had tried another tactic, posing as a potential buyer to schedule a property viewing for eleven o'clock. Instead of showing up for the appointment, she had waited down the street and then followed him back here, to a storefront that she vaguely recalled had once been a liquor store. "But speaking of phone calls, I made it pretty clear in my messages that the matter was urgent, Mr. Hunter. It's not like Hope not to answer her cell or respond to text messages. You could've at least let me know if you'd seen her or talked to her lately."

"With all due respect, Miss . . ."

"Lindsay is fine."

"With all due respect, Lindsay, you called me once Monday, and then two times yesterday, back-to-back, asking about an employee I've only known a month. It was a little out of the blue, and I've been quite busy today, in no small part because your friend went AWOL on me."

"Well, with all due respect, Evan, some people might say it's more than a little suspicious that you'd be so cavalier about the disappearance of a woman that you agreed to hire under a highly untraditional arrangement. I think this is the part of the TV show when the police start looking into your background."

He held his palms up in protest. "Wait a second. You've got this all wrong." He looked at her intently and sighed, as if coming to terms with some internal debate. "Fine. Have a seat and let me explain."

"I'd rather stand, if that's okay with you." The front of the office space was glass, so she was in plain view of passersby outside. If the situation became dangerous, she could dart out to the parking lot.

"Look, you're right. It wasn't only because of my schedule that I didn't call you back. I could tell from your message that you're genuinely concerned about your friend, and I was trying to figure out how to respond. I guess what I'm trying to say is . . . your friend suckered me. The last time she was in the office, she talked me into advancing her two thousand dollars. Then, what do you know: she no-shows all this week and seems to have turned off her phone."

Lindsay shook her head. "I've known Hope for fifteen years. She wouldn't do that. She was really excited to have this job. When did you supposedly give her this money?"

"*Supposedly?* Jeez, you're not going to believe anything I say, are you? So if you've known her fifteen years, that means you must know the abusive husband she's supposedly hiding out from under a fake name. Is that story even true?"

That was the part of Miriam's backstory that Hope had borrowed for her new life in East Hampton. Before Miriam moved to Hopewell, where she eventually married Lindsay's father, she was Karen Henderson in Fresno, California, living with a very different kind of man. She had tried leaving before, only to have him find her, drag her home, and beat her even harder to teach her a lesson. The last time she "set him off," in his words, she ended up in the emergency room with a fractured skull and a ruptured spleen. As Miriam explained it, she decided that she'd try one last time to leave, and if he ever did find her, at least one of them might just have to die. Through a contact at an underground network of resources for battered women, she was able to change her name and move to a small town where the local police chief, Lindsay's father, would keep an eye out for the newest citizen of Hopewell.

Lindsay was realizing how bad this was going to look to people who didn't understand Hope's situation. "The situation's complicated," she finally said.

"See? I knew it. A con job. And I bought it hook, line, and sinker. Sure, I was skirting some payroll taxes or whatever, but I also thought I was helping out a woman who could use a break. I knew I was taking a leap of faith giving her that cash, but she'd been working so hard, I decided that for once I wasn't going to be my usual cynical self."

"So when was this?" Lindsay asked again.

"I gave her the cash here in the office on Friday. Then Saturday night she texted me, saying she was done with a project I'd assigned to her since I had my kids for the weekend."

"What time did she text you?"

He picked up his cell from his desktop, scrolled through his screen, and handed the device to her. "See for yourself."

The place is all set. I did it tonight to make sure I didn't run into a time crunch tomorrow morning. Thanks again for trusting me, Evan. Hope you and the kids are having the best time! It was sent at 10:33 p.m.

"It was a prep for an open house. When I got there the next day, the house was close to perfect. But then she didn't show up to help with the actual event. I thought maybe I hadn't made it clear I wanted her to go, but then she didn't answer my messages. No apology. No follow-up. Then she didn't come into work Monday or any day since. Bye-bye, two grand."

"Your employee vanished, and you didn't think to tell anyone?"

"So I can get in trouble for paying her under the table, on top of getting ripped off? No, thank you."

On instinct, Lindsay took a step closer to the exit. She wasn't buying this story. If Hope needed money, she would have asked Lindsay for it. Or had she really meant it when she said she wanted to make this move on her own?

"I know you think she's some kind of scammer, but I swear, that's not who she is. Something is seriously wrong. Did she ever give any indication that she was having problems out here?"

He shook his head but then stopped, pressing his lips together with a dawning recollection. "It was a while ago. Maybe her second week working for me. She asked me not to say anything about her in the event anyone ever asked questions. I assumed it was related to the ex-husband, back when I thought that he actually existed. So I told her that of course I would never do that. But then she said, even if it was someone local from around here. I made a joke about how she was already making enemies, but she didn't seem to think it was funny. She just asked me to let her know if anyone ever came around asking about her. Then one day we were going to see a listing, and I noticed she kept checking the rearview mirror. I asked her what was wrong, but she said it was a habit—a survival instinct that all women have. I mean, maybe that's true, but again, I chalked it up to her background with the ex-husband."

"That day with the rearview mirror, did you notice anyone following you? Or did anyone ever contact you, asking questions about her?"

"No, nothing like that. See, this is why I was putting off calling you. The writing's pretty much on the wall from my perspective. She got as much as she could out of me and moved on to another town. I bet you good money she took anything that wasn't nailed down from that poor lady's cottage. She's probably trying to sell it now, along with that rug she stole from me."

"What rug?"

"Right, I left that part out. I mean, it's a cheapie from IKEA, but she probably assumed it was the real deal. She followed my instructions for the open house to a tee—better than I expected. But the area rug I gave her to cover up the wood in the foyer wasn't down. Like I said, she ripped me off."

Lindsay suddenly flashed back to the sight of Hope's rain-soaked body splayed so unnaturally at the side of the road, but now she imagined her in that same position on a cheap knockoff Persian rug, blood caking into her sandy blond hair, an unidentified man leaning over her.

"Where was this open house?"

6

Wednesday, June 16, 12:10 p.m.

According to the countdown bar at the top of her television screen, Robin Stansfield had two minutes and forty-seven seconds remaining in her hip-hop cardio workout when she heard a knock on the door. Stan, back from the driving range, too lazy to use his keys, but also an excuse for her to stop early. She hit the power button on the remote on her way to the front door, checking the peephole out of habit. She was surprised to see an unfamiliar woman, probably in her mid-thirties. Dark brown, shoulder-length hair. Big, ocean-blue eyes behind tortoiseshell glasses. A coat of nude lip gloss, if any makeup at all. Professional. Presumably she'd arrived in the white Audi station wagon that was parked at the curb.

It was probably about that darn For Sale sign in the yard. "If you're here about the listing, you can call the broker. The number's on the sign," she said through the closed door.

"It's not about the house. Or not about buying it, at least. Can I ask you a couple of questions? My friend is missing, and she was here by herself last weekend. Her name is Hope Miller."

———

THE WOMAN WHO OPENED THE front door of the For Sale house wore yoga pants, sneakers, and a "Free Britney" T-shirt and was holding a remote control. Beneath the bangs of her ashy blond bob, she eyed Lindsay suspiciously.

"I'm afraid no one was here Saturday night," the woman said, sounding slightly short of breath. "We were away on vacation."

"I was told she came by to get everything ready for an open house here the next day." Lindsay peered over the woman's head, trying to catch a glimpse of the home's interior. "Please, can I ask you a few questions? I promise I'm not an ax murderer or something." *Nothing more comforting to strangers than assuring them you're not going to hack them to pieces. Well done, Lindsay.* She reached for a business card from her purse, identifying herself as a criminal defense attorney at Kelly & Associates, and offered it with an outstretched hand. "Please."

The woman accepted it tentatively and gave the card a quick scan. In truth, the "associates" consisted of one junior lawyer—a former intern Lindsay had poached from the DA's office when she left to open a defense practice.

"So you only *represent* ax murderers."

"Well, only the one, but he was totally innocent."

The tension fell from the woman's face and she stepped back from the door, allowing Lindsay to enter. "My name's Robin. Robin Stansfield. But I don't know anyone named Hope. Our realtor is Evan Hunter."

"I know. Hope works for Evan. Or at least she did." Lindsay summarized everything she knew clearly and concisely, fighting back the panic that was building as she recited each disturbing fact.

"Oh, you must mean that adorable girl he had with her. Honestly, I think she's the only reason my Stanley picked Evan as our broker. Pretty blondes are his kryptonite—as you can see," she added with a sly smile. "But Evan didn't say anything about her working at our house on her own."

Lindsay fought to maintain an even tone. "She was working at Evan's direction. They stage the houses, I guess—make it look more generic, like no one even lives there. Don't take it the—"

"Oh, no. That's not what I meant." The woman set the remote control on a console table in the foyer. "I realize how horrible that must have sounded. Please, sit down. Can I get you something? Coffee or a soda?"

She gestured to the living room sofa, and Lindsay took a seat but waved away the offer of anything more.

"Evan mentioned that they'd be packing away some personal belongings during showings. I guess I just assumed he was doing it himself."

Now that Lindsay was here, she felt even more helpless. What exactly had she expected to find? "That's what I wanted to ask you—if anything seemed out of place. If there were any signs of, I don't know, a struggle or something."

"Nothing specific. Although . . . you know?" Robin tilted her head and paused. "When we came home, I just had this weird feeling, like I knew someone had been here. Then I remembered they were doing an open house, and it all seemed to make sense. But now your friend is missing."

Lindsay could see a genuine look of worry cross the woman's face. Maybe she had misread her. But she also saw no reason for this woman to know the real and very complicated reason Hope lived her daily life with a completely manufactured identity, so she used the same biography that Hope had borrowed from her former stepmother, Miriam. "Hope's background is . . . complicated. She can't use her real name in case her ex-husband were ever to look for her."

"I see," Robin said, a furrow working its way into her brow. "And you think he may have found her? Here, in our house?"

"I don't know," Lindsay said. "But this was one of the last places she definitely was. It's my only lead, so here I am."

"Well, have you told the police?" Robin asked.

Lindsay had driven to the East Hampton police station after talking to Evan, but then realized how the story would sound: a woman came to town a month before, using a fake name and a fabricated sad story, to fleece a man out of two grand before hitting the road again. Lindsay had come to the house instead.

"Without some sign of foul play, it's going to be hard to get their attention. I'm not family, and I don't even live here. I guess I just wanted to see your home for myself. Check for any signs of a disturbance— maybe something Evan didn't notice during the open house."

Robin was on her feet. For a second, Lindsay thought perhaps the woman had spotted something in the corner of the living room. Instead she walked to the kitchen, picked up a cell phone from the island, and placed a call.

"Are you home, Carter? I need a favor."

7

Wednesday, June 16, 12:25 p.m.

Carter turned out to be a cop named Carter Decker who lived in the guest house at the property next door to the Stansfields'. Lindsay could tell from the way he cut through the backyard and headed straight for his neighbors' back door that he was used to being called over.

Lindsay guessed he was about her age. Slim, with a long face, spiky brown hair, and three or so days of stubble. He wore a pair of faded jeans and a David Bowie T-shirt. Off duty.

Robin greeted him with a friendly hug.

"I thought you and Stan were off training for the PGA," he said.

"Let me introduce you to my new friend, Lindsay Kelly."

Carter looked at her and nodded once with a dry smile. She guessed that Carter was also used to being introduced by the Stansfields to women around his age.

"Were you around over the weekend?" Robin asked.

"In and out."

"Did you see our realtor, by any chance?" Robin asked. "Evan Hunter—a little bald, about mid-fifties? A little . . . *fat?*" She whispered the last word as if it were contagious.

"No," Carter whispered back. "Did he eat part of your house or something?"

Lindsay was aware of the passing minutes. "He has an assistant who staged the house. According to him, she definitely arrived to do the job on Saturday night, but then never came back on Sunday as expected, and no one has seen her since. She's been missing now for four days." She pulled up a photograph on her phone. It was an "ussie," as Hope called a selfie with another person, from their trip to East Hampton in April. They were each holding up an ice cream cone from Scoop du Jour.

"I'm so sorry," Carter asked. "Are you family?"

"No. Just a friend." Lindsay felt a tug at the back of her throat.

"I didn't want to believe it had anything to do with our house," Robin said, "but then I remembered the chill I felt when Stan and I first came home. I was just *certain* something was wrong. The house felt . . . off. Broken somehow. Stan accused me of acting like a woo-woo, but when Lindsay showed up today looking for her friend, I had to wonder."

Carter nodded, and Lindsay could tell he gave absolutely zero credence to Robin's intuitions.

"Her friend just moved here from Hopewell, New Jersey. Oh, listen to that: Hope from Hopewell!" Robin lowered her voice again to a whisper. "She was on the run from an abusive ex."

"Maybe she decided to go back home?" Carter suggested. "Unfortunately, women in that position often change their minds."

"No," Lindsay said. "It's a small town, and I already checked with people there." She mentally crossed her fingers that Carter would not make a call to Hopewell to verify the false backstory that Robin had just repeated to him. Would this officer worry if a domestic violence victim hiding from an abusive ex-husband suddenly disappeared? Maybe, maybe not. But he certainly wasn't going to drop everything on his day off for a woman who had only moved to town a month earlier after living fifteen years under an assumed identity and a claim of amnesia. The part about the cash advance from Evan would be the icing on the cops-won't-care cake.

"Tell you what. I've got a bag of tricks in my truck from an in-service training last week. Let me take a look and make sure we're not missing something with the naked eye. How about that?"

He was obviously humoring them, but Lindsay would take whatever help she could get at this point. "That would be great."

"Just give me a few minutes."

WELL MORE THAN A FEW minutes later, the shades in the Stansfield house were all drawn, and Carter was spraying liquid from a pump bottle onto the floor beneath the sliding kitchen door, explaining that it was a highly sensitive compound that would emit light when oxidized.

Lindsay wasn't a cop, but she was raised by one. She also considered herself a pretty talented cross-examiner when it came to challenging the processing of a crime scene. Carter had skipped every initial step—identifying and securing a perimeter, a thorough visual inspection with photographs and notes, perhaps a secondary sweep enhanced by ultra-violet light. She could have a field day with a single officer, off duty, jumping directly to what she suspected to be luminol. Because the compound had the potential to destroy certain types of evidence at a crime scene, police tended to use it sparingly and only after exploring other options.

But because Carter was humoring them, he probably didn't care about any of that. And because Lindsay was desperate for help, she said nothing.

"What is that stuff?" Robin asked. "I don't see it doing anything."

"It's luminol," Carter said. He followed up with an oversimplified explanation of the way that the liquid reacted to iron found in hemo-globin. He avoided the use of the word *blood*, but the implication was clear. "And it's not doing anything because there's nothing here that's an oxidizing agent. This way, you'll know for certain."

Lindsay could see that Carter didn't have enough of the liquid to spray every surface of the house, even if he was inclined to. An image of Hope's dead body on Evan Hunter's area rug flashed again in her mind.

"Would you mind if we checked the front hallway?" she asked.

Without even bothering to ask for her reasons, he skipped right over all the intervening square footage and began applying the liquid to the hardwood floor in the foyer. The space was halfway covered with spray when Lindsay spotted the glow of pale-blue luminescence, exactly where the missing rug should have been for the open house.

Robin Stansfield actually screamed.

8

Wednesday, June 16, 1:28 p.m.

Detective Carter Decker hit the nearest light switch as quickly as he could.

Jesus H, this was a stupid idea. He had been thinking only of the potential upsides of giving Mrs. Stansfield and her new visitor the all-clear. But now he had a glowing blue zone to deal with in the front hallway of his neighbors' house.

Robin was moving toward the place where she'd seen the blue light. "Stop," Lindsay yelled. "We've got to preserve the scene."

Great, the neighbor's new friend fancied herself a law enforcement expert. She probably had a degree in cable television crime shows.

"So is that . . . *blood?*" Robin whispered.

"No, we don't know that," Carter said. He did his best to run through a myriad of alternative explanations. "We get false positives all the time: fruit juice, cooking oil, paint, glue, cleaning liquid, horseradish. A whole lot of stuff can be mistaken for hemoglobin."

He could feel Lindsay staring at him. *Horseradish?*

"They have to follow it up with a confirmatory test," Lindsay said. "Isn't that right, Officer Decker?"

She might be a know-it-all, but this woman totally had his number. He had been looking for a way to appease Mrs. Stansfield, but one phone call to his supervisor, and he'd be left explaining why he'd hopped over to a neighbor's house with a bottle of luminol.

Carter was an ass. He knew that about himself. He was capable of playing the role of a happy-go-lucky eager-to-pleaser, but deep down, he felt absolutely no connection to 98 percent of other people. The day-to-day banter between most human beings was nails on the chalkboard to him.

So why did he always go out of his way to make the Stansfields happy?

Because they were the real deal—truly good people who were exactly as nice as they appeared to be. After Carter's father died, Robin had left him casseroles twice a week for months. Stan, he suspected, was responsible for the miraculous fact that his old man's lawn never once needed a mow until Carter started doing it himself after moving in. It had also been the Stansfields who had suggested that he could afford to keep his parents' beloved home if he were to build a small guest house in the back for himself and rent out the main house during the summer to pay for the entire year's expenses.

And they were always asking him over for movie nights and dinners, which, as sweet as they were, sounded to Carter like torture, because Carter was, sigh, an ass.

So in lieu of torturous dinners filled with mind-numbing chitchat, he found other ways to be nice to these extremely nice people. He remembered Stan coming to his door in tears four years earlier. Their daughter, Hannah, had come home from a date with her top ripped and a fat lip and wouldn't tell him or her mother what had happened. Fortunately, the Stansfields' worst fears had not come to pass, but likely only because Hannah kneed the guy in the groin and scrambled out of the car. Like so many victims in her situation, she did not want to press charges, but Carter had paid the guy a visit.

His loyalty to the Stansfields didn't extend, however, to this new visitor, Lindsay Kelly. When he stepped out for the luminol kit, he'd made a quick call to the Hopewell, New Jersey, police department to see if the town might be small enough for someone to know Lindsay's missing friend with the abusive ex. Turned out the whole story was bogus and that the woman who called herself Hope Miller had left town of her own volition. Starting over again in the Hamptons, she then suckered some real estate agent into giving her a $2,000 advance, as a second quick phone call—this one to the number on the Stansfields' For Sale sign—had revealed. It was pretty clear to Carter that the woman was a grifter who'd moved on to her next mark.

But now here he was, stuck with a positive luminol test, in front of a stranger who, if he had to bet based on the way she talked and the things she knew, was a lawyer. "I'm sure there's no reason to panic about your friend. Like I said, the spot could be anything."

Robin snapped her fingers. "Wait! Before we left town, Stan cut himself with those damn gardening shears, trying to clear the front path for the open house. He was bleeding all over. It probably just dripped when he was running to the kitchen for a towel."

"If it's even blood," Carter emphasized again.

He felt Lindsay Kelly's eyes drilling into him. "What was the point of this whole CSI reenactment if you weren't going to follow the results where they led? No one has seen Hope for days. Her last known location was *right here*, and now there's blood in the foyer—exactly where the rug would have been for the open house. A rug that has been missing ever since she went missing. So are you going to process whatever it is that lit up that luminol, or do I need to make a separate phone call?"

Yep, definitely a lawyer.

Robin started to apologize, but Carter signaled that it wasn't necessary. "I'll get someone from our CSI unit to take a closer look, just to be sure."

"Really?" Robin said, her voice brightening. "That would be amazing. I'm sure your friend is fine, Lindsay, but at least this way, you'll know for sure that nothing happened to her here."

It was obvious to everyone in the room that Lindsay had lost her ally. Robin had been briefly entertained by a mystery at her door, but once she'd seen that faint blue light, she was ready to accept any explanation that could allow her to go back to feeling safe and sound in her home again.

The lawyer thanked him, but Carter could tell that he had managed to buy himself only a temporary reprieve. This woman was going to be trouble.

9

Three Days Later

Saturday, June 19, 9:12 a.m.

Carter was asleep on his sofa, the television on but muted, when the sound of knocking at his door woke him. This was the only bad part of living in his own guest house for the summer. The rent money was sweet, but people who paid top dollar during peak season expected five-star treatment. Burned-out lightbulb? Too dumb to work the TV remote control? Go find the landlord out back!

He swore under his breath when he saw who was standing on the other side of the door. Lindsay Kelly.

He untumbled the locks and opened the door.

"Did you get the blood results back?" she asked.

He had made the mistake of telling Robin and Lindsay about advances in rapid DNA testing. Instead of waiting for days and months for an offsite lab to compare DNA from a crime scene against discarded beer cans and cigarette butts, with a rapid DNA machine police can process samples themselves, yielding results as quickly as ninety minutes. The nearly automated machines were even connected now to CODIS, the national DNA database. The sixty-three-member East

Hampton Police Department didn't have a so-called magic box of its own, but it did have access to the Suffolk County Police Department's, which typically had a forty-eight- to seventy-two-hour turnaround for results.

Carter had cashed in a favor to access the machine, hoping to get Lindsay off both his and the Stansfields' backs. But now, sixty-seven hours later, he had a criminal defense lawyer on his porch. And though he had in fact gotten the DNA results after forty-nine hours, he wasn't about to share the details.

"Good morning to you, too, Ms. Kelly. Nice keychain, by the way." He wouldn't have pegged her for something as childlike as the purple plastic cat head dangling from her car keys. "Very cute."

"Sorry," she said, slipping the keys into her purse. "You were sleeping."

She said it like it was shocking to find someone sleeping at nine on a Saturday morning. "Worked night shift." Why was he explaining himself to her? "The blood wasn't your friend's," he said.

He could see relief wash over Lindsay's face as she let out a deep sigh. "But it was blood, though? Was it Stan's? From that cut that Robin mentioned?"

Carter was so tempted to lie. It would be so easy. It would help settle this woman's fears and get her off his property. But despite all Carter's faults, dishonesty wasn't one of them. His father had always told him that a man lost a little piece of his soul every time he looked another person in the eye and told a bald-faced lie. A man who lies, his father warned, is a man who has no bottom. He never warned Carter, though, that a man who *didn't* lie might just screw up his law enforcement career, as Carter had discovered.

"The important thing is," he said, "it's not your friend's."

"No, the important thing is that Hope is still missing. So is that rug. And now you're being cagey about that blood. She would have defended herself. She was strong—physically and otherwise. And a survivor. That blood could be from the man who killed her. Or took her. The point is, she's still gone." Her voice cracked, and she swallowed before speaking again. "Do you know where that blood came from or not? Was it a man's or a woman's? I know the analysis would say."

"I promised you I'd run the DNA, and I did. You don't know me, but I am actually good at my job. You can trust me on this: I don't know what happened to your friend, but that luminol hit's a dead end."

"Well, if it was a woman's blood, but not Hope's, you'd probably tell me on the assumption that I'd see that as better news than an unidentified man's blood. So I'm going to assume it was the latter, and yet you're still convinced it has nothing to do with Hope. If I have to, I'll get a list from the Stansfields of every single man who's been in and out of that house myself. I'll track them down and swab them personally, if that's what I need to do to make you take this seriously. Until you know for sure there's an explanation, you can't just move on."

"Look. I can't tell you every link in the chain I followed in my investigation, but I assure you, I'm completely confident that the trace amount of blood that luminesced is unrelated to your friend. I know this is hard to believe, but there's stray DNA in all kinds of places, and it doesn't mean anything sinister has happened. You'd never look at a hotel room the same again if you saw it under a black light."

The woman was shaking her head, as if she knew something he did not. "You called the police in Hopewell, didn't you?"

Right after you told me that bullshit story, he wanted to say. The sergeant on duty had explained that he was going to be "perfectly frank" in the hope that he could "trust" Carter to be "discreet." According to him, the shrinks and the social workers all said that the woman's amnesia was legit, but some of the cops initially wondered if her story didn't "smell right" once they ran the plate on her overturned car and it came back as stolen from Indianapolis. They thought she might have gotten herself wrapped up in a bad situation with dangerous people and, after crashing her stolen car, concocted a story about amnesia to get a free bed and a fresh start. They were quickly shot down by their chief at the time, whose daughter had been the one to call in the accident. "She sort of made that girl her pet project while she was home from her hoity-toity college. You didn't hear it from me, but there's something weird about that friendship. Like maybe they're a little too close, if you know what I mean." Carter had asked for the former police chief's name—Jimmy Kelly. It was all the confirmation he needed.

Looking at Lindsay Kelly now, Carter wondered how representative that sergeant's opinions were. Maybe he was just a loudmouth who'd been eager to spread a little bit of gossip to a willing listener outside of his small town. "Like I said, I followed up as any investigator would have under the circumstances. I know your friend gave her boss a bogus story about hiding out from an abusive husband. And I know you played into that false impression when you came here looking for her."

They were at a stalemate, each aware that the other may have cut some corners in the interests of doing what they thought was right.

Part of him—the mean side—wanted to add that if Lindsay hounded her friends the way she was hounding him, he totally understood Hope's decision to lay low. Instead, he said, "I'm sorry you haven't heard from your friend, and your loyalty to her is admirable. But we have someone with no roots here, living under an assumed identity, with a falsified bio, who borrowed cash from her boss before what appears to be moving on. You have to admit her background is . . . suspect."

Behind him, Carter's phone buzzed against the living room coffee table. He left the front door open and went to answer it. He could tell that Lindsay was considering stepping inside, but he gave her a look that kept her in place.

"Carter."

A few seconds later, he had the excuse he needed to end the conversation. "Got a callout. A missing person report that needs a detective." He grabbed his keys from the console table next to his television and locked the door behind him.

"Are you actually going to look for that poor person?" she called after him as he walked to his car. "Unlike you did with Hope?"

As Carter backed out of his driveway, he realized that her words had landed. Would he? It was a fair enough question. He heard the echo of his own voice, a few minutes earlier: *I am actually good at my job*. There was a time when he really had believed it.

10

Saturday, June 19, 8:10 p.m.

Lindsay had never been to this restaurant before, but she could tell it was the kind of fussy place where the waiters were under strict orders to refill the wineglasses before the customer needed to. She reached for the bottle of Barbaresco anyway and gave it a tip.

"What about SP?"

It had become part of their vocabulary the first time Scott stayed at her apartment while Hope was visiting for the weekend. An hour after he'd turned in for bed, he reemerged in the living room saying he had FOMO. They assured him he need not fear. He was only missing out on SNL and gummy bears. "But what about SP?" he said, looking at the bag from Dylan's Candy Bar. It was the kind of thing that would be dorky if someone else said it, but Scott Parker had a way of making goofy seem pretty damned attractive. It helped that he was six foot three, had played college rugby, and was, let's face it, objectively good-looking.

She started to pour more wine into Scott's glass too, causing a nearby waiter to scurry to their table to take over the job.

"I'm surprised you're not exhausted," he said once they were alone again. "It was still dark out when you left this morning."

"I think the food's actually giving me a second wind." Scott had finally persuaded her to leave the apartment for dinner. She thought it would mean a quick stop for a burger or something, but now they were at this fancy place where she couldn't pour her own wine.

She had spent six hours in her car that day, driving round trip to East Hampton and back, just to have Carter Decker blow her off, claiming that the blood from the Stansfield house was a "dead end." Maybe some people would be willing to accept the officer's decision, but Lindsay wasn't in the business of allowing other people to draw conclusions for her.

Accordingly, she had sent a list of questions to Detective Decker, by voice mail and email: (1) Which databases or other resources had they relied upon to compare the genetic material? (2) What, if any, results had come from such comparisons? (3) What resources, other than DNA databases, were they utilizing to determine the source of the genetic material?

She checked her cell phone once again for email updates. Nothing.

Next to her, Scott was dragging a piece of bread through the olive oil/balsamic/basil mix at the bottom of his salad plate. "Earth to Lindsay. The whole point of going out was so you'd stop staring at your phone all night."

She set her phone next to her wineglass. "I just feel so helpless."

"You've been pulling out all the stops." He placed a hand on her knee. "I'm sorry that it's not getting the attention you want."

"They say they ran the blood, and nothing came of it. But it seems like the detective's being intentionally vague about it. It would be easy for him to say there were no hits, for example. That would be crystal clear. But when I was pressing him for details, all he said was that it was a 'dead end'? It doesn't sound right to me."

"I've got to be honest. I don't hear any difference between those two." Scott was an investment banker for institutional clients, although Lindsay still wasn't entirely sure what that meant.

"It's him giving me his conclusion, versus sharing the raw information upon which he's basing that conclusion."

"That makes sense."

She knew it was his way of validating her, but at the same time, she found the response annoying. Of course it made sense. She wasn't in the habit of saying things that didn't make sense. She realized she was also being overly defensive. She'd been trying her best not to talk so much about Hope since the move, but that seemed impossible now that she was missing.

"I don't know how to articulate it. There was just something weird about his tone. He was being evasive. And totally condescending. He even made fun of my keychain."

"Stabby Kitty? Little does he know its power."

"Exactly." A gift from Hope, who had one to match, the keychain known as Stabby Kitty was a ridiculous purple plastic cat head with pointy ears and two holes for eyes. It also doubled as a self-defense weapon. She had resisted the urge that morning to slip her index and middle fingers into place for a few quick jabs at Carter's self-satisfied grin.

"Well, from what you told me, it sounds like his neighbor roped him into doing something he didn't want to do. More of a lark than anything else, and then he happened to find some random DNA sample. You're the one who told me why you always pull the comforter off the bed every time we check into a hotel."

Everything everywhere, were her exact words. "Except it's not exactly random if it's in the house where Hope was last seen. She's been missing for a week now. I just want him to tell me that they didn't get a hit. He's being loosey-goosey with his words."

Scott studied the label on the wine bottle, avoiding her gaze.

"You want to say something," she said.

"No, I want to know where Hope is, just as you do."

"But you don't seem surprised that the police are blowing me off."

At least according to what Scott said most of the time, he personally loved Hope just as much as Lindsay did. She was a friend who was honorary family. Yada yada yada. But to the extent they ever argued about the state of their relationship, it often included him pressuring Lindsay to make more of a permanent commitment to him, and then somehow the subject always seemed to land eventually on Hope. Last fall, he'd even asked her to go to therapy with him, where he told the counselor that he feared Lindsay would never allow herself to live a complete life until Hope was able to do the same. He thought she felt too guilty about "leaving Hope behind" if—say, for example—Lindsay were to marry and have a child, or "even meet her boyfriend's daughter," he added. "I see you guys together, and you have this energy—like two puppies in a playpen, as if you've been raised together from birth. But puppies are supposed to grow up . . ."

He dropped the dog analogy the second she started laughing about it, but did not let go of his point. "It's like the two of you both got frozen in time when you found her in that car." She told him afterward that she felt bombarded by the session and wouldn't be attending anymore, but the topic resurfaced again when Hope announced that she wanted to leave Hopewell. Lindsay couldn't sleep for weeks, worried about how her friend could possibly get by somewhere else, on her own. When Hope insisted on the move, Lindsay even offered to clear her calendar so she could spend the first month in East Hampton with her, just in case. But Scott had taken Hope's side, saying that he totally "supported" Hope's decision to try to become "independent."

Independent. Meaning, without Lindsay. Meaning Lindsay might then feel free to give Scott everything he wanted from their relationship, on his timeline. All the next steps: Meet Nora, shack up, get hitched, have baby. Done.

She'd asked him early on what it was about her that made him strike up that conversation with her at the brewery, or to ask her out the very next day, and then the day after that. She worried at the time she might appear to be fishing for a compliment, but his response had nothing to do with her at all. "I'd been divorced for two years by then, and was ready for a serious relationship. And I'm determined not to mess it up this time."

Once she found out exactly how he had "messed it up," she couldn't unknow it. Lindsay's reluctance to take even that initial leap had nothing to do with Hope and everything to do with Scott. How many times had she started to tell him the reasons for her doubts, but then stopped herself? She might not be ready to go all in, but she also didn't want to lose him.

He reached across the table and placed his hand over hers. "I honestly don't know what you want me to say right now, Linds. The last thing I want to do is add to your stress."

"Look, I know you were all for her moving. And then you told me not to worry when she wasn't calling or texting. But now she's gone, Scott. Like, actually gone. I mean, how do you explain that?"

"Maybe East Hampton wasn't far enough."

"What does that mean?"

"To get the fresh start she was looking for."

And then she realized what he was saying. It wasn't far enough from Lindsay. It wasn't enough of the "space" she had asked for. All those one-sided text conversations. He was saying that maybe Hope had gotten a $2,000 advance from Evan Hunter and decided to make a clean break. The puppy finally wanted to grow up.

"There's no way she just took off like that," she said. "When I looked through the bedroom window, I could see all of her journals still on the bookshelf—years of them. Remember that horrible game your sister brought over for game night?" In Lindsay's view, it wasn't even a game. It was a box of cards containing lists of stupid questions they all had to answer, but they were allowed to use one lie per card.

"You said it didn't count as a game because there were no winners or losers, and you're the most competitive person on the planet."

"And proudly so, but that's beside the point. *What's the one thing you'd grab if your house was on fire?* I said my backup hard drive, and Hope said her journals." The doctors suggested that Hope start journaling about a month after the accident, because they noticed a prominent callus on the left side of her middle finger, a so-called writer's bump. Sure enough, it turned out that Hope was the kind of person who could pour words onto a page. It was during her very first journal entry that she decided to adopt the name Hope so she'd at least have a name other than Jane Doe. "She's obsessive about them," Lindsay said. "Have I ever told you why?"

Scott shook his head.

"She has these recurring nightmares where she wakes up with amnesia again. After years of developing a life and some kind of identity, it all suddenly disappears—poof, into thin air. She keeps those journals so she can never lose a sense of herself again. Think about that. There's no way she would leave without them. *Ever.*"

"Unless—and I'm playing devil's advocate here—unless she really did want to start all over again from scratch. How many times did she tell you that she wished no one knew about her memory loss? She could go somewhere a lot cheaper than the Hamptons and leave everything about Hopewell in the rearview mirror. She could even pick a new name. It's not like she ever made the other one official." The roll of her eyes did not stop him from completing his point. "Look at it this way: if you didn't know Hope, and all you heard was that she suddenly moved to a new town with a fake backstory, and ran off with a cash advance and a rug, what would you think?"

Lindsay could see the logic of his argument. The Becketts, Miriam, Lindsay's father . . . they all helped out Hope as an extension of Lindsay. Lindsay was probably the only person who had made affirmative efforts to check on her after she moved, and Hope had signaled that even that was too much.

"Except I do know Hope," she said.

"Or . . . you know the person Hope pretended to be around you to make you happy. Maybe she wants to be someone else."

The subject of Hope was never a comfortable one in their relationship, so she forced herself to take a few breaths to consider Scott's perspective as he reached across the table to stroke her wrist with his thumb. Something about the feeling of his strong hands against her skin always calmed her down.

"Look. It seems to me that it's the bloodstain that's really scaring you. Don't you know some magic lawyer trick to find out whatever the police know?"

Lindsay was somewhere between a decent-plus to hotshot-minus defense attorney, meaning she was far better than the average lawyer. But like her father, Scott seemed to perceive her as one of those mythical television criminal lawyers who could simply show up in a power suit and red lipstick, toting a giant handbag, and TCB—take care of business. Real life didn't work that way, at least not for Lindsay.

"No, I don't even have a client to be a lawyer for. Until the government uses its powers against someone, there's no action to fight. Basically, this Decker guy can be as lazy and apathetic as he wants, and there's nothing I can do."

"Okay. But you always say there's formal law, and there's the way things actually work. If you think this detective is holding out on you, how do you get to the heart of that?"

He already knew the answer. So did she. She stepped outside and called her father.

11

Sunday, June 20, 10:12 a.m.

Lindsay eyed her Nespresso machine impatiently as her father filled her in on what he had been able to learn from Detective Decker.

"He seems like a decent guy," he said, speaking up over the whine coming from her kitchen counter. "For what it's worth, I got the impression the neighbor called him over there to play matchmaker."

"Maybe, but trust me, Dad, even without Scott in the picture, neither of us was interested. He basically threw me off his property yesterday, and he's ghosted me ever since."

"He wasn't exactly a sieve with me, either, but I did get the basics. They ran the blood sample through CODIS. As you suspected, they did get a hit. A big one, at least at first glance. The sample is connected to a string of killings committed in Wichita, Kansas, by a serial killer called the College Hill Strangler."

She nearly dropped the cup she'd been lifting toward her lips. She knew Decker was hiding something, but a *serial killer?* She pulled her laptop from her briefcase, opened it on the kitchen island, and typed in "College Hill Strangler."

At the other end of the line, her father was employing what she called his cop voice. She was used to her father speaking quickly but casually. But now his words came slowly, in crisp, authoritative sentences.

As her father spoke, she scrolled through her screen of search results. Booking photographs of a defendant named William Summer. To her eye he looked more like a high school vice principal than a mass murderer. Photos of him as a younger man, around the time he would have killed his first victims. Black hair, and small, close-set eyes. Oddly handsome, but also menacing.

"The blood belongs to a serial killer, and he told me it was a dead end?" Lindsay said incredulously. "If the guy's free by now, he could have left the Midwest and come up here." A quick skim of a true crime website included the words *hogtie*, *strangle*, and *torture*. She tasted last night's Barbaresco at the back of her throat.

"Like I said, it looks bad at first glance. But the actual killer, William Summer, is still in prison. The DNA hit wasn't to him; it was to unidentified blood found at one of the crime scenes. The victim's name was Janice Beale."

Another Google search. Janice Beale was the killer's sixth and final victim. Long blond hair parted in the middle. Pretty.

"It's . . . complicated. I tried getting someone at the Wichita Police Department to talk to me, but no luck, so I'm just reporting what Detective Decker told me. I remember this case vaguely from the news when the guy was arrested. The lead detective's daughter is NYPD, and it got quite a bit of media attention. She did a big prime-time sitdown with one of the networks and everything. She's also the reason that the blood sample was in the database to begin with. So, long story short, a detective named Jerry Hatcher was in charge of the College Hill Strangler investigation. The case went cold, but he kept digging. Fast-forward four years after William Summer's last kill, and Jerry was found dead in his car from what looked to be a self-inflicted gun wound from his own service weapon. His family was adamant that he would never take his own life. For years, they promoted the countertheory that the College Hill Strangler had killed him because he was close to cracking the case."

"So where does the blood sample come in?"

"Hang on with me here, okay? So, the detective's family got into a dispute with the police department about the cause of his death. The police department wanted to label it a suicide. The family said it was in the line of duty. Obviously, no family wants to believe that a husband and father would take his own life, but there was also money on the line. If a cop dies on the job, they get a death benefit, and well, you know the drill."

Once Lindsay became a lawyer, her dad had insisted on sharing the details of his will, life insurance, and bank accounts in the event anything happened to him, whether on the job or off.

"I'm looking up the case right now," she said. "It's like something out of a horror movie. How in the world did Decker tell me this was a dead end?"

"Because the DNA entry they hit on is itself problematic. Honestly, from what I heard, it shouldn't have even been there." He began to deliver a lecture about the management of law enforcement databases that was worthy of a law-school classroom.

"What was so unusual about this one?" she prodded, trying to hurry him along.

"Right. Okay. It goes back to the dispute between this detective's family and the police department about how to label his death, whether he'd get a line-of-duty benefit, and so on. The family eventually reached a settlement with the department, but one of the conditions was that the police department enter any and all trace evidence from the College Hill Strangler case into all available databases, just in case any new leads eventually surfaced."

"And now we have an actual cold hit," Lindsay said. She found herself wishing she hadn't read the details of the College Hill Strangler's modus operandi. She pictured Hope running for the front door of the

Stansfields' house. A masked man grabbing her from behind. A rope. A gag. She took a deep breath. "There must be some process that gets kick-started when you get a match."

"Except they already have their guy," her father said. "They caught him four years ago. They matched his DNA to every crime scene. A full confession, the works. And the DNA from that house in East Hampton isn't his. Trace evidence could be from anyone. If you scratch a mosquito bite a little too much, there's a spot of blood on the sofa. A paper cut. An accident with a kitchen knife. Someone who left behind a little bit of blood in a house in Kansas did it again on Long Island twenty-three years later. The odds of it having anything to do with Hope are pretty low."

"But it's all I've got, Dad. Did it sound like the police are even looking for her?"

There was a long pause before he spoke. "This Decker guy put in a missing person report based on the information you gave him, but you got to remember, Hope Miller doesn't even exist on paper. It's a missing person report filed under an alias. I did my best to personally vouch for her, explaining the whole situation with her memory and the car accident. But honestly? He sounded skeptical."

Over the years, Lindsay had researched whether a Jane Doe could establish a legal identity under a new name. She was stunned to learn that it was all but impossible. The scenario wasn't common enough, and the concerns about fraud were too strong. The federal government didn't even have a process for tracking unidentified people who were still alive. A few years earlier, New Jersey had introduced such a database. So far, it contained only three entries—Hope, a toddler who was left as a newborn in the parking lot of a Newark fire station, and a mentally ill homeless man. Until there was a way to connect those local cases to data gathered nationwide, the state system was unlikely to provide any answers. Lindsay thought they could try to use Hope's existence in an official state database, though, as a way to force New Jersey to issue a state identification card. Maybe if she at least had a legal ID, the cops would be taking her disappearance more seriously.

"This is exactly why I didn't want her to leave Hopewell. At least there, people got to know her." That wasn't to say that every town resident believed that Hope was telling the truth about her condition. At least one cop, Sergeant Prescott Hanson, had made his suspicions known on several occasions, but Lindsay knew for a fact that it was because Hope had shot that jerk down when he made the moves on her at a party. As a general matter, though, the people of Hopewell treated Hope as a known quantity.

"You could report the car stolen," he said. "It's in your name. It would guarantee that any cop who happened to run the plate would take action."

"Yeah, but the kind of action that would end with Hope getting arrested."

"And then you wouldn't press charges, and at least we'd know where she is. If someone spotted her in the car, it would be a way to have the police make a stop."

"I'll think about it." Lindsay felt like she was running out of options. She still hadn't been able to get inside Hope's cottage, and Decker hadn't shown the slightest inclination to help with that either. She had gotten the cottage owner's name—Catherine Gondelman—from city property records, but hadn't been able to reach her yet. She thought of mailing a letter that might get forwarded, but the cottage was on a street without mail service, and the post office had refused to tell her the landlady's PO box number. Lindsay had sent a Facebook message to the only account she found under that name, but had received no response. She would have gotten into that house four days ago if Hope had gotten a spare key made for her, like she had suggested when they did the move.

"I'm sorry. I know how worried you are."

She thanked her dad again for his help and went back to reading about the string of murders in Wichita, Kansas, when she was still a child. Her coffee was long cold by the time Scott emerged from the bedroom, wearing boxer briefs and a Yale T-shirt he kept in one of his drawers.

"I think that second bottle of wine got the best of me last night." He moved behind her and dropped a kiss on the nape of her neck. "I heard you on the phone. Jimmy K?" Scott's nickname for her father. It was a mutual lovefest between those two.

"Uh-huh."

"Any news?"

It took only a few minutes to relay what she had learned, but she realized when she was done how gruesome her description of the Kansas murders had been.

"Well, if the killer guy's in prison, at least you don't need to worry about that part. It does kind of sound like a coincidence—two different houses, plus a thousand miles and a couple of decades apart. And it seems like neither bloodstain would have been of any interest to the police if it weren't for the unusual circumstances. I mean . . . you basically forced that Long Island cop to go all CSI on a house that had been hosting construction workers and realtors for weeks, because who could say no to you?" He gave her a playful grin.

"And of course you mean because of my mad lawyering skills."

"Obviously. And it sounds like that Kansas detective's family did something hinky, forcing blood samples that might not be connected to any crimes into the databases."

"The daughter apparently followed in her father's footsteps. She's an NYPD detective. About my age, I think. Several years ago, before they caught the killer, she did a big media blitz trying to drum up new leads on the case. From the little I've read, it sounds like her father killed himself, but she wouldn't accept it. She comes across as pretty obsessed."

Scott flashed that goofy, flirty grin again. "Sounds like someone else I know—which could mean that she's absolutely brilliant."

"Basically they want me to believe that some random person who cut themselves in that house in East Hampton also randomly left some blood in a house in Kansas twenty-three years ago. And that none of it has anything to do with Hope, or with this serial killer."

He gave her shoulders a quick squeeze. "It is possible."

"Or . . . there's a connection." Her focus returned to her laptop.

She found herself stopping on a quote from Ellie Hatcher about her father's death. *I'm telling you, I knew my father at a fundamental level. He wasn't perfect, but he understood that my brother and I needed him. He wouldn't have left us voluntarily. And he was also a homicide detective to the core. I am not exaggerating when I say that he was haunted by the College Hill Strangler case. He believed he had a solemn duty to the victims to find their killer. Even if he wouldn't stay alive for us, he would have stuck it out to see that promise kept.*

Maybe Lindsay didn't know Hope's background up to fifteen years ago, but for fifteen years, she had known Hope at a fundamental level. And she knew Hope would not shut her out unless she was in serious danger.

She was going to find her friend.

12

Monday, June 21, 8:52 a.m.

NYPD detective Ellie Hatcher entered the Thirteenth Precinct to the sound of raised voices and the sight of her partner, J. J. Rogan, waving his palms, demanding that the couple in front of him "get control over yourselves."

The man was broad-shouldered, with wisps of curly salt-and-pepper hair escaping from the edges of a baseball cap. The woman was hunched, her hands in the pockets of a cardigan sweater, even though it was warm outside. They looked old, even from behind.

"I just need you to reinforce a few rules with my wife."

"You can't tell me what to do!" the woman yelled. "You're not the boss of me."

Salt and Pepper Man flinched as the woman raised her right hand to smack him. With a clear look at their faces, Ellie recognized the couple. For the seven years that Ellie had lived alone in a sublet near the precinct, Hank and Edna had lived in the complex next door.

"Whoa, whoa, whoa," Rogan said. He was dressed impeccably as usual—Canali or Zegna, most likely, more Wall Street than police station. "You can't be laying hands on each other. We've got mandatory arrest for domestic violence in New York. Every one of us in here is obligated to hook you both up if you start getting physical."

As Ellie quickened her pace in their direction, Hank removed his cap and smoothed his hair, expressing his gratitude at the sight of a familiar face.

The first time Hank spoke to Ellie at the coffee shop around the corner, his wife had apologized, explaining that her husband was "a born flirt." Ellie had assured her that he'd said nothing to offend. "Maybe not aloud," Edna had said, "but I can read the man's mind, and trust me— you don't want to know. I suppose I should be flattered, though. I used to look a lot like you in my day."

"Don't scare the nice woman," Hank had joked, and they had both laughed, pleased with their comedic timing.

That was probably six years before, and over time, Ellie had noticed the changes. Hank's ears and nose grew bigger. Edna had shrunk. But age was not imposing on them equally. Hank had slowed physically, grimacing noticeably when he sat and rose from his favorite corner table at the coffee shop. Still, he remained a constant flirt and a fierce intellect, reading both the *Times* and the *Wall Street Journal* every morning, leading the discussion group among any of the regulars interested in chiming in. It was clear even to Ellie, a casual neighbor, that Edna's mind wasn't faring as well.

"Edna," she asked, "what did Hank do this time? Together we'll set him straight."

The older woman's face brightened momentarily, but she quickly grew confused.

"You remember Ellie, don't you?" Hank's voice had changed, as if he were talking to a child. "The detective. She's from Kansas. You call her Dorothy."

Ellie was having a hard time processing how much Edna had changed. Her blond hair was brown with grease. Her lips were slightly parted as she stared vacantly, revealing black gaps between her remaining teeth.

"I know you," Edna finally said. It was hard to tell whether some part of her actually recalled Ellie, or if she had learned how to fake it in response to cues.

"What brought you in today?" Ellie asked, focusing the question on Hank.

"*She* did," Hank declared. "I went to the CVS, gone maybe fifteen minutes, tops. I told her, we'll get breakfast when I get home. But I do a double take as I pass our bank. She's in there with the teller, and I see there's a problem. She's upset." Hank mimicked the body language, waving his arms around animatedly. "I go in, and apparently she tried to withdraw twenty thousand dollars, which we don't exactly have sitting around like jellybeans. Then she asked the teller, 'Well, how much *do* we have?' and says, fine, she'll take that instead. When I got there, they were explaining she needed permission from the other person on the account—namely, me."

Edna was still glaring at them, arms crossed. "You're not my boss," she pronounced.

"As you can see, she's not a happy camper. She marched straight here, saying she was going to have me arrested for stealing her money and kidnapping her in the apartment. I figured she'd calm down and forget the whole thing by the time we got here. But no. *This* she can focus on."

Ellie placed an arm gently around Edna's shoulder. "You don't really think Hank is stealing anything from you, right? Or kidnapping?"

"But he won't let me go where I want. I'm a grown woman."

Hank lowered his voice. "Early on, when things were—clearer—we talked about her wishes. She wants to stay in the apartment, with me, as long as possible. I shouldn't have gone to the pharmacy alone."

"He told me I'm not allowed to go to the bank anymore, but it's my money."

"She's still able to go places like the coffee shop and deli. It's habit for her. *Familiar.* But I told her yesterday there were two places she absolutely shouldn't go alone: to the bank and to the Logans' apartment on the fourth floor. They're our closest friends in the building, but they don't always lock their door, and they don't need Edna walking in and out of their home at all hours. As for the bank, God knows what would have happened if they had allowed her to withdraw all our money. She could've thrown it in the corner trash, for all I know."

He was speaking more quickly and loudly with each new phrase. Ellie placed her hand gently on his forearm.

"Edna, what were you planning to do with all that money?"

"Buy more of this." When she removed her hand from her cardigan pocket, it held a red silk bag with a black drawstring. As she opened it, Ellie was hit with the smell of unlit marijuana. Rogan placed a hand over his mouth to hide the smile breaking out across his face as he made his way to the staircase that led to the homicide squad. Ellie grabbed the bag, stuffed it in her purse, and led the older couple to an unoccupied corner of the lobby.

"See what I mean?" Hank asked. "That's why she goes to the Logans', to steal the doobie." He pantomimed raising a joint to his lips.

Ellie and Hank reached an agreement that she'd send them home with the red bag on the condition that they'd return it to the Logans and never mention Ellie's role in the discussion. Ellie also tracked down a list of phone numbers for eldercare resources, including a doctor who could hook up Edna with the good stuff through proper channels. And despite her better instincts, she gave Hank her business card, with her cell number jotted on the back.

WHEN ELLIE FOUND ROGAN AT his desk, he was already hunched over paperwork.

"Why do I have a feeling you're carrying some old woman's stash?"

"Consider it squared away."

"This is what happens when you're all nice and sweet to strangers. You can take the girl out of Kansas, but . . ."

"Please. I happen to know you take a chicken-and-potatoes dinner to Miss Celia two floors up from you every Tuesday night."

"Fucking Rain Man shit," he said, shaking his head in disbelief.

He had mentioned that factoid only one time, two years earlier, after he placed an extra-large takeout order when they'd grabbed a bite at the end of shift. Ellie had one of those memories that trapped random details.

"I finished the write-up for the Bunning interrogation," he said, pushing a document on his desk over to hers. "I figured you could take care of the report for the cousin, and then we'll send it over to the ADA."

"Sounds good."

They had cleared the murder case the night before. Four years into their partnership, splitting up their work came in a natural rhythm.

"Still not used to seeing you with that tan," he muttered.

"Trust me. I'll be back to my usual envelope color any day." She had been home from vacation for nearly a week.

She was almost done with her report when a call came to her desk phone. She could tell from the screen that it had been connected through the switchboard.

"This is Hatcher."

"Detective Hatcher. This is Lindsay Kelly, I'm a defense attorney."

"I coordinate all of my case inquiries through the DA's office."

"It's not about the NYPD," the lawyer said. "I'm calling about one of your father's cases. His name came up as I was researching an old investigation that dates back to Wichita, Kansas."

Ellie felt a chill run up her spine. Her father. The College Hill Strangler. Somehow she'd always known that eventually this phone call would come.

"Is this about William Summer?"

ROGAN HANDED ELLIE A VENTI latte from Starbucks as she replaced the handset. She hadn't realized she'd been on the phone long enough for him to make a coffee run.

"You're an angel on earth, Jeffrey James."

"Figured you'd want your privacy." Rogan had left his desk shortly after she uttered the name William Summer. "You want to talk?"

"That was a defense attorney. She wants to meet with me about the case."

"He's trying to appeal his conviction or something? Get the fuck out. He pleaded guilty on a mountain of evidence."

There was an era in Wichita, Kansas, when children lived in the midst of a real-life bogeyman. Someone who appeared inside homes to kill women and children. He didn't simply kill them, either. He controlled them. Positioned, posed, and staged them. He took his time with them. They were his entertainment as long as he could drag it out until the final moment when he ended their lives.

Children her age, in that place, were taught to check the phone lines intermittently to be sure no one had cut them. They knew how to turn the series of multiple locks installed on all entries to the house, including from the basement. Eventually, when the killings stopped, the College Hill Strangler became more regional folklore than a constant fear. But for Ellie, his shadow lingered.

The basement that used to be the space where she and her brother, Jess, could play Ping-Pong or produce their own impromptu talent shows became her father's makeshift office away from the precinct. Long after the task force shut down, he continued to work the case, adding bigger whiteboards for his ever-expanding list of theories. Detective Jerry Hatcher was determined to find the killer who had eluded him for nearly a decade.

"No, it's an attorney here in the city. A friend of hers hasn't been heard from in more than a week. They found some blood spatter in the house where she was last seen, and it matched to one of the samples from the case."

She waited a moment for him to digest the information that she had already processed. "Okay, but the bad guy confessed and is locked up for life. The rest of it's noise."

With almost anyone else, Ellie would have shut down the conversation. But maybe more than anyone—besides Jess—Rogan understood the balance she had tried to strike between putting up a good fight for her father's legacy and forcing herself to accept the hard truth.

"Unless it isn't," she said.

"Nothing I say is gonna convince you to move on without knowing more about that DNA hit. Sound about right?"

"I'm meeting her as soon as this report gets filed."

13

Monday, June 21, 11:15 a.m.

A re you sure you don't want to order something else, Ellie?"
The name sounded overly familiar to Lindsay's ear, but Detective
Hatcher had insisted on first names, making clear that she was here in
a personal capacity, not as a cop. When Ellie suggested meeting at the
Bluebell Café, Lindsay had assumed they were eating lunch and ordered
accordingly, but then the detective asked only for a cup of coffee. Now
she felt weird, fumbling with this stupid avocado toast while talking
about serial murder.

She had already laid out everything she knew about the blood sample
from the Stansfields' house and its connection to trace evidence found
at the home of Janice Beale. "The police in East Hampton, at least, are
chalking it up to coincidence."

"I worked an interstate case once with an older detective from the
LAPD. He said there was no such thing as coincidence. The longer I've
been on the job, the more I agree. You're a lawyer: What's your gut?"

"That it's connected. I might be willing to say otherwise, except
Hope is missing. One possibility is that it's a person from her past—
someone who's been looking for her this entire time and finally found

her. Another possibility is that it has nothing to do with her or her amnesia, but it's connected with this College Hill Strangler case. But the
odds that it's a completely random coincidence that has nothing to do
with either Hope's disappearance or your father's case?"

Ellie shook her head. "Would be weird."

"William Summer could have had an accomplice," Lindsay said.
"Maybe when Summer went inactive, the accomplice left the region.
Who knows how many places he has lived since then, and how many
women he could have killed."

"It's an interesting theory."

Lindsay waited for the detective to say more, but Ellie simply took
another sip of her coffee. Lindsay was familiar with the tactic. Say nothing and force the other person to fill the silence. She could play the game
as well as any police officer, but in this situation, she was the one who
needed the detective's help.

Fine.

"In some ways," Lindsay said, "the modus operandi itself suggests
the possibility. The amount of control. The time spent with the victims. It all seems slow and methodical. That could mean more than one
person."

Ellie nodded. At least it was some kind of feedback. But instead of
working the angle with Lindsay, the detective abruptly changed the
subject. "Tell me more about your friend."

Still my turn, Lindsay thought. This woman didn't share in the
sandbox.

"Well, we certainly met in the strangest way." The detective listened
as Lindsay chronicled the history of finding Hope after the car accident and the years Hope had spent building a new life. "She wanted to
start over again where no one knew her history. She'd only been in East
Hampton about a month."

Lindsay pulled up a photograph on her phone. It was a selfie of
her and Hope, an ocean view barely visible in the background of the

close-up shot. "That's the last picture I have of her—from when we visited East Hampton together, in fact."

"She's pretty."

Lindsay felt her throat tighten as she glanced down at her screen. "I always joke that I want to do a Freaky Friday switch with her for one day—just to know what it feels like to be that beautiful."

Lindsay knew that she was also attractive, to an extent. With shiny dark hair, pale skin, and bright blue eyes, she had a look that matched her Irish last name. She might be described as cute or pretty or—what had Scott's mother called her? *Delightful.* But she wasn't the kind of gorgeous that turned men stupid. Focusing on the woman across the table, she realized that Detective Ellie Hatcher probably knew what it was like to attract that kind of attention. On closer inspection, she concluded that the detective intentionally frumped herself up for the job. She knew from the profile she'd read that Ellie had put herself through college with prize money from midwestern beauty pageants.

When she stopped speaking, Lindsay was already prepared for an onslaught of skeptical questions. What if Hope faked the amnesia? Why was she in a stolen car? What if she simply decided to disappear and start all over again? All of the reasons Carter Decker had used to rationalize his indifference. Instead, Ellie asked if Lindsay had spoken to anyone who knew Hope on Long Island. When Lindsay got to the part about Hope sending a text message to Evan from the Stansfield house on Saturday night, a look of surprise crossed Ellie's face. "This was two Saturdays ago?" she asked. "What time?"

"Ten thirty-three, to be exact."

The answer seemed to bother the detective, but she said nothing more about it. She did, however, finally speak about the College Hill Strangler case.

"William Summer targeted women who were the sole adult in their household," she said. "He called the victims his 'projects.' He'd spend weeks stalking them before closing in. He'd figure out their schedules, their habits. He'd watch through open windows, planning where he would position them once he was inside. What he would do to them. The kids, too, if that was the case. I'm sorry. That must be upsetting to hear."

Lindsay did her best to mirror the other woman's matter-of-fact attitude. "If he did have an accomplice, he'd be pretty old by now. That would be rare, wouldn't it?"

"There's a theory that some serial killers just stop—they age out. But there are exceptions. If your theory panned out, my guess is that the accomplice would be a younger person. Almost like an apprentice. Summer could have even groomed a vulnerable child he had access to in some manner. Exposed him to violence early on. Encouraged him to inflict it on others. If the accomplice was in his early twenties during Summer's killings, or even a teenager, he'd only be in his forties today, max, and could definitely still be active. You said your dad managed to get this information from that detective in East Hampton. Have either of you contacted the WPD?"

"My father did. They wouldn't give him the time of day. That's why I called you. From what I can tell, you really poured yourself into the case. I'm very sorry, by the way, about your father. Having a cop as a dad isn't easy. Luckily, mine never had to deal with anything so gruesome."

"But he did the job," Ellie said. "It's more dangerous for an officer to go out on a domestic call or initiate a traffic stop than to work a homicide investigation. You know what it's like to see someone you love leave for work and know that it could all go south."

"Though to be clear," Lindsay said, "I've learned as a defense attorney that a whole lot of Americans who *aren't* cops have to worry that this might be the day it all goes south—for selling loose cigarettes, having a barbecue, or asking some lady to put her dog on a leash while watching the birds at a park. All because someone calls the police on them." Lindsay immediately wondered if she might have sabotaged any chance she had of forging an alliance.

"You're not wrong," Ellie said.

"Hope wasn't vulnerable to that danger in the usual sense," Lindsay said, "but I'm still worried about her." It was why Lindsay had not taken up her father's suggestion of reporting the Honda Civic stolen.

"You really don't have any other theories as to what happened to your friend?" Ellie asked.

"I have a million theories, but this is the one I keep coming back to."

"Humor me with one of the others."

She knew Scott's leading theory. *She dumped everything from her past, including me.* That one she wasn't willing to share.

"It's possible that she had been running from trouble before her car accident, and it finally caught up to her."

When Lindsay finally came up with a potential strategy to get Hope a state ID card, she couldn't understand why Hope didn't jump at the chance, even if it was a long shot. Lindsay had kept pushing until Hope finally revealed that she'd always had a gut feeling that she might have been involved in something dangerous before the accident. It explained why she had always seemed distrustful of police—except, eventually, Lindsay's father. She was driving a stolen car when she was found, after all, with no wallet in her purse and only a Hefty bag filled with clothes in the trunk. For all she knew, she could be wanted—by the police or worse—and she wasn't willing to risk it.

"You think someone was looking for her all this time?"

"Some people never quit. But even if that's the case, the blood sample's still my best lead. It belongs to someone who lived in Wichita, Kansas, at some point twenty-some-odd years ago. I guess this leads me to the reason I called you in the first place: Any chance you know someone down there who can shed some light into whatever they know about that DNA?"

"Let me see what I can do."

Lindsay had no way to know that for the first time in years, Detective Ellie Hatcher was allowing herself to believe once again that maybe she didn't know the truth about her father's death after all.

14

Monday, June 21, 1:18 p.m.

Carter flipped down the sun visor of his department-issued Dodge Charger to cut the glare reflecting off the water as he turned onto Star Island Road. Carter was born and bred on the East End, but he could count on one hand the number of times he'd been to this tiny island in Lake Montauk—once for a bar mitzvah and twice for weddings. The flashing lights of two marked police cars and an ambulance in a parking lot next to the yacht club tennis courts were a stark contrast to the rest of the scenery.

Carter badged the uniformed Suffolk County Police officers who were unspooling a roll of crime scene tape across the entrance to the path to the marina and made his way to the cluster of activity on the nearest boat dock, next to a boat marked "Marine Patrol." He recognized the officer who hopped effortlessly from the police boat and began to make her way toward him. Her name was Lisa Robbins, and Carter knew for a fact that she liked him, even though she shouldn't.

"Carter, what are you doing here?" she asked. It sounded flirty, and he noticed her adjusting the navy-blue polo shirt of her uniform.

"You just had to be the smarty pants to call in the guy's name, didn't you, Lisa?" he said, holding his hand above his eyes, wishing like hell he'd grabbed his shades when he got the callout. "Couldn't just be lazy and phone it in as an unidentified floater?"

A boater preparing to launch had spotted what he feared was a body, washed up between his boat and the neighboring one. The initial dispatch went to paramedics and the Marine Patrol. Without a name, an on-duty detective from the interagency major crimes team would have gotten the callout. But Lisa Robbins had managed to get a name to match the body: Alex Lopez.

"Wait. They told me they were sending out the detective who took a missing person report on this guy a few days ago."

"Yep. Lucky me."

"No, they told me it was Decker. Wow, it dawns on me I don't even know your first name."

"Sure you do."

"Fine, you don't want to tell me. How bad can it be? My middle name's Eugenia, not that you asked. My uncle Eugene always gave me extra cash for Christmas to make it up to me."

Not that you asked. The passive-aggressiveness wasn't lost on Carter. He and Lisa Eugenia Robbins had gone out on one and a half dates last year. The second dinner was cut short, supposedly by a callout, and then Carter had never made it up to her. "My name's Carter."

"Yeah, I get it. You want to be called Carter. No first names allowed, I guess."

I guess. This was why he'd feigned the appearance of a callout with a glance at his cell phone on that second date. And he was beginning to feel like he was in the middle of a bad version of Who's on First. "Lisa, you do realize my first name—my actual first name—is Carter, don't you?"

The expression on her face told him that she did not, in fact, realize that. "So what's your last name?"

"Decker."

"No, Decker's got the hairy neck and always smells like deodorant."

"Nope. That would be Kinderwood. Anyway, I'm Carter Decker. Nice to meet you. Again. Let me guess: You thought I was the one who pulled that little girl from the path of an oncoming car on Abe's Path last summer?"

Her blank stare was confirmation.

"That'd be one Sergeant Deborah Carter." He could see Lisa's disappointment. "So, what've we got here?"

"No visible sign of distress. The ME will have to call it, obviously, but looks like a drowning. He's in swim trunks and a rash guard, and we had a couple days of twelve-foot swells last week. Those kinds of waves are no joke."

"Those kinds of waves aren't on the shores of Lake Montauk, though."

Lake Montauk wasn't even an actual lake. It used to be, back when it was called Lake Wyandanch, until a real estate developer blasted a gap on the northern slice of shore to connect the lake to the Atlantic Ocean in 1927. He dreamed of transforming the port of Montauk into the Miami Beach of the North. Instead, as Carter understood it, he went bankrupt in the Great Crash. This was the kind of shit he knew thanks to his old man, who had loved both history and the only home he knew outside of Poland, coming straight to the East End from Ellis Island to work a farm. Filip Dankowski the teenaged farmhand eventually became Philip Decker, the electrician who married a bank teller whose parents had come from Ireland. Carter was named for the man who was in the White House when he was born, not because his parents shared that President's party or policies but because they loved being citizens of the greatest country in the world.

Lisa Robbins was still talking about the water patterns. "The current could definitely carry him from the ocean to here."

Carter nodded. "How'd you get an ID so fast? The guy swam with a wallet?"

"The rash guard. The logo's from Reel Deal Fishing. I pulled it up online, and there's his picture. Sorry, but what a waste." She held up her cell phone. He recognized the photograph as the same one Lopez's girlfriend had provided when he took her missing person report. The "what a waste" comment clearly referred to the fact that Lopez had been an attractive man. Carter was confident enough to recognize objective facts. "Seems like a small operation. Not like Jack's or Hot Rods or anything, but a legit outfit. I found an *East Hampton Star* article online announcing Lopez's purchase of the business from the previous owner. How long's he been missing?"

"His sort-of girlfriend filed the report Saturday, but she hadn't talked to him since Thursday. It's not clear they spoke on the regular, though."

"Anything of note in your missing person investigation so far?" she asked.

An honest answer would have been "What investigation?" After taking the girlfriend's report, he had used up some time on the clock to swing by Lopez's business and house, but saw nothing out of the ordinary. He had also run Lopez's criminal history: a speeding ticket three months earlier for going fifty on Town Lane, which, based on what Carter knew about the officer who issued the ticket, probably had something to do with Lopez's skin color.

He also found reports of two separate anonymous phone calls to the police department, claiming that Lopez's fishing guide business was a cover for a drug-dealing operation. The first call had come in four months earlier, not long after Lopez had moved to the area. The tipster claimed that Lopez was a "known" dealer, whose apparent financial resources far exceeded any reasonable income from his one-boat tourism outfit. The information lacked the kind of specifics that police generally look for in deciding whether to pursue an investigation, and no action was taken. More intriguingly, a second anonymous call came in only four days before Lopez's girlfriend reported him missing. This time, the informant claimed to be a heroin user who had bought drugs from Lopez multiple times. Believing that Lopez had shorted her in their two most recent transactions, the user decided to "blow the whistle" on Lopez's illegal side hustle. "He gets his product from a guy he used to fish salmon with up in Alaska."

Unlike the first tipster, the second caller had provided details about the source of her information, claiming to be a direct participant in drug transactions. Her mention of Lopez's prior work and its location also suggested inside information. The tip had been passed on to the Suffolk County Police Department's drug investigation unit but, according to detectives there, not yet assigned for follow-up before Lopez's disappearance. "If you find him," the sergeant had said, "let us know, and we'll check him out."

All of this was more detail than Lisa Robbins needed. "A few whispers that he might have been involved in the drug trade," he said, "but nothing concrete."

"For what it's worth, someone posted a one-star Yelp review on Sunday, saying he stood them up for a charter reservation that day and wasn't answering his phone, so he was probably dead or missing by then."

"Look at you being all sleuthy."

"You're the investigator. I just keep the water safe—or try to, at least. This will be our third drowning this summer, and it's only June."

Carter said nothing.

"You look dubious. There's some reason you think it's not a drowning, isn't there? Something about it seems . . . fishy?"

She looked proud of herself, and Carter wondered if he'd made a mistake, cutting short that second date.

"Too soon to tell," he said. He couldn't put his finger on it, but something in the back of his mind was tugging at him. He pushed the nagging feeling away, knowing his job would be a whole lot easier if Alex Lopez was just another drowning victim.

15

Monday, June 21, 5:38 p.m.

Ellie had just stepped out of the precinct when her cell phone rang. The screen read Uncle Steve. Steve Thompson, her father's former partner.

"Hey, Steve. You get anything?" He had been the second person she called after meeting with Lindsay Kelly that morning. He had retired from the WPD years ago, accepting a job as the on-site head of security for LockeHome, the largest home improvement retailer in the United States, headquartered in little old Wichita, Kansas. Whereas most cops in Kansas retired for good, or kept a small side hustle working security at concerts and sporting events, Steve was living the dream of a full-blown double-dipper, pulling in a healthy six-figure salary on top of his pension.

"A little, but it's not too late to stay out of the rabbit hole," Steve warned. "I lived there myself a long time, but no one got sucked in worse than your dad. I was pretty worried about you, too, not all that long ago."

Like Ellie's father, Steve had been a member of the College Hill Strangler task force. Unlike her father, he had been able to move on after the case seemingly went cold and the task force was disbanded. While her father was slowly sidelined to less important cases, Steve went on to become the department's most prolific homicide detective. After her father's suicide, Steve filled the void as well as he could, acting as an honorary uncle.

"I need to know," she said. "If there's any chance at all. I fought to have those samples added to the DNA database. I didn't do all of that for nothing."

"The sample that got a hit was blood on the edge of a sofa cushion in Janice Beale's living room. I remember when your dad spotted the stain. I don't think I would've caught it. More like a little smudge—could have been makeup, food, or a dog's butt print until the labs came back. That's all I got."

"And what are they doing about it?"

"Other than getting annoyed with me for calling? And saying they-told-you-so about dumping every last bit of trace DNA evidence into the database? Jack squat. Or if they're working the case, they're not going to tell a private security guy like me."

Steve was sometimes apologetic for his fancy corporate gig, but it had been a natural transition. He'd gotten to know the Lockes personally after the family's son-in-law was shot to death in his driveway and Steve was assigned to the case. Fortunately, Steve's reputation within the department was rock solid. If they were following up on the blood match, they would tell him.

"Why am I the only one who thinks this needs an explanation?" she asked.

"Look, there's a certain risk to DNA testing being as good as it is now. You touch a doorknob, and ten years later, they can pick up the DNA. That little smudge on the sofa wasn't enough to pull DNA from at the time. It was only when they went retesting everything with new technology after Summer's arrest that they got it. And then you and your mom had them dump all that into the database as a condition to settling. And that was your right, granted, and you were looking out for Jerry—"

"But now you can understand why the cops there are saying 'I told you so.'"

"People move around, Ellie, especially from Wichita, as you and Jess certainly know. Sometimes it feels like the highways here only run one way. Your DNA was probably all over other people's houses when you were kids, and now it's all over New York City—especially your brother's, if I had to guess."

She found herself smiling. She only talked to Steve a few times a year, plus the occasional quick text message, but he sent them overly generous Christmas checks when he got a good bonus at work, and sometimes he'd even tack on a side trip to New York when he visited his brother in Boston. Like the best kinds of aunts and uncles, Steve was often more willing to see and to accept imperfections in Jess and Ellie than were their own parents. When Jess got caught smoking pot in the alley behind the high school, Steve vouched for him to the school resource officer, saving him from a drug bust. He gave Jess the required lecture, but never told their mother about it.

"Speaking of which . . ." She'd turned the corner to spot a familiar silhouette leaning against the brick exterior of Plug Uglies. From the ground up: black ankle boots, black jeans, black Clash T-shirt, cigarette in mouth. Jess, her first call after seeing Lindsay today. "I'm about to meet him."

"Tell him I said rock on."

"I will, and I'll keep you posted if I find anything new."

"And vice versa. Your dad would be damn proud of you, Ellie. Both of you."

JESS GREETED HER WITH A nod and a smoke-filled exhale.

"What happened to the Nicorette?" she asked. Her big brother had started smoking—to her knowledge, at least—when he was fourteen. A quarter century or so later, he was still at it.

"That you decided to buy for me, even though I would have preferred a pack of Camels? Gave them to Darla."

"And who pray tell is Darla?"

"Behind the bar at work, Tuesday and Thursday nights. Her father's finally trying to quit. She was very appreciative, by the way. Wants me to tell you you're a good person."

Jess's profession by choice was the lead of a band called Dog Park. His profession according to his W-2s varied wildly, but his current job as a bouncer at a "gentlemen's club" on the West Side Highway had established his longest employment streak since he tore ticket stubs at the Wichita Mall movie theater in high school. Jess had been the one to make the sudden move to New York City fifteen years before. Ellie might have spent the rest of her life in Kansas if it weren't for her brother—or at least their mother's certainty that his rebellious ways would catch up to him in a big, tempting city without a bunch of cops looking out for the boy they'd known since he was in diapers. Two years later, with Steve's encouragement, Ellie made the move too, realizing that the best way to help her mother was to leave town and keep an eye on her brother.

She made a point of waving away the smoke wafting in her direction, but simultaneously allowed herself a deep breath. Damn, she still missed it. Jess ground out the butt against the bottom of his boot and dropped it in the garbage can at the curb as she pulled open the door to Plug Uglies.

Leo, the bar manager, flashed a broad smile as he wiped down the counter. "My favorite siblings."

A customer Ellie didn't recognize complained that the title belonged to him and his brother, Jack.

"Take a look at these two, Benny. Two freaking beautiful specimens. Sorry, but no contest."

Jess ordered a beer Ellie had never heard of. Leo held up a bottle of Johnnie Walker Black to confirm Ellie's order, and then poured her two fingers over two ice cubes.

In theory, a known cop hangout would be the last establishment where Jess might want to be a regular, but it was around the corner from Ellie's precinct. And since Jess had taken over the lease on Ellie's old apartment, it was now only a ten-minute walk from his place. And with $4 happy hour drinks, it was one of the few spots where Jess could occasionally pick up a tab. But like all of New York City, even an old Irish-style tavern had changed over time. Leo still winced whenever a customer ordered a frosé from the giant blender he referred to disdainfully as the Pink Slushee Machine.

She took a first sip of her drink.

"I expected you to down the whole thing in one gulp," Jess said.

"Trust me, I want to."

"You went poking around, didn't you?" She held his gaze, confirming his suspicion. He shook his head. "Els, the case is solved. William Summer's the serial-killing creepazoid. And our dad, as much as we didn't want to believe it, went bonkers and called it quits. That's it. End of story."

Jess had always been more willing to accept that their dad did the selfish thing and took his own life. Maybe because he was older, he had been more aware of their father's emotional absence even when he was alive. Where Ellie felt protective of her father's memory, Jess didn't mask his resentment.

Four years earlier, they'd received the news that the Wichita police had finally arrested a suspect. Ellie had been so certain that the breakthrough in the case would finally answer her family's questions about her father's death. But by the time William Summer pleaded guilty, two things were certain.

One: William Summer was definitely the College Hill Strangler. Over the course of nearly two hours, he had chronicled each murder on the record in the courtroom, reciting from memory the horrific and previously undisclosed details that only the killer could possibly know. The proceedings were both gruesome and televised, but the prosecutors justified both decisions, saying it was important the local community be convinced that they had finally caught the man who had terrorized an entire generation of Wichitans.

And two: the College Hill Strangler had a rock-solid alibi for the night Wichita Police Department detective Jerry Hatcher died. At the moment Ellie's father was killed by a single gunshot from his service weapon, William Summer was in Olathe, Kansas, 175 miles away, serving as the best man at his sister's wedding.

Jess, halfway done with his beer, signaled Leo for another. "You were a mess when you went back to Wichita," he said, referring to Ellie's decision to drop everything and fly home after Summer's arrest to pore over whatever evidence she could get her hands on. "You told me it was like burying Dad all over again. You really want to relive that a third time?"

"Look, I know I told you that I was finally on board. I made myself accept the fact that Dad . . . well, Dad made that final decision. But maybe Summer didn't act alone, which changes everything. If Dad figured it out, the second killer could be the one who shot him. The accomplice could have remained active this entire time." She waited as Leo switched out the beer pints before continuing. "This woman missing from East Hampton might be his latest victim."

"I lost count, but that was, like, five different ifs and maybes you blew through there. I'm afraid to ask, but just how much poking did you do today?"

"Don't worry. I didn't call Mom." When it came to dealing with the past, their mother was fragile on a good day.

"But you did call . . ."

"Steve."

"Of course. And what did Steve tell you?"

"That the blood came from Janice Beale's house, which I already knew from that lawyer, Lindsay."

In some ways, Beale's death had haunted her father even more than the others. By that time, it had been six years since the first set of murders. If they had made an arrest by then, or at least warned the public that a series of unsolved murders were believed to be connected, maybe Janice Beale would have lived. On the days when Ellie was willing to accept the idea of her father pulling his own trigger, she imagined that he was thinking not about her or Jess or their mother, but about Janice Beale.

Jess nodded. As much as he tried to distance himself from her obsession with the case, she could tell he recognized the name.

"Any chance I can talk you out of getting any more involved with this Lindsay person? I'm worried you're going back to the dark place again."

"Rogan told me the same thing."

"And what does Max say?" he asked.

Max. Her first call had been to Jess. The second to Steve. She had exchanged a few rounds of texts with Max about what they were going to do for dinner, and to see if he knew Lindsay Kelly, but she hadn't told him why she had asked.

"He was in trial all day."

She couldn't tell if he believed her, and then his phone buzzed against the bar. He glanced at the screen and held it up. "Add another vote for letting this drop." It was a text from Steve. I'm worried about your sister. Look after our best girl, OK? Here for you guys.

"There's one more thing I haven't told you," she said.

"Okay . . ."

She downed the rest of her whisky. "Lindsay's friend Hope went missing two Saturdays ago. The last text she sent anyone was at ten thirty-three p.m."

"And? What am I missing?" Clearly the announcement was a letdown.

"That was when I was in St. Barts."

"So damn bougie," he said, shaking his head in mock judgment. "Plus you went off-season, which is just kind of sad."

"There's some truth there, but focus. That was the night I texted you—when I woke up thinking about Dad, about when we went to the hospital."

She waited for him to make the connection. She wasn't going to say it out loud.

"Jesus, Ellie. You sound like Mom or something. That's crazy."

"I know. But seriously, I hadn't had a nightmare like that in . . . probably at least a year."

"So, you think . . . what? Dad was sending you a message? If he could do that, why doesn't he just pick up the phone and tell us what happened that night? Or what? It was this woman Hope, reaching out to you from the beyond? Waking you up so you'd somehow figure out that her disappearance had something to do with Dad?"

"Come on, Jess. You're being really harsh right now."

"That's rich, Ellie. How many times have you torn me a new one when I was being a dumb-ass?"

"Great. First I'm crazy. Now I'm stupid."

He took a deep breath, which was usually more her style than his. "What I think is that you're grasping at straws to search for some kind of sign from the universe that justifies jumping right back into that spiral you were lost in. Not because it's logical. Or rational. Or smart. But because it's exactly what you want to do, regardless of what anyone tells you."

16

Monday, June 21, 7:20 p.m.

L indsay felt sets of eyes on her as she tucked another flyer onto yet another car windshield in the Atlantic Beach parking lot. She gave a friendly wave to the wary family walking past, beach chairs beneath their arms, towing umbrellas and a cooler.

"Don't mind me," she said. "Just an informational bulletin."

Once they were out of earshot, she muttered her true feelings beneath her breath. *Nothing to see here. Just a human being who might be kidnapped or murdered. But have a great time at the beach.*

Scott pulled her into a quick hug and kissed the top of her head. "We're pretty much done with all the copies we printed at Staples. That was our goal for the day."

They had also finally found a neighbor on Hope's street who had a cell phone number for the cottage owner, who promised to call her handyman so Lindsay could finally get inside.

"But the sun's still up. We might have time to go back and run more."

"I'm worried about you, babe. It's hot out, and you haven't eaten anything all day, or had any water. You're running on empty."

"Let me just finish the cars in the overflow lot for now."

Lindsay had a sudden flashback to the day she was helping Hope move. "I know this feels drastic," Hope had said, "but once I'm gone, it will be as if I were never here. Not that I know from experience, but I was reading about change as a source of stress. Whether change is positive or negative—a marriage or a divorce, the birth of a child or a death in the family—all change is a form of trauma. But it's only a stressor until it no longer feels like change. Until it's no longer a difference from the status quo. Once the change is over, it's just a new normal."

Had Hope been trying to tell her something? Was she already planning to disappear? She shook the possibility from her mind, knowing that other people's doubts were slowly affecting her judgment. Lindsay didn't want Hope's absence to be the new normal. Scott may have had a point about her current state. She was exhausted and running out of . . . well, hope.

"You okay?" Scott asked. "You spaced out for a couple of seconds there."

"No, I'm good. You're right. Let's get something to eat." She reached into her purse and handed him her keys. They had taken her car from the city, but she was always happy to let someone else drive.

They were almost to the Audi when a black Dodge Charger pulled into the parking lot, slowing as it approached them. The driver's tinted window rolled down, and she recognized Carter Decker.

"Someone called in a complaint about leaflets littering the beach."

"You've got to be kidding me. Fine. Write me a ticket then."

"Hey, it's nothing like that, okay? The only reason I even heard about the complaint was it's yet another 'summer people are fucking assholes' stories making the rounds in the department. When I heard it was a missing person flyer for Hope, I figured I'd find you here. Email me the PDF, and I'll have some of our high school volunteers post some more of them around town tonight, okay?"

Next to her, Scott held out his hand toward the open car window. "Hi. Scott Parker."

"Oh sorry," Lindsay said. "This is Detective Decker. I've mentioned him to you."

Decker gave Scott's hand a quick shake. "I can only imagine."

"Why are you suddenly helping me?" Lindsay asked.

He tapped the steering wheel a few times before answering. "Look, I'm sorry we got off on the wrong foot. Hope's case may not meet the markers for the response you're looking for from the police department, but we also serve a community caretaking function, and you're still looking for your friend. I'm not your enemy here."

"Did you even bother to look into the College Hill Strangler case?"

Lindsay could see that Scott was thinking of intervening, but she gave him a look that made him stand down.

"Not that I'd normally share this information," Decker said, "but yes, I've been in contact with the Wichita Police Department, our own major crimes team, and the FBI. As I explained to your father, there's no reason to believe that particular case is connected."

"So you just let women disappear under your jurisdiction and don't give a rip?"

"I never said that. But maybe it's possible you're paying too much attention to a random DNA sample."

She shook her head. "And maybe you're not paying enough attention . . . to anything."

"Well, you've got my email for those flyers if you want to use it."

As he drove away, Scott finally spoke. "So that's Decker."

"I told you he was an ass. He's already made up his mind about Hope. I don't trust him. And what was that 'Hi, Scott Parker' thing?"

"You didn't tell me that he's hot for you."

"You have to be kidding me."

"Lindsay, come on. That guy was totally flirting with you."

"He's cocky and arrogant. I think what you see as flirting is his default position. That's not why you came out here today, is it? To scope out the competition?"

"Oh my god, of course not. I came because I know I've upset you by not being more worried about Hope, and I wanted to make it right."

"I mean, not everyone is capable of cheating." She regretted the words the second she heard them leave her mouth.

"Wow. Okay, so you *are* mad at me."

The first time Lindsay asked why his marriage didn't work out, Scott had said all the right things. That he had fallen in love with someone else. That it didn't justify crossing that line while he was still married. That he had ended up hurting two women he cared about and breaking up his daughter's family. That he would never forgive himself and wished he could go back in time and change it all. And that it was a mistake he would never, ever make again. Lindsay could not have asked for more honesty.

But here's the thing: sometimes she wished she didn't know. It changed how she saw him. If he could fall in love with someone else while he had a wife and a baby, who was to say he wouldn't do the same to her? What had he been missing in his marriage that allowed him to accept his attractive coworker's invitation for a nightcap at the hotel bar in the first place? It made her wonder if at some level, Scott would always need more love, more assurances, more adoration, more whatever-it-was-that-certain-men-needed, than she could ever possibly give him. Was that the reason he always joked that she'd never love him the way she loved Hope? Or why he insisted that some cop was flirting with her? How long before whatever justification he had used to rationalize his betrayal of his ex-wife might be wielded against her as well?

"I'm sorry. I'm . . . frustrated. I didn't ask you to come out here with me, and I can't forget that until now you've been sounding pretty convinced that Hope just up and left because she wanted to get away from me. Honestly, I think part of you is actually happy that she's gone.

I'm killing myself trying to find her, and you've made these passive-aggressive comments like we never give each other space."

"It's not passive-aggressive. It's just . . . *true*." He opened his mouth to say even more, but caught himself and pressed his lips together instead.

"What?"

He shook his head as if he were already regretting his next words. "Let's just say that I'm not the only person who thinks you and Hope are sort of codependent."

"That's such a gaslighting thing to say, Scott. 'I hear people saying. . . . Everybody tells me. . . .' Who, Scott? Who thinks Hope and I are so screwed up?"

"Your father."

She scoffed. "My father *loves* Hope."

"No. He loves *you*. And he knows I love you too. It was on your birthday, when we were handling cleanup in the kitchen after dinner. He told me that for fifteen years, he had watched you treat that woman like you can't even breathe without her. He thought maybe it had something to do with losing your mom at such a young age."

"Oh Jesus."

"Come on, Lindsay, you have to admit there's something weird about your friendship. She literally doesn't have anyone in her life except you."

"Of course she does. Miriam. Rebecca. The Becketts."

"Her boss. Her therapist. Her landlords. In fifteen years, she couldn't make another friend? Or date someone for more than a few months? And I've got to be honest, I think you like it that way. She needs you so much that you can be a hundred percent confident that she will never leave you."

"Like my mom did? Is that what you're saying, Sigmund Freud?"

"Yeah, I guess I am. Sometimes I think I never should have told you about how I screwed up my marriage. I'm just a little too messy for you, but not Hope. You never have to wonder if she'll betray you. You don't have the tiniest sliver of doubt? Even before she went silent, you said she wasn't texting or calling you as much as normal. You can't open your mind to the slightest possibility that she wanted to go on with her life without you in it?"

"Because she wouldn't."

"Look, we're both exhausted, okay? I'm on your side here."

"There are no *sides*, Scott. I'm telling you that I'm right about this. Something is seriously wrong."

He nodded. "Okay. You know your friend."

"Yes. I do."

"But . . . that cop was totally flirting with you."

She found herself smiling. "Well, whether he was or not, I have no interest in that man."

"Yes, I think you made that pretty clear." That grin. It melted her every time. "So what do you want to do? About his offer with the flyers." Apparently they were moving on.

"I'll send him the file. But that guy gets under my skin."

"I also think you're hangry," he said, hitting the unlock button on the key fob. "Let's get some food in you."

"AH, I LIKE THE LOOK of a satisfied customer." Rowdy Hall was packed, but they got lucky and scored two seats at the bar. The bartender was a large, bald man with thick black glasses. The gray soul patch beneath his lower lip somehow suited his friendly face.

The margarita she ordered was perfect. She'd had at least a drink a day since Hope went missing, but it helped calm her nerves.

"The designated driver is officially jealous," Scott said, using his finger to taste the salted rim.

She didn't realize how hungry she was until she opened the menu. Scott ordered the burger, while she went with the Croque Madame, described as a grilled ham and cheese with a fried egg on top and a salad on the side.

The bartender was telling her she was going to be very happy with her selection when her phone buzzed with a new message. Carter Decker. Got the flyers. She held it up for Scott to see before dropping it into her purse. "He probably wants me to thank him. Again. For offering to do the laziest version of his actual job." At Scott's urging, she had sent him a polite email with the file, moderating her tone and expressing her "sincere gratitude" for his help.

"Look, I know I only met the guy for half a second, and you've had more of a chance to form an impression than I have . . ."

"But?"

"I can at least understand why he's not totally convinced there's some accomplice serial killer out there who's gone undetected for twenty years and counting."

When Lindsay learned of the DNA match to the College Hill Strangler case, of course she assumed there was a connection. And when she read in an old newspaper article that the woman who was killed was a volunteer at a nearby summer camp, she had even imagined a teenage camp counselor who might have been the one to choose Janice Beale as the duo's next target. "It does sound a little crazy," she conceded. It was just as likely that the blood belonged to some kid who ran to Beale's house when he cut himself on the playground. "If I had to guess, when Decker heard about the cash advance from Evan, his mind was made up."

"Well, what if you could find a way to make her past actually work in her favor?" Scott suggested. She knew he was trying to make up for the things he had said about Hope earlier. "If you could offer the police a theory where Hope's background makes it more likely she's in danger, rather than a runaway, maybe they'd be more willing to take it seriously. You always thought Hope's memory loss was from some kind of trauma."

Because the earliest anyone could account for Hope's existence was the moment of her car crash, the obvious explanation for her memory loss was the physical impact of the accident. But Lindsay had learned that psychological trauma or post-traumatic stress disorder could also induce dissociative fugue, or what used to be called a fugue state—a psychological condition characterized by an inability to recall one's identity or personality. Usually these were relatively short-lived black-outs, but there were reported cases that lasted decades.

If Hope had suffered an extraordinary trauma before her car accident, it might explain not only her absence of recall but also her reasons for being in New Jersey, driving a stolen car from Indianapolis. It could even be the cause of the car accident itself, if she had blacked out behind the wheel. Hope had undergone hypnotherapy in an effort to draw out any buried memories, but, like everything else, it had yielded no further clues to her identity. Scott, of course, knew all of this.

"Did I ever tell you about going to the shooting range with Dad last year?" Lindsay asked.

"Maybe. I assume you go to the range with your father, like, every time you visit."

After Lindsay left behind roommate living and got her own apartment in the city, her father had pleaded with her to get a gun and a permit. She finally relented, which meant learning how to shoot, something she had resisted until then. The truth was that she kept the gun in a locked safe and didn't even own any ammunition, but now she and her father finally had a second joint activity to add to jigsaw puzzles when she visited Hopewell.

"But I'm talking about the time we took Hope with us. It was last Christmas, after you went back to the city. Hope tagged along to the range, and Dad talked her into trying it out. He walked her through all the basics. Well, you know his usual spiel." Her father had dragged Scott to the range the first weekend she brought him home to Hopewell.

"'Never point your gun at anything you don't intend to shoot,'" Scott recited from memory. It was one of many safety tips that her father reviewed before letting anyone handle a gun for the first time. He also had a simple process for explaining the mechanics of firing a weapon. He boasted that every one of his pupils managed to hit within the circle of their paper target the very first time.

Until Hope.

"I could tell Hope was nervous, so I assured her she didn't need to try it if she didn't want to. But she said she was fine and assumed her isosceles stance, just as Dad showed her. And then she pulled the trigger. He had given her a nine-millimeter, because she has those super tiny baby hands, plus that weird wrist thing." Hope had recovered from the physical injuries sustained in the accident, with the exception of what was called partial radial nerve palsy in her left hand. She had regained most of the hand's function over the years, but still had problems with her wrist strength. "Dad had warned her about the recoil, but it obviously caught her off guard. Dad felt awful, saying he should have started her off with a .22 to be safe. Even the mild kickback was so bad that she wasn't remotely close to the paper target. But it was more than that. She was seriously rattled. I hadn't seen her like that since the early days right after the car accident. She was physically trembling. I rushed her out of there as if we were under fire."

"You think it triggered something in her? So to speak," he added.

She knew she should probably take a break from talking about Hope, but she was on a roll. "I pressed her on it, wondering if her subconscious was reacting to the sound of the gun, but she insisted it didn't feel like a lost memory. She said she was just upset that her left hand had let her down so badly. She's learned so well to compensate for it, she didn't even realize how weak it was. But now I'm replaying it all in my head. Maybe she pushed the idea away, not wanting to remember. She could have witnessed a shooting, or maybe someone threatened her with a gun, or even took a shot at her? They might have finally found her. The odds of anyone running into her in Hopewell were pretty low, but then she left the bubble. The move here could have been the thing to put her back on someone's radar."

Lindsay felt like she was on the right track, but something still felt wrong. Then she saw it. "The cause and effect could be the other way around. Maybe something scared her *away* from Hopewell. If someone turned up in Hopewell looking for her, maybe her gut told her to run. She asked Evan to tell her if anyone ever came around with questions about her."

"But wouldn't she tell you? She'd be safer in Hopewell where people know her. And your dad's the former police chief."

"Unless she panicked. As much as she has tried to get her old memories back, I know there's a part of her that's always been afraid to find out what she might have been running from."

The bartender reappeared carrying two giant oval diner-style plates loaded with food. Hers was especially mountainous. "That's crazy," she said.

"It's a doozie. Occasionally someone will put down the whole thing, but it's enough to feed three normal people."

"The bottomless sandwich," Lindsay muttered. When Hope told her that she was close to achieving "regular" status at one of the restaurant bars, she referred to a gigantic sandwich that she could buy and eat for another two meals.

"Yep. I've heard someone else call it that exactly."

Lindsay fumbled in her purse for her phone and pulled up a picture of Hope. "Was it this woman, by any chance?"

"Yeah, that's Hope. You know her? I'm Joe, by the way."

"Lindsay. And Scott. Hope's my best friend. No one's heard from her for more than a week."

Joe looked up at the ceiling before responding. "I saw her maybe two weeks ago. Definitely not last week. Come to think of it, that's unusual for her. She's usually here once or twice a week."

"She was new in town, and I can't get the police to give two shits about it."

Joe sighed. "This is a place where people come and go like a turnstile, especially in the summer. But you know what?" he said, the breeziness leaving his tone, "she asked me to walk her to her car, now that I think about it. Usually she was an early bird, so this was a late dinner for her. It was quiet and she was doing a crossword puzzle, chilling out. I think she lost track of time because she was surprised when I told her I was ready to lock up. When I was walking her out, she said she thought someone had been following her. I wanted her to call the police, but she insisted it wasn't necessary. She made it sound like it was probably her imagination, and she didn't want to make a big deal out of it. I know my wife does that all the time. If the dogs bark when she's home alone at night, she's convinced someone must be breaking in, but not convinced enough to call nine-one-one. But, man—I really hope there wasn't more to it."

"Did she say who it was? Or when? Or how often?"

Joe shook his head. "No, that was the last time I saw her."

Joe's report lined up with Evan's. But for some reason, Hope hadn't mentioned any of this to Lindsay. She suddenly wasn't interested in her sandwich.

Scott placed a palm on her knee. "You okay?"

"Just really confused."

Her phone buzzed in her hand. Please stop looking for me. You're putting me in danger.

The text was from an email address made up of seemingly random numbers and letters.

She typed a reply as fast as she could. Where are you? How do I know this is you?

We left the armoire.

Her fingers began to tremble. She forced herself to focus on typing the letters accurately and quickly. Where are you?

No reply. Lindsay clicked out of her text messages and into email, trying to use that format instead. She immediately received an auto-mated reply. Your message wasn't delivered because the address could not be found or is unable to receive mail.

Just like that, Hope was gone again.

17

Monday, June 21, 7:30 p.m.

When Ellie walked into her apartment, Max had CNN muted on the television, Smashing Pumpkins streaming on the speakers, and the apartment already smelling like really good tomato sauce. In their texts about dinner, they had decided to stay in and make spaghetti pomodoro. It was fast, cheap, and delicious, and had butter as the final ingredient, making it a perfect at-home meal, as far as Ellie was concerned.

Max gestured to the TV screen. "Hey, did you see that Kansas might get itself a new senator? Any chance she'll take Uncle Steve with her?"

She had gotten the *New York Times* alert on her phone before she jumped on the subway. The CEO of LockeHome, where Steve was the head of security, was running for the Senate as an independent. Speculation was that it might be an initial step toward an eventual presidential campaign.

"Zilch. Steve would rather live at the bottom of the ocean than in Washington, DC."

She pinched away a tiny pop of sauce that had made its way from the pan into Max's dark wavy hair. "You started without me?" Another reason Ellie liked the recipe was that it was one of the only things she could actually cook by herself without thinking Max would have made it taste a lot better.

"Figured I was here, might as well. Sauce is done except for your favorite part." He knew she doubled the butter when he wasn't looking. He gestured to a half-consumed Manhattan on the countertop and asked if she wanted one.

"Better go straight to wine."

"I take it you and Jess had fun, then?"

Fun. She wouldn't call it that.

She had spent most of her life wondering if she was destined to turn out exactly like her father—distracted, distant, consumed by thoughts that could not be shared with others. It wasn't until William Summer was behind bars that she had allowed herself to be open to the idea of a life in the light with the happy, normal people. Now she was living with a man she loved, and still hadn't told him about the bombshell that had been dropped on her day. Through no fault of Max's own, some part of her was still afraid to let him see the darkness that still resided within her.

She was about to fill him in when Max beat her to it. "Oh, you asked about Lindsay Kelly this morning. What was that about? Did Bunning hire her?"

She liked the way Max could recite the name of her most recent arrestee as if it were one of his own cases.

"No, actually, it's not about any case I'm working." Not any current case, at least. "It was about my dad and William Summer."

He stirred the sauce, but said nothing, waiting for her to explain. It didn't take her long. She realized how little she actually knew. A missing woman with a mysterious background. A DNA match. And from that, both she and Lindsay Kelly had contemplated an apprentice serial killer, staging a detective's suicide twenty years earlier so he could continue his murderous spree for years to come.

Unlike Steve and Jess, Max allowed her to speak without interrupting her to argue. It all sounded different now. She began to form her own dissenting opinion.

"Summer was adamant that he acted alone," she said, thinking aloud.

"But isn't that consistent with his psychological profile? You said that once he knew he was caught, it became a point of pride with him. He was eager to take credit for his work."

"Yes, but he also loved to play cat-and-mouse games with the police. If there had been a second person to offer, he would have dangled the idea in front of the investigators like a piece of raw meat. He would have dragged it out endlessly, making them beg for a name. You're a prosecutor. Wouldn't the DA's office have been willing to make a deal with him to give up the second person, if there had been one to offer?"

When they first met, Max was on the go-to list of ADAs entrusted with homicide trials at the Manhattan District Attorney's Office. When they moved in together, he had voluntarily transferred to the white-collar unit to avoid any conflicts with Ellie's police work.

"I assume. Could give the possibility of parole at least. But he never once even mentioned the possibility?"

She shook her head. Ellie had used her mother's lawsuit against the city as leverage to get access to the case evidence. She remembered the pride in Summer's voice as he took credit, on tape, for each and every one of the murders. He not only denied involvement by anyone else but seemed almost offended by the suggestion.

And for the first time, she saw the largest hole in what had felt like a plausible theory just two hours earlier. "And this DNA profile was only at one of Summer's crime scenes, and it was definitely from blood," she said. "Summer left semen behind at almost every scene."

She knew she didn't need to spell out the rest of the argument to Max. If the blood sample belonged to William Summer's imagined co-conspirator, it meant that the accomplice had somehow left behind DNA evidence at only one victim's house, and only with one small spot of blood, even though Summer himself had been unconcerned about leaving behind his own bodily fluids.

Ellie realized that she had developed a classic case of tunnel vision. When she first heard from Lindsay Kelly, they had reinforced each other's suspicions, allowing them both to see what they had wanted to see. When Steve and Jess tried to expose the holes in the theory, she had dug in her heels, pushing herself further into the tunnel.

If only her first phone call had been to Max, who had never attempted to steer her in either direction. She said as much to Max.

"We had a training last year at the office," he said. "A Hofstra law professor came in to talk about how mental shortcuts can lead to wrongful convictions. Anyway, she said one way to prevent tunnel vision is to force yourself to do the opposite. You heard about a DNA hit from the College Hill Strangler samples in the database and naturally assumed there was a connection. But think of all the other explanations for a blood sample from that house turning up now in East Hampton."

She pulled up what she could recall about Janice Beale while Max filled a large pot with water and turned on a burner. "She was single and lived alone. She had broken up with her boyfriend a few months before she was killed. It's certainly possible he cut himself at some point." In his confession, Summer described to the police how he had first spotted her buying toothpaste at Target and had selected her as a potential new "subject." When he followed her home and saw that her house was adjacent to Edgemoor Park, he thought it was a sign that she was a perfect target. He could watch her from the park for hours, planning his attack. But then a man had arrived. She kissed him. A boyfriend. He shifted his focus, searching for another subject, but still continued his strolls through the park. After three months without a single sighting of a male visitor to Janice's house, Summer decided that he was finally ready to make his move. He had joked that his only fear was that an overly protective parent might call the cops on the middle-aged man who kept showing up at the summer camp to stare across the park.

Then she saw it.

"The rec center," Ellie said. "The backyard of Janice Beale's house essentially ran directly into Edgemoor Park, which has a big rec center on the opposite side of the park. She used to bring juice and snacks out to the kids if they were playing ball on that edge of the field. If they needed to go to the bathroom, they'd run into her house instead of schlepping all the way back to the building. The police ran a kids' sports program out of the park, so the cops took her death especially hard."

"So did your father actually know her?"

She shook her head. "No. He and his partner both used to volunteer there, but by the time Janice Beale moved to the neighborhood, Dad was so obsessed with the investigation that he barely had the energy to pay attention to Jess and me, let alone a bunch of other kids." Ellie had a vague memory of talking to her father about the camp a few weeks before he died. A girl at school was gossiping on the playground that her older sister got a "pervert" vibe from one of the volunteers, and Ellie had passed the story on to her father. In retrospect, she realized it was simply a rumor, but having something potentially police-related to report to her distracted father had been Ellie's way of trying to get his attention. She shook away the memory. "Anyway, Janice Beale was like a de facto den mother to all the camp kids, which means she had rug rats running in and out of that house on a regular basis."

"So if a kid cut his leg or something . . ."

He let her finish the thought. "Her house would have been the natural place to run to. And the kid with the skinned knee might be a carpenter in East Hampton now and cut himself again in someone else's house."

"Or he could be a bad guy who had some kind of altercation with that missing woman—"

"Hope Miller," she reminded him.

"Right."

"But either way, it doesn't have anything to do with William Summer," she concluded. *Or my father.*

She started to reach for her cell phone to call Lindsay Kelly, but decided it could wait until morning. Maybe by then, Lindsay Kelly would have moved on to another theory about her missing friend. Better yet, maybe Hope Miller would already be home, safe and with a simple explanation.

18

Monday, June 21, 8:20 p.m.

Carter was swiping much more left than right on Tinder, the Mets game playing out on his muted television, when his cell rang. He didn't recognize the number.

"Decker."

"Carter, it's Harvey from Truth Training." The Irish lilt on the other end of the line belonged to Harvey O'Brien.

"Hey man. I'm overdue for a session, I know."

"Tell me about it. Your belly must be jelly by now. I'm calling about that fishing guide who drowned this morning. Chris told me about it this afternoon. He said you were involved somehow. Does that mean it wasn't a drowning?"

The Chris in question was a reputable journalist who was also part of the gym crowd. He was a national cable anchor, but always seemed to know every local development as well. An "anonymous police source" had confirmed that a body was pulled from the water near Star Island in a suspected drowning, but the department had not yet released the man's name or the fact that he was a fishing guide.

"Nah. I took the initial report when he went missing. Must have taken a couple days for his body to wash up."

"But it's an accidental drowning? Nothing . . . fishy?"

"Harvey, would you believe you're the very first person to have used that pun today?"

"Not at all. I was asking because one of my clients owns a dive shop out in Montauk. This is crazy, but he found a twenty-four-kilo kettlebell at the bottom of Fort Pond Bay yesterday. He assumed someone was goofing off on their boat and lost their grip. Anyway, he managed to get it out of the water and dropped it off at the gym today, thinking we could always use an extra bell. But then I hear a dude's body floated to shore, so I want to make sure I don't have some kind of murder weapon sitting on my gym floor right now."

"I doubt it. Bodies sunk with fifty-pound weights tend to stay missing."

"Maybe the tie came loose or something. All I know is I'm not touching that bell now. Gives me the heebie-jeebies."

"Yeah, okay, set it aside. I'll pick it up from you tomorrow, just in case."

Carter had returned to his profile-scrolling when he found himself thinking about Alex Lopez again. Damn it. The nagging feeling Carter had about Alex Lopez as he left Star Island had long passed, but now Harvey's phone call had him wondering again. He closed the dating app and pulled up the number for the Suffolk County Medical Examiner's Office. He was soon connected to Dr. Loretta Mason, the deputy chief.

"Hi, Doc. I know you said the autopsy on Alex Lopez would probably be tomorrow, but I was calling to see if anything was out of the ordinary so far."

"Well, first of all, thank you for not saying 'something fishy.' But perfect timing, because I was actually about to call you. This definitely wasn't an accidental drowning."

"I got a call about a weight found in Fort Pond Bay. Maybe—"

"It's a GSW."

"What? I saw the body." Granted, Carter had been phoning it in lately, but he'd notice a freaking gunshot wound. Or would he? How much attention had he really paid? Even though something about the case had bothered him that morning, he'd done nothing to follow up on his instincts. Instead, he had passed on a flyer from Lindsay Kelly to a few high school students and tried to tell himself he'd done his job for the day.

"Don't blame yourself. He's got very thick hair, and it was plastered to his scalp with water. It's one shot at the base of his skull. Twenty-two caliber. Didn't go through and through, so no damage to his face or the rest of his skull. It wasn't until I really started examining him closely that I saw it. He's got two small gashes above his left temple as well, but they were also covered by his hair."

"Do you have a sense of when he was killed?"

"The water makes it tricky. Submersion slows decomposition, and that varies with temperature, and as you know, our water temperatures vary greatly depending on location and depth. My guess is he was in the water about a week, but there's a big margin for error."

Carter turned up the volume on the baseball game after the call, but his mind remained elsewhere. He should have listened to his gut that morning, but he'd convinced himself that the odds of a murder in the Hamptons were far lower than the odds of a drowning.

Why? he thought. Why had the case bothered him as he was leaving Star Island? The reason he was the detective assigned to the callout: he had been the one to take a missing person report from Lopez's girlfriend. He had a sudden image of Lindsay Kelly standing in front of his house three mornings before. He'd told her why he had to leave.

Are you actually going to look for that poor person? she had asked. *Unlike you did with Hope?* She saw through his superficial charm and had no reluctance to call him out. It was why he had driven to the beach today to help out with her missing person flyers. He used to be a good cop—the one who believed his father when he said a man who lies is a man who has no bottom. But then Carter saw three fellow cops "teach a lesson" to a suspect who "made us chase him," and had committed the cultural crime of telling the truth during the investigation that ensued.

The knuckleheads who had abused the power of their badges paid not a single penalty thanks to the police union that defended them, but it quickly became clear that Carter had reached the end of the road when it came to the department.

Two missing person reports in a week, and he'd blown off both of them. Was it possible?

He scrolled through his email trash until he found what he was looking for, jotted down a number, and then made another call to Dr. Mason. "Hey, Doc, this is weird, but I submitted a DNA sample for databank hits on June sixteenth." He recited the sample number from the blood collected from the Stansfields' foyer. "Can you compare that profile against Alex Lopez?"

"Easy-peasy, but what's the connection?"

One missing woman and one murdered man, where the local paper's usual crime blotter fare might be a DUI or a house alarm set off by possums. "Probably nothing."

"Can't be nothing, or you wouldn't be asking. I'll run it now. Usually takes a couple hours."

That night, the Applied Biosystems RapidHIT ID System was especially rapid. Mason called Carter precisely ninety-two minutes later. The blood he had located at Hope Miller's last known location belonged to Alex Lopez. One missing woman, one murdered man, now connected.

He found himself wanting to call Lindsay Kelly. He wanted to prove to her that he was doing the job, that he wasn't the complete sack of shit she assumed him to be. The blood from the Stansfield home did indeed suggest that something terribly wrong had occurred after her friend staged that open house. But criminal defense lawyer Lindsay Kelly was now the last person with whom he'd be sharing information regarding either Alex Lopez or Hope Miller. If he owed an apology to anyone, it was Jocelyn Hodge, who had reported her boyfriend missing.

One murdered man. One missing murder suspect with a two-week head start.

19

Tuesday, June 22, 10:22 a.m.

Jocelyn Hodge pressed the two ziplock ice bags against her eyes. Oof. Bitter, burning cold. She tried a washcloth as a buffer, but lost the chilling effect altogether.

She took another quick look in the bathroom mirror. She looked rough. Her face was bee-stung. Not like glamorous, sexy swollen lips. Her entire face, like the elephant man. She could not take appointments looking like this, especially in the summer. Seasonal clients expected her to look Insta-ready, or how could she possibly do the same for them? Her Yelp rating would be toast if she reported to work looking like ass.

She pulled two tissues from the box on the vanity and placed them between her eyes and the ice packs. Almost there. Then she added a tiny bit of water to the ziplocks and . . . bliss.

What do they say about the mind-body connection? It's the link between a person's thoughts and emotions, on the one hand, and their behaviors and physical condition, on the other. She usually believed it was a big load of mumbo-jumbo bullshit. Her lower back pain, for example, had nothing to do with negative thoughts and everything to do with ten hours a day on her feet, cutting, dyeing, processing, blowing, and curling other women's hair. But today? Yes, there was a connection. Her face looked like a lumpy autumn gourd because she had been crying all night.

Crying about Alex.

Knowing it was futile, she tried his cell phone again. Straight to voice mail. As she disconnected, her phone buzzed with an incoming call. She didn't recognize the number, but it was a 631 area code. She answered, just in case. Just in case it was him, despite the truth she was still trying to process.

"Is this Jocelyn Hodges?" the man asked. It definitely wasn't Alex. Alex had an accent. Not the one everyone expected him to have. It wasn't identifiable, or even really an accent, as he had noted repeatedly. Jocelyn thought of it as an accent because she was so used to hearing *actual* accents—Long Island (Nassau and Suffolk Counties, slightly different), Staten Island, Brooklyn, Jersey, Boston, and of course the accents of those who, unlike Alex, spoke English as a second language. Alex's accent sounded like an accent—at least to her, born and bred on the East End—because it was utterly neutral. Like he was a TV anchor or something.

"This is she," Jocelyn said. She had dated a writer two summers back, one who wrote one huge best seller that got adapted into a movie, and three other books that maybe no one read. He was the one who told Jocelyn that it was incorrect to say "This is her." He then took another seven minutes to explain why that was the rule, given the difference between subjects and objects and whatever. She had pretended to be interested and then stopped answering his phone calls. "But it's Hodge," she now corrected her current caller. "Not Hodges."

The caller identified himself as Carter Decker from the East Hampton Police Department. "We spoke Saturday about Alex's missing person report."

This motherfucker. Like she needed a reminder. Since then, she had heard about the unidentified man pulled from the water off Star Island.

On the East End, in the circles that really truly mattered, year-round at least, Jocelyn was an insider. She was one of the original families, the fishers and the farmers. This cop didn't think she already knew after an entire day? Please. Jocelyn had been crying since she got the call in the middle of the Brazilian blowout she was processing the previous afternoon.

Alex had gone from working a commercial fishing boat to a charter. An Alaskan fishing boat doesn't mean jumping into the water. He never seemed like a strong swimmer to her. Just a few weeks ago, she had yelled at him to come back to the beach when the waves were tossing him around and around like tumbling laundry.

She decided not to tell the detective that she already knew that Alex had drowned. "I keep calling him." It was a true statement. "Still no return call. And as of last night, his pickup truck still hasn't moved from the lot. Something's not right."

She had looked for Alex at his house first, then checked the docks, then began circling past his usual haunts. She eventually found his truck parked in the public lot off West Lake Drive in Montauk, but no Alex.

In retrospect, she had been too honest with Detective Decker when she initially filed the report. Too defensive. It was her own inner voice, judging her. Maybe if she had lied and said they were engaged, or if she had not mentioned her family's animosity toward Alex, the cops would have treated it more seriously.

Her family—the Hodges. It wasn't a name that meant much west of the Shinnecock Canal, but here on the East End, it was backed by a tiny bit of power. Her father was one of five siblings who all had their little piece of the industries that mattered—a land surveyor, a contractor, a pool builder, a realtor (the one sister in the family), and, in her father's case, a mason. They deserved to be listed in a local dictionary under the word *synergy*—enough long-term roots, contacts with the city folks, and goodwill with everyone else that they carried some weight. And it was no small secret that her family deeply disapproved of her relation-ship with Alex.

"Actually, we impounded the truck this morning," Decker said. "I'm just down the street from your house. Are you home now? Can we talk?"

This is it, she thought. At least he's finally going to tell me that my boyfriend is dead.

DECKER ARRIVED WEARING SHADES ON his head, which an-noyed her. She opened the door and led him to the kitchen table. She didn't offer him coffee, even though she already had a mug for herself.

"I have a few follow-up questions," he said.

Go ahead and tell me, she thought. *Pull off the Band-Aid. Maybe I won't even cry again. I might be all out of tears.*

"You mentioned before that you thought something bad may have happened to Alex," Decker said. "That someone might have had ill will toward him."

In broad strokes, the East End's population was largely a blend of three distinctive communities: the city people with second and third homes, the multigenerational old-timers like the Hodges, and the more recent influx of Latino immigrants. None of them could exist without the others, given the realities of the home building, landscaping, agri-cultural, and service industries that drove the local economy. But the divisions and resentments among the factions always simmered beneath the surface.

Alex was what too many of the people she knew would still casually call "a brown guy," but he wasn't a handyman or a landscaper or a day laborer that they could treat as the help. He didn't even speak Spanish. He simply showed up in Montauk last year as the new owner of Reel Deal Fishing. There must have been ten long-term guides who would have killed to make a deal when Frank announced he was finally retiring to Florida. But Frank had sold the operation to an outsider. A stranger. And a brown one at that.

She explained all of this again to the detective.

"Seems pretty shaky as a motive to harm him," he said.

"Racism's not rational."

"There's a lot of Latino business owners on the East End. Most of them don't go missing."

He isn't merely missing anymore, is he? Just tell me. He drowned. "Well, only one of them was dating me. Trust me: some people were upset."

"Our department had received two anonymous tips claiming Alex was involved in the drug trade."

"That's bullshit. Alex is the last person who'd get wrapped up in anything illegal."

"Well, the tips came in, I assure you. Whether they were true or not's another question. Do you know Ed Young?"

Of course she did. Everyone did. Former chief of East Hampton Police. "Sure."

"Apparently your father told him a few months ago that he thought Alex Lopez was dealing cocaine and speed to the usual suspects. He said the guide business was just a cover for the drug dealing. Your father was pressing the department to look into it. Is it possible he was behind those anonymous tips?"

Was it? She realized she couldn't rule it out. "My father wasn't exactly cheering on my relationship with Alex."

"Because he was a fishing guide?" Decker asked.

"Please. You know that wouldn't be the reason."

"So it was a race thing? Just how angry was he?"

She shook her head. Why was he asking all these questions when Alex had drowned? Hadn't he drowned? Or was Decker trying to suggest that someone drowned him?

"This is like asking someone 'When was the last time you beat your wife?' My dad's feelings toward Alex were awful. I called him out on it, but he really convinced himself it was because Alex was supposedly a drug dealer. Or appeared out of nowhere buying a business that should be locally owned. Or because he didn't make an effort to get to know my family. But all of that would have been fine with my father, if Alex hadn't been Mexican. Or 'a Mexican,' as my dad would say. But that doesn't make my dad a killer." But was it possible she knew someone else who might be? One of the uncles? She shook the thought from her head. Fact one: Alex couldn't swim. Fact two: Her family was bigoted. Didn't mean there was a connection. "My father never really liked anyone I dated. So Alex was batting average, all things considered."

"Do you know where Alex was from before he moved out here?"

"He worked on Alaskan commercial fishing boats for years. That's where he met Frank." She could tell the name meant nothing to the detective. "Frank Garner. Owned Reel Deal Fishing until last winter, when he sold it to Alex, whom he met, like, a decade ago." *Whom*. The same writer who had told her about *she* versus *her*.

"So, we didn't talk about that before," the detective said. "Alex was from Alaska?"

We didn't talk about anything before, she thought. *You barely listened to me. You wrote me off as some kind of ditzy hairdresser sidepiece. You never asked me a single question.*

"I told you that on Saturday," she said. "I told you he saved up all his money from work catching salmon, and that Frank became a kind of mentor. They stayed in touch. And when Frank decided to retire, he sold the guide business to Alex. Six months ago, but that was, like, New Year's. So this was really Alex just getting started on running the place during a season."

"Did he grow up in Alaska?" Decker asked.

She shook her head. "Phoenix. He told me he moved to Alaska because it was basically the exact opposite of where he grew up."

"What about his family?"

For his next of kin. That's why you're asking, right?

"They were undocumented—his family, I mean. He had DACA

protection. That's how the subject came up. He told me . . ." She started
to say "once." *He told me once* . . . She realized how fleeting it made their
relationship seem, but it wasn't like that. And she realized how stupid
she'd sound if she tried to explain "It wasn't like that." She'd had short,
dramatic, intense flings before—ugh—but Alex hadn't been that. She
left out the *once* and embellished a bit. "He told me all the time how unsettling it was to grow up with undocumented"—her father would have
said *illegal*—"parents. It wasn't until he got registered with Dreamer
protection that he started to, well, dream, I guess, that he could be
something other than pure under-the-table labor. Like he'd been living
in an invisible prison, and the bars were suddenly gone. And Frank was
the one who encouraged him. For Alex to be a business owner here? In
the Hamptons? It was major to him." She felt a lump in her throat again
and a sudden urge to crawl back under the blankets. She was exhausted
from the pure physical act of crying.

"Did he ever mention living anywhere other than Phoenix or
Alaska?"

She shook her head.

She could tell that Decker was contemplating whether to ask another
question. "Not the Midwest?" he asked.

She shook her head again, even as she thought about that neutral
accent.

"Kansas, maybe?" Decker asked, clearly revealing more information than he had initially intended. "Wichita, Kansas."

"He just said Phoenix. And Alaska."

"Did he ever tell you where his parents currently lived? Any siblings? Anything?"

"His parents are gone. He told me that even with DACA protection,
it wasn't until his parents passed away that he felt comfortable owning
anything in his name. He called it 'coming out from the shadows.'"

"Do you know when his parents died? Or where they were before
they passed? Nothing about Kansas?"

"I'm sorry. No."

"When you filed the missing person report, you mentioned that he had seemed distracted lately."

Suddenly, you're interested. "He was normally one hundred percent in the moment." Unlike anyone else she had ever dated, she thought. "But for the past few weeks, I'd notice him not listening, kind of with a vacant stare. Checking his phone a couple times. I'd ask him about it, but he'd brush it off and tune back in."

"It doesn't sound like he was the most open boyfriend."

This was the judgmental detective she remembered from Saturday. He'd clearly had some preexisting idea of what a "real" girlfriend should know about a man. Her exact words were, "He'd been distant lately. Worried. Distracted." She had offered the observation as evidence that something was terribly wrong. Instead, this overaged frat boy had reached a final opinion, writing her off as some thirsty chick whose man wasn't that into her.

"Just go ahead and tell me," she said now. "He drowned out there in the ocean. I already heard. He's the guy who was in the paper this morning. I don't understand why you didn't tell me that from the beginning."

For the first time since she had encountered Detective Decker, he seemed like an actual person. He looked pained.

"That's why we haven't made a formal announcement yet about the body pulled from the water yesterday. I wanted to make sure you were notified first, not just about his identity but also about the actual cause of death." And then he delivered the news. Alex's body was the one found at Star Island, but he had been killed by a small-caliber bullet to the base of his skull.

The wail that broke from her throat surprised even her. It was raw and visceral, unleashing a new flood of sobs that felt like the riptide she had imagined Alex trapped in. She was surprised when she felt the detective's hand on her back, patting her gently in a steady rhythm to help slow her breath.

"Why is this so much worse?" she managed between gulps of air.

"Not my place to say, but maybe because it's unnatural—which means someone out there is responsible? And that's why I have to ask you another question, even though it might be painful. You said that when you reported Alex missing, he had seemed distant."

"And worried," she emphasized.

"Do you think it was possible he was seeing another woman?"

"No, he would never." She could only imagine how many times this detective heard naive people claim the same faith in their partners.

Decker pulled a phone from his shirt pocket, fiddled with it, and then showed her a photograph on the screen. "Any chance you've seen this woman before?"

The photograph had been cropped, a second person visible only because of an arm wrapped loosely around the woman's tank-topped shoulder. The woman's smile was broad, her teeth shiny and white. Her long hair cascaded in waves to her toned biceps. And Jocelyn knew for a fact that the bright sandy blond was the woman's natural color.

"Oh my god. I know her. That's that woman I told Alex about."

"Her name is Hope Miller," Decker said.

"No." It came out almost as a scream, because Jocelyn was so certain. "No, that wasn't it. She told me . . . Lynn, I think. Or Linda."

"Lindsay?" Decker asked.

"That's it. She said her name was Lindsay."

20

Tuesday, June 22, 10:52 a.m.

The messages had come from an account created on VeilMail, an app that could be used to send encrypted text and email messages.

Please stop looking for me. You're putting me in danger.

Where are you? How do I know this is you?

We left the armoire.

Where are you?

That was all she had.

Lindsay had a client last year who had used—or "allegedly used"—the service to communicate with a man who claimed the client hired him to burn down his restaurant. At least at that time, there had been no way to trace the origins of incoming messages.

Lindsay had spent most of the morning calling tech experts to confirm that VeilMail remained a black box, which meant it was impossible to know for certain who sent the messages. She was pretty sure she had mentioned VeilMail to Hope when she was prepping for that arson trial, but anyone could find the service on their own with a little research on the dark web.

We left the armoire. If someone had been watching Hope in New Jersey, they could have easily seen the two of them through the open curtains at the garage apartment, struggling to move the large piece of furniture.

And even if Hope was the one who sent the messages, she might not be doing so voluntarily.

Or it was just like Scott said, and whatever Hope was going through, she wanted to go through it on her own.

Scott had taken the early train back to the city for a big deal he was closing that day, but Lindsay had cleared her calendar for the entire week after finally getting word from Mrs. Gondelman that the handyman could meet her at Hope's cottage that afternoon with an extra key. The hotel had given her a late checkout, so she at least had a place to work until then.

She was cranking through all of the emails she had deferred the day before when a new call came in. She didn't recognize the number.

"This is Lindsay," she said.

"This is Detective Decker. Just checking in. Did you hear anything from Hope?"

Had she? There was no way to know. But she did know that as an officer of the court, she shouldn't outright lie to a police officer. And she also knew she didn't trust this guy, and that he was certain to interpret the text messages from the previous night as surefire proof that Hope had taken off and didn't want to be found.

"I'm still looking for her," she said. It was an unresponsive reply, but truthful. He didn't seem to notice she hadn't technically answered his question. "Are you?" she added.

"Of course," he said warmly. "I told you that when I saw you yesterday."

She started to say that he had not, in fact, told her any such thing. He'd offered to help Lindsay by having some flyers posted, which wasn't the same as actively searching. She decided to keep the peace and thanked him instead.

"On that note, do you know what exactly led Hope to move here for her fresh start? I mean, there are probably easier places to live than the East End in the summer."

"We came here together for a visit a couple of months ago. I was thinking about taking a rental. As it turned out, she was the one who fell in love and wanted to make the move. She loves being near a beach."

"And why was that?"

Even though Lindsay didn't owe the detective any further explanation, she stopped to ponder the question.

"I'm not sure," she said. "But I noticed a long time ago that she seemed totally at peace whenever we were around water. I started wondering whether she might have grown up in a beach town. I pressured her to take a paddle-boarding lesson to see if perhaps it came naturally. The first big wave knocked her over, almost like she'd never even been in the ocean before."

She suddenly imagined a map of America, Kansas smack-dab in the very oceanless middle. Maybe the trauma that had led to Hope's memory loss had originated in Kansas. Maybe something involving guns, explaining Hope's reaction at the shooting range. Someone had finally found her in Hopewell—a stranger spending too much time at the restaurant, asking too many questions. Her instincts told her to leave . . .

She realized she hadn't been listening to Decker. "I'm sorry, what?"

"You said she liked being on the water," Decker said. "But she wasn't a good swimmer? Did you spend any time in the water when you took that trip here together?"

"We went on a fishing trip. I was surprised she wanted to go."

"So it was her idea? Maybe she used to fish . . . in her former life."

Surprisingly, Lindsay noted no sarcasm in his voice.

"She never expressed an interest," she said. "We had tons of fishing not far from Hopewell, but she said it was more about wanting to be out on a boat."

"Did she keep up with it?" Decker asked. "The fishing, I mean? Or any other activities? Might be helpful to talk to any people out here who got to know her."

"It's not like she could afford regular fishing excursions with a guide," Lindsay said. "But she was a semi-regular at Rowdy Hall. A bartender named Joe said Hope asked him to walk her to her car once. She was worried someone was following her. It lines up with what her boss said."

"I know Joe," Decker said. "I'll swing by and have a talk with him."

"Really?" Lindsay asked.

"Don't sound so surprised," Decker said. "I never thought that DNA hit was any kind of smoking gun, but like I said, I'm looking for your friend. If nothing else, maybe Joe can point me in the direction of other locals who might have known her."

"Okay, thanks."

Lindsay was about to hang up, unsure what else to say, when Decker asked another question. "Oh hey, I was thinking about taking my dad on a fishing trip the next time he visits. Did you have a good time?"

"Yeah, I guess. For us it was more about the experience than actually learning how to fish."

"But did you catch anything?"

"A seven-pound blackfish, in fact." Granted, it was some teenager on the boat who actually caught it, but close enough.

He let out a whistle. "Which shop did you use?"

She pursed her lips, trying to remember. "Hope found it on Yelp. It had some kind of pun in the name."

"Reel Deal Fishing?" Decker asked.

"That sounds right."

Decker thanked her for the recommendation and assured her again that he was going to reach out to Joe the bartender. At last it seemed that the detective might finally be taking her concerns seriously. But as she hung up, Lindsay found herself remembering that horrible Sunday afternoon two Novembers before. She and Scott were eating burgers and drinking bloodies at J.G. Melon when Scott's cell buzzed on the table, the word Mom appearing at the top of the screen. Scott's dad, in the city for an engineering conference at the Grand Hyatt, was in an ambulance headed to Lenox Hill. A heart attack.

The nurse at the front desk assured them there was no Ned Parker in the computer. Annoyed at the request that she double-check, she began listing all the other hospitals in Manhattan, insisting that Scott and Lindsay were in the wrong place. Lindsay was the one to suggest that they probably beat the ambulance to the hospital and would wait a few minutes, if that was okay.

When the nurse found them in the waiting room to confirm that Scott's father had in fact just arrived, she seemed like a different person. Her voice was low and kind. Her face even seemed softer somehow. "The doctors will be ready to see you in a little while."

Lindsay said nothing, but she'd taken Scott's hand in hers, knowing that he would soon learn that his father was gone. And now Lindsay realized that the shift in Detective Decker's attitude wasn't necessarily a good sign.

21

Tuesday, June 22, 1:08 p.m.

Carter Decker pushed the keyboard away in frustration and cracked his knuckles.

After he spoke with Jocelyn Hodge that morning, he'd thought he felt the boom—that singular moment when a case suddenly bursts open and pieces of evidence explode into view. Then he got Lindsay Kelly to give up the fact that Hope had been the one to suggest the fishing trip and choose the guide company. He was on fire.

But now, back at the station, he was down to embers. He had snapshots of a story, but he was missing the context he needed to see the bigger picture.

Lopez had left behind no real electronic footprints. Jocelyn said he had zero interest in social media. He had both a Gmail account and an address linked to his business, but the messages there suggested nothing unusual. Carter knew from an *East Hampton Star* write-up in January that Lopez had moved to the East End to take over Reel Deal Fishing from Frank Garner. The piece described Lopez as a longtime friend of Garner and included a photograph of the two men to mark the passing of the torch.

But it was as if Garner were the one and only person who had known

Alex Lopez before he appeared on Long Island. When Carter called the older man in Florida, he'd said the two met thirteen years earlier working on an Alaskan salmon boat. Garner had become something of a mentor. The two would go their separate ways off-season, but always link back up to work the same boats when it came time to make money again. Lopez apparently lived a nomadic life, sometimes staying put in Anchorage but often taking short-term rentals in other parts of the country. Like Lopez's girlfriend, Jocelyn Hodge, Garner was under the impression that Lopez had grown up in Arizona; he had never mentioned Wichita, Kansas. "He talked a couple of times about a sister, though," Garner added. "He told me he wished he could see her more, but I didn't press as to why he couldn't."

To Carter, it didn't sound like the kind of close friendship that would lead to handing over the keys to the man's business, and he said as much. Garner's response had been straightforward. "He was a lot like me. A loner. Quiet. But just a good, nice, trustworthy man. Rock solid. Hard to explain it better than that."

Jocelyn Hodge had given a similar depiction, as if they were both innately able to recognize a person's fundamental goodness. What neither of them could do, however, was offer Carter a bead on who the man actually was and why Hope Miller might have killed him.

Lopez's cell phone activity consisted primarily of texts to customers about fishing trips, plus regular—though not exactly daily—communication with Jocelyn. To judge from the scarcity of actual calls, he wasn't much of a talker. Three calls to a number Carter hadn't been able to trace stood out. Chicago area code, and by all indications so far, a burner phone that was now disconnected. It could be confirmation of Lopez's involvement in drug activity. In addition to the two anonymous tips the department received, the former police chief had contacted Carter this morning to tell him that Jocelyn's father had reached out with concerns about Lopez. So was Jocelyn's father right about Lopez? Or was he behind the anonymous tips?

The only other call that intrigued Carter was from Lopez's cell to the main corporate number for LockeHome, placed two months earlier. Carter had certainly heard of the company, because who hadn't? When Carter was a kid, the chain store's long-running TV ads always featured the company's folksy owner, imploring customers to "Locke in our low, low prices." When big-box retailers came along with even cheaper offerings, LockeHome not only survived but grew to eclipse all the other chains. Widely credited for the surprising success story was the folksy owner's daughter, who joined and eventually replaced her father as the face of the company. The stores' ads featured women at all stages of a home improvement project—from planning and purchasing to painting and plastering. While the other big outfits largely hired men for the sales floor, relegating women to lower-paid cashier positions, LockeHome publicly committed to ensuring equal pay and representation at every level of employment. The stores grew to include not just hardware and building supplies but furniture and high-end kitchenware—one-stop shopping for the dream home.

As a result of the corporation's evolution, Melanie Locke—maiden name retained, of course—was now a leading role model for working women, an unapologetically ambitious corporate executive who firmly believed that gender equity and profits went hand in hand. A committed philanthropist who raised her young daughter on her own after her husband was killed, she also had a compelling personal biography. And now that she was a candidate for the Senate, it was probably only a matter of time before she ran for president too.

Carter had no interest in either corporate business or politics. What mattered to him was Melanie Locke's city of origin. The one where the folksy patriarch was born and raised and where the company's headquarters still remained. The one to which Alex Lopez had made a phone call just two months before he died. That city? Wichita, Kansas.

The call had been to the main number; Carter had no way of

knowing where Lopez was transferred from there. But it was one indication that Alex Lopez's connections to Wichita were not entirely in
the past, which meant they might possibly explain his connection to
Hope Miller.

Carter thought he was onto something when he pulled up the driving route between Wichita, Kansas, and Long Island and found that it
would pass directly through Indianapolis. Hope Miller had been found
in a crashed 1999 Toyota 4Runner, stolen from Indianapolis.

But then Carter had entered a new map search, this time for direc-
tions from Phoenix to Long Island, and ended up on the same exact
route from St. Louis on. So if Hope's car crash had anything to do with
Alex Lopez, the two of them could have met in Kansas, Arizona, or just
about anywhere south or west of Indianapolis.

His thoughts were interrupted by the buzz of his phone against the
desk. A new text message. Detective Carter. Again with people messing up his name. This is Jocelyn Hodge. He rued the day the department
started "encouraging" detectives to give victims their direct cell phone
numbers. When do you think I can get that necklace? You can understand
why it would mean a great deal to me. Thank you.

The necklace in question was a silver chain with two small hearts
dangling from a pendant. The chain itself had even smaller hearts em-
bedded every few inches among the links. Carter had found it wrapped
in a piece of tissue paper, tucked inside a tackle box on Lopez's boat.
With the help of the zoom lens on his cell phone, he'd been able to make
out the tiny letters on the clasp: Tiffany & Co. Shown a photograph of it,
Jocelyn said she had never seen it before. She also immediately jumped
to the conclusion that it was meant for her, perhaps for her birthday the
next month. He could tell she took comfort in that theory—those two
silver hearts dangling side by side—but Carter wasn't ready to release
the jewelry yet. Unable to locate the necklace on the Tiffany website,
he had contacted the general manager at the Fifth Avenue store, who
offered to research the matter and get back to him. He was also waiting

for Lopez's credit card statements to see if he could locate the purchase details.

> I'm sorry, Ms. Hodge. It's logged in evidence for now. Thx.

He hit the send key and then resumed tapping a pen against his desktop. He knew that Alex Lopez was the source of the blood in the Stansfields' entryway, where Hope Miller was last seen. He knew that Lopez had been murdered. And he was pretty sure he could prove that Hope Miller had come to East Hampton for the express purpose of finding Alex Lopez. But he still didn't feel the boom.

The sound of his desk phone broke his train of thought. "Decker."

"Hi, Detective Decker. My name's Ellie Hatcher. I'm a detective with the NYPD."

Hatcher had started to explain her connection to Lindsay Kelly when he interrupted. "Ms. Kelly told me she reached out to you. She was convinced that the bad guy must have had an accomplice who had targeted Hope Miller twenty-three years later. She gave me the impression you agreed."

He felt a little guilty for misleading Lindsay earlier, asking her all those questions without telling her what he knew about Lopez. Fuck it, he thought. She's a defense lawyer. She should know better than to trust him.

"'Convinced' is an overstatement. It was a possibility, but it was always conjecture. Having noodled it over for a while, I'm inclined to contact Lindsay and tell her I think any connection between her friend and the College Hill Strangler is a stretch. I just wanted to make sure I wasn't missing anything before I made the call. Don't suppose Hope Miller has turned up?"

"Definitely not." He looked again at his computer screen, wishing he knew more about Alex Lopez. "Actually, I do have a name to match to the blood samples, but you'll understand once I tell you that this information definitely can't go to a defense lawyer who's also Hope Miller's BFF."

He could almost picture the detective sitting up straighter on the other end of the line. "Of course," she said.

"A thirty-six-year-old Hispanic male named Alex Lopez." He recited the date of birth from Lopez's Alaska driver's license. "Someone shot him in the head and dumped his body in the water."

"Sometime after his blood wound up on the floor where Hope Miller was last seen."

"Correct. We haven't made the announcement yet. I'm hoping we'll be able to put out a search for Hope Miller as a person of interest at the same time."

"So he was only a kid when his blood was found inside Janice Beale's house," Hatcher said.

"Thirteen, to be exact. And of course his blood could have been there however long before that." The implication was clear. Alex Lopez was far too young to have been wrapped up with a serial killer more than two decades earlier. "Anyway, I don't have a bead on the guy yet. He only moved here in January, and told his girlfriend he grew up in Phoenix before moving to Alaska. But obviously he was in Kansas at some point. Problem is, Lopez is a pretty common name, and little kids don't exactly have driver's licenses. Got any local knowledge to impart? If the shoe were on the other foot, I'd send you to the YMCA summer program and two grade-school principals, and you'd probably be able to track down eighty percent of the kids who grew up out here."

"Wichita may be small, but it's a lot bigger than East Hampton."

"Figured it was a shot in the dark."

"Not that dark, as it turns out. There's another reason I was calling you. Janice Beale's house backed up to one of the city parks, with a big family rec center. The police helped run a summer camp program there, and Beale used to come outside to play with the kids, give them lemonade, that kind of thing. After she was killed, the kids made it sound like her house was almost like an extension of the camp."

Carter gave a quick pump of his free fist.

"I was going to pass that on as a possible explanation for the blood, but now that you've got a name and an age—"

"It feels right," Carter said. "Don't suppose this camp is the kind of place that keeps records from twenty-three years ago?"

"No clue, but it's at the Edgemoor Park Rec Center, and at least at that time, it was called the COP Youth Camp."

"Sounds like a euphemism for a juvenile detention center."

She chuckled on the other end of the line. "The COP part of the name is an acronym—Community Oriented Police. But, yes, it doesn't exactly scream carefree summer fun."

"What about LockeHome? Lopez made a call to their main corporate number a couple of months ago."

"That could be anything. I assume you've heard of the company. It's huge."

"But this wasn't a call to a customer-service eight-hundred number. He used the three-one-six area code, a direct call to the headquarters in Wichita."

"Unless the switchboard system has a way to track the transfer to a specific extension, it's going to be a needle in a haystack. Locke is probably one of the top five employers in Wichita—more jobs than the city, state, feds, or university. I probably know at least fifteen people who work there now. Actually, let me give one of them a call and see what I can find for you."

Carter accepted the offer, remembering when he used to be the kind of cop who would have volunteered to help out if the tables were turned.

22

Tuesday, June 22, 1:19 p.m.

Steve picked up after two rings. "Two calls in two days. Lucky me."

"Except you might not like the reason I'm calling," Ellie said.

"Unless something's wrong with you, Jess, or your mom, whatever reason you have for calling always makes me happy."

"It's about that case we talked about."

"No . . . *really?*" he asked, making no attempt to conceal the sarcasm. "I might keel over from shock."

"I know you told me to leave it alone, but—"

"And I also knew that you wouldn't. No apologies necessary as long as you're okay. What'd you find out?"

"Long Island's got a name to go with the DNA hit. Alex Lopez." She recited his date of birth, and then explained her idea that he might have been one of the kids from the COP camp who'd hung out at Janice Beale's house.

"It's a good theory," Steve said. "Regardless, given the guy's age, no way he could have anything to do with Summer."

Ellie didn't know whether to feel relieved or disappointed. She realized she had gotten her hopes up about finding an alternative explanation for her father's death.

"Lopez apparently made a call to the main headquarters at Locke-Home a couple of months before he died. Do you know if there's a way to track whether a call was transferred to a direct line from there?"

"I do know, and unfortunately, the answer is no. We just investigated a former employee for stealing intellectual property and selling it to a competitor. He was definitely working with someone who was still inside, but he was calling the main switchboard and transferring the call from there. We're getting the system modified, but the changeover hasn't happened yet."

"Got it. Any chance Alex Lopez's name rings a bell from the COP camp?"

"No, but when you get to be my age, you've forgotten five times the number of people you currently know. You want me to make a call? See if my name still means a thing there?"

"That would be great."

"Any other work you want to pawn off on me while we're at it?"

She snickered. "You're the best. I owe you beers the next time you visit. Hey, did you know about Melanie's Senate run before it was announced?"

"You seriously overestimate my importance to the organization."

"Max was wondering if you'd be going to DC with her."

"Only if it's in a casket. You should bring him to Wichita, you know. Your mom would be over the moon. She keeps saying she wants to meet the man you're living in sin with. Didn't have the heart to tell her I met him over Christmas."

"Another reason I owe you."

When she hung up the phone, Rogan was giving her the side-eye.

"Woman, you told me earlier that you had come to your senses and were staying away from this mess. Your version of staying out of something looks a whole lot like doing some other cop's job."

"And this looks a whole lot like my partner getting all up in my business by eavesdropping on my phone calls." Decker had been awfully quick to let her work his case, but she got the impression he was in over his head.

Rogan's face lit up. "All up in your business, huh? You're all street now?"

"Word."

He shook his head, not satisfied with her response.

"Fine, I admit it. I'm doing that thing I do where I take on everyone else's problems."

He placed an index finger to his nose, and then pointed it at her. "Ding ding. We have a winner."

"It's not the worst fault a person could have."

"This is true, and I have certainly benefited from your dragon-slaying tendencies over the years. But first you were helping the defense lawyer with the missing amnesia friend. And now you're helping the cop who obviously thinks the missing friend went and killed someone."

"What can I say? I like being in the middle of a mystery. Probably explains why I have this job."

"Speaking of your job, you do actually still have one." He gave a pointed look toward an untouched stack of E-ZPass records on her desk. They belonged to Ralph Bunning, whom they had arrested Sunday night for hiring a convicted ex-con to murder the man who'd been having an affair with Bunning's wife. Without a confession from either defendant, they were trying to prove their meetings indirectly, aligning their movements with cell-phone pings and bridge-and-tunnel charges.

She was on page three when her cell rang. It was Steve. "Hey there," she said. "That was quick."

Rogan scribbled something on a legal pad and pushed it in her direction. *I.e., lazy bum on Long Island could've done it.*

"Only took a phone call," Steve said. "The community policing unit has a database going back years, I guess. There was an Alex Lopez in the camp for the three summers before Janice Beale was killed."

There it was: confirmation that the bloodstain found in the house had nothing to do with Beale's murder and therefore nothing to do with her father. "Do they have contact information for the family, by any chance?"

"Shoot, I didn't even ask. I'm losing my chops. Want me to call back and see what I can find?"

"Nice of you to offer, but that's okay. It's another cop's case to work." She smiled knowingly in Rogan's direction, and he flashed a thumbs-up.

One more phone call to close the loop, and she could forget the names Alex Lopez and Hope Miller forever.

"Decker."

"Good news and bad." She began with the fact that LockeHome wouldn't be able to identify the route Alex Lopez's phone call had made from the company's general number, and then moved on to the new information she'd gathered. "Lopez was definitely enrolled in the COP camp for the three years before that blood sample was found. My friend didn't get any other information, but I assume you can follow up with them. It's the WPD community policing department that keeps the records."

"Will do," he said. "Thanks again, and thanks for not tipping off Lindsay Kelly. She'll find out about Lopez soon enough, though. I just got the okay from our DA. They're announcing Lopez's murder at a press conference this afternoon, and we're also putting out an APB for Kelly's friend as a person of interest—as a potential witness who might be in danger . . . of course."

"Of course." Ellie knew what that language in a police department press release actually meant. Though investigators weren't yet ready to say as much, Hope Miller was their primary suspect in the murder of Alex Lopez.

23

Tuesday, June 22, 1:47 p.m.

Bing. Another new message alert. From Ed Carpenter—again.

Lindsay glanced at the top of her laptop screen: 1:47. Shit. She should have been in the car seven minutes ago.

By her count, this was email round five with the same client in the last twenty minutes. She knew he was slamming her with questions because he was still aggrieved that she'd handed over a court hearing this morning to "some person I've never even met before." She had explained that it was a simple request for a trial setover—one that he had sought—but he replied by threatening to hire another lawyer if she didn't handle his case personally at every stage. Now he was asking whether his pending DUI charges could affect the ongoing fight with his ex over child support. She typed "Late for a meeting, but the short answer is no" and hit send. Terse, but a lot cheaper than if she'd billed him for researching and writing a responsive memo, which is what most lawyers would do.

She was zipping up her roller bag on the hotel bed when the handyman sent her a text saying he was running late. With extra time suddenly on her hands, she pulled up the number for Detective Ellie Hatcher.

"Hey, Ellie, this is Lindsay Kelly. I was calling to see if you might have learned any more about that blood match from the Wichita crime scene. I found out that Hope thought someone out here might have been following her."

There was a pause on the other end of the line. "Look, I'll be honest with you," Ellie finally said. "Your call, bringing up William Summer, and everything that happened with my father? I was probably a little too quick to jump at the possibility your friend's disappearance might be connected to that case. But taking a step back? There's nothing there, Lindsay. There's not a shred of evidence that the College Hill killings were committed by more than one man. Plus, Summer made it clear after he was caught that he was terrified of being executed. As it turned out, none of his crimes were committed when Kansas had capital punishment as a sentencing option, but he didn't know that when he was first interrogated. If he had an accomplice, he would have offered him up in exchange for leniency. I don't want you focusing only on William Summer to the detriment of other possibilities about what's going on with your friend."

"I guess that's good to hear. The blood belonging to a killer would probably be the worst explanation." She still hadn't told anyone other than Scott about the messages she had received from someone claiming to be Hope. "It would just be nice to have a definite account for that DNA match. I saw that Janice Beale lived next to a park with a rec center, and she became a kind of den mother to the whole crew. Maybe one of the kids skinned a knee or something, and is now one of the people who did work on the Stansfields' house."

There was another pause, and Lindsay wondered if perhaps Ellie was distracted now that she had decided she had no personal connection to Hope's case. "It's possible, but in any event, I'd leave the William Summer thing alone. The fewer heads that man lives in, the better. And best of luck to you and your friend."

Lindsay had a gut feeling that the detective was holding something back, but she couldn't imagine what it might be, so she thanked her once again for trying to help.

She slid her laptop from her briefcase and pulled up the article that mentioned Beale's connection to the summer camp. She then searched for "COP camp Edgemoor Park Wichita Kansas." In her fourth page of search results, she found a series of Facebook pages dedicated to "alumni" groups, arranged by five-year spans of summer "classes." Enrollment in the groups was sparse, drawing low double digits of members and no ongoing activity.

She clicked on the group that covered the years immediately before Janice Beale was murdered. Only fourteen members of the group. The few posts were typically vacuous social media fare.

Wow. Blast from the past. Such great memories!

Shout-out to my former kickball homies. We ruled!!

Anyone know whatever happened to Officer Simpson? Man, I had such a crush.

What exactly had Lindsay been hoping to find here? Maybe a member who was currently living on Long Island's East End, one who might confirm he had recently been at the Stansfields'. At least she could check the blood sample off her long list of worries.

She jumped one "class" group forward, covering her bases. More of the same.

She scanned the annual fundraising pleas, checking out the current cities listed for the few people who posted in response.

So glad to hear that COP camp is still around. Best days of my summers!

We should have a reunion.

LOL. Can't believe you're hitting us up for money when you let us be preyed upon by a sexual predator with no consequences. But that was all about the money too, wasn't it?

Lindsay felt a jolt of energy as she reread the message. The woman who posted it was named Katy Barnes. Lindsay clicked on Katy's photo, but the resulting profile page was set to private.

She hit the back button and read the replies to Katy's post.

WTF are you talking about? That camp saved my life.

OMG I heard a rumor YEARS later but had no idea it was true. I'm so sorry if that happened to you.

And a final message from the camp administrator who had organized the reunion groups. We are distraught and saddened to hear this allegation for the first time. We have no knowledge of any current or prior misconduct at the Community Oriented Police Youth Camp and are eager to listen to you fully and to complete an investigation. I am also sending you a private message with contact information for both myself and the police department's bureau of internal affairs.

The message was posted two days after the original remark. Lindsay had no doubt the camp administrator had been waiting for guidance from the city's legal department.

If Katy Barnes had responded to the post, she hadn't done so publicly, at least not on this page.

What did any of this have to do with Hope? She pulled a legal pad from her bag and started jotting down every piece of information she had gathered.

The blood at the camp den mother's house. Sexual abuse at the camp. Lindsay's long-held suspicion that Hope's amnesia could be the result of psychological trauma.

Lindsay had only once asked Hope directly whether she believed she might have been sexually abused. It was after Hope's longest relationship—almost two years—had ended. Carl Walsh was Hopewell's best mechanic, the older brother of one of Lindsay's childhood classmates. He was nice and loved Hope like crazy. Lindsay thought he'd be around for the long haul. Instead, Hope showed up at Lindsay's apartment in New York City, saying she needed to get out of Hopewell for a few days. She and Carl were over.

Only after three nights of avoiding the subject did Hope finally tell her that the problem was sex. Carl needed it. Hope hated it. He'd been patient, and she had tried, but frustration had evolved into resentment and, at least in Carl's case, sufficient blame and rationalization that he had started up with the garage office manager. There was no going back.

Lindsay's immediate response came in the form of twenty ways Carl could fuck himself, but then the conversation took a turn. She and Hope never spent much time talking about sex or men, whether there were boyfriends in the picture or not. "Was he just bad at it or something?" Lindsay had asked. "Like a jackrabbit on meth? Because I could totally picture that."

Instead of eliciting the expected laugh, the question made Hope break out in tears. She explained that she was utterly incapable of enjoying sex. She thought of it as a chore. She'd try to feign pleasure, but she must have been a bad faker, because with time, men always realized she wasn't into it. She had no problem experiencing pleasure on her own, but simply shut down when she was with another person.

"Hope, I don't want to upset you, but that's similar to what I've heard from clients who were abused as children. Do you think that's possible?"

"Of course. I've talked about it with Rebecca over the years, but I just don't remember, because—well, obviously. And then it becomes this chicken/egg question. Is my amnesia from abuse? Or do I not remember the abuse because I have amnesia? Either way, I have no way to know for certain. Maybe I'm just a bad lay."

Lindsay didn't know how to respond to Hope's self-deprecating laugh. Instead, they drank another bottle of outrageously expensive cabernet.

What if Hope was abused at the summer camp in Wichita? The blood at Janice Beale's house could have belonged to the abuser. If the abuser now lived on Long Island, he might have spotted Hope when she moved to East Hampton and recognized her as his former victim. Had Hope started to remember? Had she confronted him? Or maybe she hadn't recognized him at all. Perhaps the abuser, with no knowledge of Hope's amnesia, had become convinced that she was going to expose him. Either way, Lindsay imagined a faceless man following Hope to the Stansfield house, pushing her inside as she opened the door to leave.

She went back to Facebook and sent a friend request to Katy Barnes, along with a message request: I am a lawyer in New York City and saw your post on the Wichita COP camp page about past abuse at the camp. I am terribly sorry to raise what I am sure is a traumatic topic for you, but I assure you that the matter is urgent. She left her contact information and hit send.

If Lindsay was right, and Hope's childhood abuser had confronted her, perhaps Hope was in shock. Or hiding for her own safety. Or maybe the message Lindsay had received wasn't from Hope at all. Maybe Hope was dead, and the abuser was covering his tracks.

Her cell phone buzzed, rescuing her from her own thoughts. It was the handyman. He was ten minutes out.

24

Tuesday, June 22, 2:40 p.m.

Hope's computer was nowhere to be found in the cottage. Lindsay didn't know what to make of that. Her best guess was that Hope had taken the laptop with her to the open house, but she knew its disappearance was another point on the board for the runaway theory.

A second, closer inspection of all the drawers and closets was inconclusive. She wasn't sure what she had expected to find. The aftermath of a ransacking? It looked exactly as it had when Lindsay left after the move.

Her journals appeared to be untouched, lined neatly to fill the bottom two shelves of a bookcase across from the meticulously made bed. She knew that her friend had kept all of them, going back to when she was still at the hospital. Hope thought of the journals as a safe place for her to interrogate herself, trying to shake a memory loose from her old life, while documenting her efforts to build a new one. She joked that someday she'd use them to write a best-selling memoir when she finally knew who she was and could accept a royalty check in her actual name.

To read these personal thoughts under any other circumstance would feel like the worst betrayal, but to leave them unread in the face of Hope's disappearance was unfathomable. Lindsay wasn't spying, she assured herself. She was investigating. If the police had taken her case seriously from the outset, the journals would have been a logical starting point.

She opened the nightstand drawer to find a Tiffany-blue notebook in a butter-smooth calfskin, a Christmas gift from Lindsay last year.

The first page was dated May 15—the day Hope moved to East Hampton. Lindsay smiled as she read, remembering the hours they'd spent setting up the cottage together. She sat on the edge of the bed and flipped to the next entry.

May 18

Day four, and the cottage is beginning to feel more like home. It's nice to have a place that's more than a crash pad above a garage, but at least my place at the Becketts' was completely mine. Here, it's pretty clear that I'm staying in someone else's house, just a temporary caretaker. But today I was inspired after a meeting with one of Evan's new sellers. Evan told the client that houses sell fastest when a buyer can look at a property and imagine it as theirs, which is easiest when rooms are stripped bare. So long, family photos. Goodbye, tchotchkes. After taking thorough photos of every surface, I took the liberty of packing away every visible piece of evidence that Mrs. Gondelman is the actual owner of the cottage. Upon her eventual return, I'll put every last knickknack back into place, but for now, it's sufficiently generic for me to pretend that it's truly mine. I'm trying to decide whether to be bold enough to install curtains over the front windows. Tonight while I was watching TV after dinner, I could have sworn that I saw movement inside a car that had been parked across the street for at least twenty minutes. I got so freaked out that I even pretended to be shutting things down for the night, turning off all the lights and going to the bedroom, only to crawl across the living room (yes, I realize how crazy this sounds) to peek out the window. The car didn't budge, and the street was too dark to see whether anyone was actually inside, or if my eyes had been playing tricks on me. I hid in the bedroom for an hour before checking again. By then, the car was gone. It was a white (I think) pickup truck, but those are everywhere out here. Anyway, note to self: shop for opaque curtains that I can install and uninstall without Mrs. Gondelman being any the wiser upon her return.

Lindsay turned her head and looked through the bedroom door into the cottage living room. She remembered Hope telling her about the shopping trip to IKEA for the cheapest "good" curtains she'd been able to find in her online research. She boasted that she had managed to install the rods herself with nothing but a chair, a hammer, and a screwdriver, then hung the drapes "high and wide," the way they tell you to do it on all the DIY shows. She had even texted before-and-after photographs to show off her handiwork. It was one of their lengthier communications since the move, and felt much more like their usual and frequent back-and-forths.

But she'd said nothing about a white pickup. Lindsay rose from the bed, walked to the front of the house, and drew the dark gray cotton curtains closed before reading on.

June 6

Treated myself to a haircut at a chichi salon today. Cost three times more than Tammy's trims back home—oops, I mean in Hopewell, because this is home now, this is home now, this is home now (sigh)— but the accompanying scalp massage was heaven, and the blowout made me tempted to open an Instagram account just so I could take a hundred selfies with perfect hair and plenty of wardrobe changes.

Unfortunately, the little bounce in my well-coiffed step vanished

*outside the salon. I saw a man across the street parked in—guess
what? A white pickup truck—and he was definitely looking toward
the salon. That probably wouldn't have freaked me out by itself, but
the guy definitely looked familiar. It's always an infuriating feeling
when someone or something looks familiar. It would probably be annoying for anyone, like your memory is betraying you, like you feel
like the answer is right at the tip of your brain but keeps getting lost.
But for <u>me</u>? I don't know if he looks familiar because I saw him on
the street last week, or because he looks like an actor in some movie I
saw once, or because . . . 15+ years ago? If I see something that feels
familiar and can't pull up the connection, it turns into yet another
reminder that I don't really know who I am. Or who I <u>was</u>, at least.
And can I know who Hope is today if I don't know who she was—
Ugh, see I'm doing it. Fifteen years later, and I'm calling Hope—
ME!!!—a third person <u>she</u>.*

    *OK, just took some deep breaths to calm down. Anyway, white-
pickup-truck guy: parallel parked at a crowded curb, so I couldn't
get his plate. But the fear factor is apparently getting to me. Went
to Rowdy Hall for dinner. Ate my weight in ham and Swiss while I
worked the crossword. When I realized how late it was when it was
time to leave, I asked poor Joe to walk me to my car. He probably
thought I was crazy. My eyes darted toward every passing car, searching for the white pickup. So . . . yoo-hoo, if someone finds my body
chopped to bits in the woods, look for a handsome dark-haired man
who I may or may not know from either the recent or distant past, who
drives a white pickup.*

Lindsay flipped the page to blank white space, then turned to the
next pages and the next. Was that Hope's last entry, or had she started in
on another notebook?

She sat cross-legged in front of the bookcase and skimmed through
the final journal on the bottom shelf. She recognized the blue-and-white

polka-dotted cover of the notebook Hope had been scribbling in the weekend they came out here in April. She found herself smiling as she read her friend's account of the trip—ice cream, real estate prowling, fishing—it was all there. She studied an entry from the end of the month more closely as Hope recounted a second trip to East Hampton—this time alone to recon her living and employment options. Lindsay realized she hadn't given Hope nearly enough credit for pulling it all together so quickly. She blinked back tears when she reached the final sentence: *I just hope Lindsay will understand that this isn't about her.* She closed the notebook and returned it to its rightful spot.

What else could she do here?

She eyed the bed next to her, and then stood up to pull the quilt back tentatively with two fingers. Nothing of note, at least to the naked eye, but depending on how the facts unfolded, the police would eventually want the sheets as potential evidence. She had bought them for Hope's birthday two years ago. Of course, there was only a 1 in 365 chance that the date was her actual birthday, but it did mark the date of her arrival in Hopewell. It was also the anniversary of the day Lindsay first found Hope.

She stripped the sheets from the bed and replaced them with fresh linens she had spotted in the small closet outside the bathroom. As she was inserting the used sheets into a garbage bag, she paused on the final pillowcase and held it to her face. It still smelled a little like Hope's shampoo. She spread it out over a pillow on the bed and rested her head on it.

So far, she could justify her intrusions into Hope's private thoughts. To dig further into the past felt like a deeper violation of trust. There was no way the diary entry she wanted to read would include any information related to Hope's disappearance. But she needed to know. If she never saw Hope again, she would at least know.

Two notebooks back. She got out of the bed, pulled it from the shelf, and thumbed to a date committed to memory, nearly a year earlier.

Tried to go to sleep but too much adrenaline. And the bed was spin-
ning because . . . too much tequila. Oh wow, even my handwriting's
drunk. Will I even be able to read this in the morning? L is in town.
Picked her up from the train station at 3 and she was hangry so we
went straight to Picante for tacos and margaritas. Turned into a four-
hour day-drinking situation, and then we came back here and made
the tequila-soaked decision to open a bottle of wine, which I promptly
spilled on my white shirt. I took it off as I ran for the sink. She came
over to help, saying I needed dishwashing liquid and hydrogen per-
oxide, which of course I didn't have, so we used salt because the in-
ternet said so. Anyway, the stain came out and . . . wow, I'm afraid
to even write it down, because that will make it real. She kissed me.
Or maybe I kissed her. But she definitely kissed me back. Finally,
after all these years, it happened. And it was good. Really, really
good. Gentle at first, but then she was the one who took it to the next
level, pushing into me. When her hands started to explore, I was the
one who stopped it. Like an idiot. And now of course I can't sleep.
Idiots don't deserve sleep. They deserve to replay the entire scene over
and over again, knowing it would have gone further. Imagining what
we'd be doing right now. Knowing she's in the next room, wondering
what she's thinking?

Well, I just got up the nerve to open my door under the guise of
trying to convince her one more time to sleep in the bed instead of the
pullout. She's out cold. Lucky woman. Will she even remember in the
morning?

Lindsay noticed that Hope's handwriting became more even as she
wrote. She was sobering up.

Maybe she'll tap on my door in the middle of the night and slip in
beside me. Or maybe in the morning, she'll tell me that tonight was
what she'd been wanting to do for years, too. But if I had to guess?

She'll laugh it off and blame the booze, and I'll just play along like it's mutual. And that is why I pulled away and ran to my dresser for a clean shirt, saying I was drunk and tired and needed aspirin, water, and sleep. The way she makes me feel scares me. And most of all, I don't want to lose her. That's what it comes down to. I'm that contestant on Deal or No Deal who'd rather keep the suitcase they have than go for the cool mil.

The base of Lindsay's stomach began to burn. She felt like she was back on that pullout sofa again, nearly shaking at the possibility that Hope might reappear from the bedroom. When she finally did, Lindsay pretended to be asleep, faking deep, loud breaths even as her heart raced. And in the morning, she did exactly what Hope had predicted—brushed it off with a joke. "Wow, I guess there really is such a thing as too much tequila. Sorry about that."

The truth was that Lindsay had wanted it to go further. How many times had Scott—and other men before him—complained that she seemed most attentive, most *happy*, when she was with her best friend? If someone were to poll the handful of Lindsay's past boyfriends, the results would be unanimous: they were always second to Hope for Lindsay's affections. While Hope was always welcome to crash a couple's night, or even entire vacations, Lindsay and Hope protected their girls' nights like the most sacred ceremonies of a secret society. Lindsay always defended herself by saying that female friendships were simply different, and it was clingy for men to compare themselves to their girlfriend's girlfriends. But then that night happened, and the truth was undeniable. Lindsay loved Hope more than she'd ever love anyone else.

But when they had the chance to see if they might be something other than best friends, Lindsay let the moment slip by. She knew Hope feared she could never be in a serious relationship until she knew the truth about her own past, not to mention the anxiety she had described over physical intimacy. Better not to ruin a good thing, Lindsay told herself at the time.

Or, Lindsay thought now, I was too chickenshit to deal with the truth about the feelings I kept trying to deny.

She was clutching Hope's journal to her chest, tears streaming down her cheeks, when her phone rang. It was Scott. She almost let it go to voice mail, but that felt like another betrayal.

"Hey," she said, wiping her face dry with the palm of her free hand.

"You need to turn on the news. Now. New York One."

Lindsay hopped up from the floor and scrambled for the remote control in the living room. "Wait, there's no New York One here."

"Well, find the Long Island equivalent. If it's running in the city, it's got to be on there."

"Damn it, there's no cable. What's going on?"

"It's about Hope. Lindsay, it's really bad."

"Scott, you're killing me. Just tell me."

"They found a dead body in the water, and now they're looking for Hope."

She sucked in her breath. "So she's dead."

"That's not what it sounded like to me. Shit, Lindsay, I gotta go. I saw the story in the break room, but they're yelling at me to get back to the conference room for this closing. I'm really sorry though, okay?"

"Sorry about what?

"Just find the press conference online."

She opened her laptop browser on the coffee table, typed in "Hope Miller East Hampton," and hit enter. There was a video posted by the Long Island ABC affiliate twelve minutes earlier. Lindsay clicked on the link, and a young male correspondent standing outside the Suffolk County Police Department appeared on the screen.

"At a press conference held in Islip this afternoon, Suffolk County's Homicide Squad, working with East Hampton Town

Police, announced that a death that had been widely rumored to be an accidental drowning has, in fact, been ruled a homicide. Thirty-six-year-old Alex Lopez's body was pulled from the water near Star Island at the eastern end of Suffolk County early yesterday morning. His pickup truck was found in a public parking lot in Montauk, not far from the docks where Lopez operated a fishing tour operation. Though investigators released no official statement regarding Mr. Lopez's cause of death until today, news of the discovery of his body spread quickly in the bustling Hamptons. On the heels of two other drownings already in this very early summer, it appeared likely that Mr. Lopez's death was yet another warning about the potential dangers of unusually rough ocean waves this year.

"However, in a press conference that just ended moments ago, Marcia, police officials made a shocking announcement: Alex Lopez died of a gunshot wound. No other details about his injuries were provided, but police made clear that they are investigating this case as a homicide. They also announced, Marcia, that they are looking for this woman, who has been known for years as Hope Miller, and who only recently moved to East Hampton in May."

The photograph that appeared next to the correspondent's face on the screen was the same one that Lindsay had been using for her missing-person flyers.

"Police say that a friend of this woman reported her missing almost exactly one week ago today."

Marcia at the studio had a question: "You said she's been 'known for years' by that name, Reggie. What do you mean by that?"

"Now that's when this story gets even more intriguing. I asked police the same question because the wording seemed unusual. It turns out that fifteen years ago, this woman, for whom police are now looking as a person of interest, was involved in a very serious car accident in central New Jersey. When she regained consciousness at the hospital, she was unable to recall her name or any other details regarding her identity. And, get this: all these years later, her past remains a complete mystery."

Marcia widened her eyes in a pantomime of shock. "That's pretty mind-blowing."

"It certainly is, Marcia. In addition to looking to question Hope Miller, police also alerted the public that they are seeking any information about this specific rug."

Hope's photograph was replaced by a photograph of a cream-colored Persian-style rug with green accents. "They say this is a mass-produced rug that sells for less than two hundred dollars and that it was missing from a location where Alex Lopez is thought to have been seen last. They also said that it may have been stained with blood, and that it's possible someone could have tried to hide or dispose of it in the last two weeks."

"Wow, that paints a dark picture, Reggie."

"The police did not connect the dots explicitly, but, yes, they certainly seem to have a theory about how that rug may have been used. Police were also coy about why they are looking for Hope Miller in connection with Alex Lopez's murder, and they were careful to say that she was not a suspect at this point, but simply a person who might have relevant information for their investigation. It seems safe to say, though, that we're likely to be hearing more about this fascinating case in the near future."

"Fascinating, indeed."

LINDSAY RETURNED TO HER BROWSER and searched for "Alex Lopez." Too broad a search. She tried "Alex Lopez East Hampton," but the top results were all local news summaries of the press conference announcing his murder.

"Alex Lopez Wichita Kansas." A restaurant owner. Obituary from eight years earlier. A bunch of high-school track times for some kid named Alex Lopez who was apparently quite a runner.

Who the hell was Alex Lopez, and why were police looking for Hope in connection with his death?

The DNA hit. It was the only explanation.

The reporter said that Alex Lopez was thirty-six years old, meaning he was thirteen when Janice Beale was killed. Definitely not an accomplice to a serial killer.

Lindsay leaped from the sofa at the sound of the bolt turning inside the front door. She ran faster than she knew she could and lunged so hard against the door that she cried out in pain from the impact against her right shoulder. She fought to reengage the lock, but it wouldn't turn. Whoever was breaking in had a key.

"I have a gun," she cried out in desperation, even though her Glock was locked in its safe in Manhattan. She heard two thumps of a fist against the wood, then the sound of a woman's voice.

"Lindsay, it's me."

Lindsay stepped back and allowed the door to fling open.

Hope's eyes were bloodshot, and her cheeks were streaked with tears. "I messed up, Lindsay. I really fucked up."

25

Tuesday, June 22, 3:12 p.m.

I don't think anyone followed me." Hope kept her voice low as Lindsay bolted the door shut.

Lindsay was frozen in place, unable to find her words. When she realized that she was face-to-face now with her friend, she also realized just how certain she had been that she would never see Hope again. Hope looked pale and exhausted. She had also lost several pounds and was apparently trying to disguise herself with a low bun and a navy-blue Montauk baseball cap. But she was here, alive.

Hope threw her arms around Lindsay's shoulders, and Lindsay returned the hug. Hope was the one to let go first, moving into the bedroom.

Lindsay noticed her friend's gaze pause on the open journal on the bed. "I'm sorry. I was looking for anything that might explain what happened to you."

Hope's eyes moved to the row of journals still neatly shelved together, then nodded. Did she know which entry Lindsay had intruded upon? Did she understand why?

"Hope, where have you been?" Lindsay asked. "Are you okay?"

"I've been hiding at one of the rental houses Evan manages. I told you not to look for me," she said, shaking her head.

"So those texts *were* from you."

"Of course. I even mentioned the armoire. It's a reference from, literally, the last time I saw you. Remember? When we left the armoire at the Becketts'?"

"I thought if someone had been watching us move, they could have known. And I didn't understand why you'd tell me not to look for you—"

"Because I didn't want to be found, Lindsay. And I didn't want you to be in danger. I thought I could figure it out by myself. I thought I could find out what he wanted and why, and then it would all be okay. But now . . ." She closed her eyes and exhaled. "He's dead. How is he possibly dead? They said I'm wanted on TV."

"They only said they were looking for you. As a witness. Someone who might have relevant information."

Hope clenched her jaw and held her gaze. "Are you honestly telling me as a defense attorney that I don't need to be scared right now?"

Lindsay looked away and shook her head. "So do you know this Alex Lopez person?" she eventually asked, her voice low.

"No!" Hope cried out. "At least, I don't think so. Or I mean, I didn't. But I think I know who he is now. And I hit him. I like basically stabbed him, and now they think I killed him."

Lindsay led Hope to the sofa. "Sit down, and start from the beginning."

IT TOOK A FEW FALSE starts, Hope getting bogged down in details Lindsay couldn't follow, but she finally steered Hope in a clear direction. "You said in your journal a couple of times that you thought someone was following you. Someone in a white pickup. Was that Alex Lopez?"

Hope nodded. "At least, I think so. I didn't know that at the time. I mean, I didn't even know for sure that anyone was following me, let alone who the guy was. I just sensed that I was being watched one night, but the cottage feels like a fishbowl without the curtains drawn, especially after living at the Becketts' for so many years." In New Jersey, Hope had lived in a second-floor garage apartment behind the main house on a wooded lot, whereas her current rental was only feet from the sidewalk, with no privacy. "Anyway, one time I got creeped out and saw a white pickup out there. And then another time, I thought I saw the same truck parked outside while I was getting a haircut, and I thought he looked a little familiar, but I wasn't sure."

"That was the last entry in your journal," Lindsay said. "I was convinced the guy had you locked in a basement or something. I've basically been going crazy. Why didn't you tell me when it was happening?"

"Because I didn't want to worry you. You've got to understand that the only place I can remember living is little tiny Hopewell. I'm not used to all these people, or to every single face belonging to a stranger. And I knew how much you disapproved of my decision to move here, and I assumed it was just my imagination going wild. I thought if I said anything to you, you'd drive out here and convince me to go back home."

She wasn't wrong. Lindsay realized she had broken her own practice of letting a client or a witness give their complete account of the facts, uninterrupted, before asking follow-up questions. "I get it. So then what happened?"

"I had an open house to stage in Sagaponack. I was in the house alone."

"Two Saturdays ago? The Stansfield house?" Another violation of her usual protocol, but she wanted to make sure they were talking about the same night.

"Yeah. How do you know—"

"I'll explain. Just go on."

"Anyway, I finished up the job. When I opened the front door to leave, he was standing there. It took me a second to realize it was the guy I'd seen with the white pickup truck. I tried to run back into the house, but he pushed his way inside and grabbed me. And then he said something like I was playing some kind of game." Hope was gazing at a spot on the wall, as if she was in a trance. "I just kept trying to fight him off, and he was saying crazy things like he wasn't going to let me ruin his life with my games. I tried explaining that I didn't even know who he was. I said he could look it up—that I've had amnesia for fifteen years—but he was looking at me like I was insane. And I'm saying this while I'm trying to get distance from him, and he's following me all over the room. I finally got hold of my keys in my purse." She returned her gaze to Lindsay. "I swear, I thought he was going to kill me."

Lindsay arched a brow and glanced toward the end table next to the sofa, where her own keys rested, complete with a purple, cat-head-shaped self-defense keychain that she knew matched Hope's. AKA Stabby Kitty.

Hope looked more like herself as she flashed a brief smile. "I can't believe I even thought to grab for it, but it actually worked. I managed to get two of my fingers into the holes and just began swinging. I aimed for his face. It drew blood. A lot. I don't know if it was his head or his eye, or what, but there was all this blood." She ran her fingertips against her own left temple. "He kind of stumbled backward and fell. All I could think about was getting out of there. I grabbed my purse and ran. I also took this."

She reached inside her purse and retrieved an iPhone, which she placed on the sofa between them.

"Is that his?" Lindsay asked.

Hope nodded, wincing. "It dropped out of his shirt pocket when he fell."

Lindsay knew her expression revealed her immediate analysis of the situation: *Not good.*

"I just wanted to know who he was," Hope explained. "I drove until I was sure he wasn't following me, and then pulled over to look through it real fast."

"Wait, how did you even get into his phone?" Any evidence that Hope was able to get past a locked phone screen would undermine her claim not to have known Alex Lopez.

"When I finally felt safe enough to pull over, I realized that could be a problem, but I guess he didn't have it protected. It was just on."

"And you've had it this whole time?" By now, the police would have triangulated the location information. The coverage in the Hamptons was notoriously spotty due to a scarcity of cell phone towers. She had to hope that it decreased the accuracy of the pings.

Hope nodded. "But I turned it off after I went through it in the car. Most of the emails were to Alex Lopez at ReelDeal.com. That's the name of the guide shop we used for the boat trip. I know this is crazy, but I'm almost positive he was our fishing guide."

"And you didn't recognize him when he showed up at the house?" Lindsay realized how judgmental she sounded, but she needed to know if Hope would be able to answer these questions when the police inevitably asked them.

"No. I barely paid him any attention. It's not like we were actually fishing—just enjoying the boat ride. And remember, he was wearing shades and that safari hat or whatever? You said something about how it wasn't fair because we couldn't tell if he was hot or not."

Lindsay summoned a memory of a dark-haired, olive-skinned man in mirrored aviator sunglasses and a tan cotton hat with flaps that covered the ears and neck from sun. Practical gear for someone who spent most days on the water, but also a hindrance to forming a clear impression of his appearance. If she could find photographs of Lopez in his usual guide attire, it could back up Hope's explanation.

Her mind skipped back to Lopez's mirrored sunglasses. She closed her eyes, drilling down on a vague memory. A floppy-haired kid—the one who caught the big blackfish—showing the fishing guide how to turn off the screen lock on his iPhone after the guide complained that he was constantly pulling off his shades to get his device's facial recognition to work. The kid offering to change the settings and then making fun of the guide for having such an obvious password. The guide joking that he was too boring for anyone to want to snoop through his cell.

"Did you learn anything else from his phone?" Lindsay asked. In a perfect world, she'd have an investigator conduct a full data analysis, but she knew that powering up the device was too risky.

"All the emails were about fishing trips. Most of the texts too. I jotted down a bunch of the phone numbers from the call log. I also looked through the contacts really fast, but nothing jumped out. I've been too afraid to turn it back on since then. If he had tracked his phone, it would have led him right to me. And I was obviously too afraid to come back here, so I went to one of the rental properties my boss manages. I knew the renters took off for a month to Napa Valley, and I knew where the spare key was hidden. I've been staying there."

"What about your car?"

"It's in the garage at the rental. I rode one of the house bikes here." Lindsay started to stand up, but Hope told her not to worry. "I locked it up near the train station and then walked the rest of the way. Figured it would be easier to dash inside someplace on foot if someone seemed to be following me."

Lindsay reached for Hope's hand and gave it a squeeze. "It's like you've been living inside a Netflix show for two weeks. Are you okay?"

"It's not as easy to be invisible as they make it look on TV."

"I'm just glad you're safe. And alive. I thought I'd never see you again."

"I can't believe he's dead. Or that the police think I killed him. I mean, even if I had, it would have been self-defense when he attacked me, and I would have called the police. But I'm absolutely positive he was alive when I left that house. I heard him kind of groaning and cussing as I ran out the door. They said on the news that he was shot, and his body was found in the water. They . . . what? Think I somehow got a gun, killed him, and threw him in the ocean? How would I get a full-grown dead man's body into a car by myself? And I don't even know how to shoot a gun—as I'm sure you remember."

The shooting range. What was it about firing that gun that had rattled her so badly?

"Look, we don't know for sure what the police think. They said for now you're a person of interest. I do know the police found Alex Lopez's blood in the foyer of the Stansfield house. I was the one who brought them there when I first reported you missing."

Hope pressed her eyes shut and bit her lip.

"Hope, I had no idea. How could I?"

"I'm not blaming you. At all, I promise. I just . . . I didn't know what to do. I could see how it would look. They'd ask all kinds of questions about who I am, where I came from, what I know. It was everything you warned me about when I moved." Her shoulders shook as she began to cry. "I didn't want to drag you into this until I at least figured out what was going on. I thought all I had to do was keep myself safe until I could figure out whatever connection I must have had to this guy. I have no idea why he'd start following me around town, or what kind of game he was accusing me of playing."

That asshole, Carter Decker, had pretended to be on Lindsay's side, to want her to make nice with him. She replayed the conversation in her head, realizing the damage she had inflicted.

We took a fishing guide trip. I was surprised she wanted to go.

So it was her idea?

She wanted to jump back in time to tell herself to stop talking.

"And you haven't seen Alex since you left him at the Stansfield house?"

"Not once. I swear."

"Did his face spark any kind of recognition? Maybe shake something loose from the past?"

She shook her head.

"What about the idea of Wichita, Kansas? Do you think it's possible you used to live there?"

"Why would you— Oh, wait. Whoa, this is bizarre."

"What? Are you remembering something?"

"Don't ask me why, but when you said Wichita, I immediately thought, Doo Dah. What does that even mean?"

Lindsay reached for her laptop on the coffee table and searched online for "Wichita Doo Dah."

"It says here that's what locals call their city. 'Doo Dah.' Origins unknown."

Hope's brow furrowed. "How in the world would I know that?"

"If you grew up there," Lindsay said, "which is what I think. It's a long story, but Alex Lopez definitely used to live there as a child. You two must have known each other."

Hope reached into her back pocket and pulled out a scrap of paper. "These are the phone numbers I jotted down from Alex's cell—every number in the log since we went on that boat trip. There actually aren't that many. Looks like he did most of his guide business by email. I googled all the numbers to see what I could find. This is the one I was most interested in: three calls back and forth to some number with a Chicago area code. I tried calling it using the landline at the rental after hitting star six seven, but now the number's disconnected."

"Okay, that's weird." Lindsay could see that Hope had scribbled three different dates and the note "disc-x" next to a number with an 873 prefix.

"Super weird. I'm thinking that has to be the person who killed him." Hope mimicked a shiver going down her spine. "But now you've got me wondering more about this other call," she said, pointing to a 316 number on the list. "That's the corporate headquarters of LockeHome in . . . guess where? Wichita, Kansas."

Lindsay knew the company well. She had even read Melanie Locke's book, *How to Be a Lady Boss.*

Hope had written "LockeHome" next to the number, along with "April 12," approximately two months earlier and, more interestingly, exactly one day after their fishing trip with Alex Lopez. Lindsay pointed out the timing to Hope.

"I didn't think anything of it until you started asking me about Wichita. It has to be connected, right? Maybe he recognized me on the boat, and then called someone we both used to know?"

"Does Edgemoor Park ring a bell for you? Or COP summer camp? It's a summer camp through the police department in Wichita."

"Not really, but we do know I'm good at softball." It was one of the many tiny clues that hinted at Hope's past. Her writer's bump. Her unexpected crushing of the ball when they were goofing around at the batting cages at Chelsea Piers. The fact that she knew how to make homemade lemonade that was so freaking good that people who drove through Hopewell would swing by the diner for a to-go cup. "Why?"

Why, indeed. The camp was just one of a thousand ways that Alex and Hope might have known each other in Wichita. "Just a theory I've been working on. First things first, we've got to figure out a way for you to turn yourself in—" Hope rose from the sofa, but Lindsay grabbed her forearm. "They're going to argue that hiding shows consciousness of guilt. Right now, you've got an explanation for it. This crazy person attacked you, and you had no way of knowing whether the police here would believe you. But now that they've got an alert out for you, I promise: the best move is for you to present yourself voluntarily."

They were interrupted by a ringing sound coming from the bedroom. "Don't go anywhere," Lindsay said, heading for her cell phone. Seeing it was a call from the local area code, she picked up.

"Hello? I got this number from a flyer on the beach—about a missing woman?"

Not missing anymore, Lindsay thought. "Yes, I posted those. You've seen her?"

"She's . . . what?" the woman asked. "Your daughter or something?"

The *s* in *something* was slightly slurred. A nut job, or a little help from a bottle? From the heavy background sounds of wind, Lindsay's best guess was that the woman was calling from a beach.

"A friend," Lindsay said. "A very dear friend. So you've seen her?" she asked again.

"Indeed, I have. And I'm trying to figure out why the hell she was stalking my boyfriend."

26

Tuesday, June 22, 3:40 p.m.

As he entered the East End Senior Thriftshop, Carter Decker inhaled a mouthful of dust and mothballs. A dying fluorescent light buzzed loudly. Racks of clothing and tables of clutter were scattered sparsely throughout the otherwise barren space.

"Hello?" he called out.

A woman with close-cropped silver hair appeared through a swinging door at the back of the shop. "Can I help you?" She was probably in her late seventies but seemed to have no problem managing the large cardboard box in her lean, unsleeved arms. Nevertheless, Carter rushed to offer his assistance, which she gladly accepted.

"Are you Mrs. Streeter? I'm Detective Carter Decker. We spoke on the phone."

"Well, of course you are. Sorry if you were waiting. I'm here by myself today, and we've got a lot of new inventory in the back that needed processing."

"I just got here, not to worry. Do you have the rug ready?"

"Oh, I've still got it in the back. We hadn't made the decision yet whether it was worth sending out to get professionally cleaned or not. We weren't going to sell it in its current state. And, well . . . none of us was willing to clean up someone else's bodily fluids." She made an ick face that he found absolutely delightful.

Carter's request to release a photograph of Evan Hunter's rug might have panned out. When Hope Miller was initially reported missing, Carter suspected that she had run off with the cash advance she had borrowed from her boss, along with the rug she was supposed to have placed in the Stansfields' foyer. The discovery of Alex Lopez's body had changed that theory. The area rug was about the right size to pull a corpse from a house.

Fifteen minutes after the press conference announcing that they were looking for both Hope Miller and the rug, Carter had received a phone call from a volunteer at one of the local charitable thrift shops, identifying herself as "Mrs. Streeter, the supervisor of operations" and saying she was "ninety-nine percent certain" they had the rug in question. The IKEA label was still attached to the back of the rug, and there was a bloodstain that she described as being "wine red, about the size of an index card."

Carter's plan was to inspect the rug for himself and then call out a crime scene technician to transport it to the lab and complete the chain of custody record. "So one of your volunteers pulled this out of the dump?" he asked.

East Hampton did not provide public trash services. Residents either paid a private company or schlepped their own garbage and recycling to the processing center. As a result, the crowds there on weekends were a combination of some of the poorest and wealthiest people in town—those who couldn't afford the alternative, and those who could, but took pleasure in the sense of self-reliance that came from taking out their own trash.

Knowing the physical setup of the local dump, Carter hadn't understood exactly where the rug had been discovered. To his knowledge, once something was dropped in the dumpster, it was beyond access to the public.

"Oh no, trust me," Mrs. Streeter said, "these aren't our employees or officially sanctioned volunteers. It's a small group of seniors who have taken it upon themselves to scour the dump for possible donations. To tell you the truth, though, most of what they bring to us ends up right back in the dumpster. You know that drop-off center next to the trash cans where you can leave things that others might be interested in?"

Carter nodded. He called it "zombie land." Every weekend, crowds of people would linger in the area, hoping some multimillionaire would swing by with a truckload of lightly used luxury goods. If a Porsche SUV stopped at the curb, the crowd would swarm toward the fresh meat. A beat-up jalopy? The zombies might not bother to rise from their beach chairs.

"A couple of years ago," Mrs. Streeter went on to explain, "a few folks began bringing in donations from the drop-off area. Then if they saw anyone tossing something salvageable, they'd ask if they could have it for us instead. But now one of them goes even further and hassles the workers to pull stuff from the dumpsters. I mean, it's very sweet of them to try, but the other day, they brought in a laminate card table that was missing two legs. Give me a break."

"So do you know where the rug came from?"

"Oh sure. Bob brought it in himself. Bob Taylor. I've got his number written down for you already and told him you'd likely be calling. I think he's pretty excited about it, to tell you the truth. He's a hoot, but also a Chatty Cathy, so prepare yourself. He was so proud when he brought in the rug. I got the impression he thought it was a real Persian carpet. He also thought it was a wine stain, but when I saw it for myself . . . well, I wasn't going to risk it. Like I said, we weren't real sure what to do with it, and then I saw the press conference playing on the TV."

"Do you know when he found it?"

"He got to the dump that Sunday at eight a.m. to get first dibs on the drop-offs, and it was close to the top of the big trash dumpster."

"Which Sunday was that?"

She calculated the date in her head. It was the morning of the open house at the Stansfields'.

Carter knew that the garbage processing center did not have any surveillance cameras near the dumpsters themselves, but they did have a camera at the entrance's check-in booth. Maybe he'd get lucky.

Back in his car, Carter reached out to a crime scene technician to follow up with Mrs. Streeter. Next up was the recycling center, to ask them to pull all camera footage from the morning the rug was discovered. He was seven minutes into a conversation with Bob Taylor when he heard the sound of another call coming in. A Manhattan area code. He let it go to voice mail. Mrs. Streeter hadn't been lying about Bob Taylor's loquaciousness.

Another six minutes later, he finally hung up. He'd learned nothing new from Bob Taylor but had been able to confirm his account of the rug's discovery. He hit his phone screen to play the latest voice-mail message.

"Detective Decker, this is Ashley Banks from Tiffany and Company on Fifth Avenue. You sent me that photograph of the double heart sterling silver necklace. I went through our catalogue archives and was able to locate it. We discontinued that piece twelve years ago and launched it five years before that."

If Alex Lopez had bought the necklace, he certainly hadn't done so for his current girlfriend. He would have been at most twenty-four years old at the time of the purchase. It occurred to Decker that Lopez could have simply found a lost necklace dropped on his boat and stashed it in a tackle box in case a customer came forward to claim it.

He started his engine, letting Ashley Banks's message play to the end. "It's what we call a 'starter' necklace, meaning it retailed at a hundred and ten for the basic stainless-steel version you showed me. But here's the thing, Detective. We have a resident institutionalist—our archivist. He's been here nearly forty years and knows our merchandise like the back of his hand. I showed him the old catalogue picture, and I thought he was going to have a stroke. It turns out you're not the first detective to have asked about this necklace. It has to do with a murder fifteen years ago in Wichita, Kansas." Carter felt a humming in his ears. "Have you ever heard of Melanie Locke?" This was it. The boom. Finally. "The only thing missing from the house after her husband's murder was this same piece of jewelry. Anyway, I have no idea if it's connected, and we sold thousands of these over the years, but call me for the details if you're interested."

Carter was definitely interested.

27

Tuesday, June 22, 3:58 p.m.

Lindsay spotted the black Ford Bronco at the far end of the parking lot, as Alex Lopez's girlfriend had promised. *You're out there looking for your missing friend,* she'd said, *but the love of my life is dead, and the police won't even tell me anything, but I know it's got something to do with that woman.*

When Lindsay asked why she would say such a thing, the woman had lashed out. *Are you deaf? Because she was stalking him, and now he's dead! One plus one equals two.*

The woman had refused to give her name or any other details. *Not unless you tell me who she is. In person. I want to see you and know who you are, too.*

Lindsay had a decision to make. Get Hope's version first, or go talk to the drunk woman. The clear preference was the former, but she needed to get to Atlantic Beach before the woman heard the police alert or sobered up enough to realize that sharing information with a likely suspect's best friend was a bad move. If this woman was going to claim that Hope had been stalking Alex before his murder—instead of the other way around—Lindsay needed to know that before she arranged for Hope to turn herself in.

Keeping her facial expression neutral, she had told Hope that the call was from a woman who might know why Lopez was interested in Hope. It wasn't a dishonest answer. Now she had to pray that Hope would keep her promise to stay put at the cottage until Lindsay returned.

Lindsay pulled up next to the SUV, rolled down her window, and waved. The woman at the wheel had plump, suntanned cheeks and bloodshot eyes. She leaned in Lindsay's direction, and the passenger side door of the SUV opened. Lindsay climbed in.

"Lindsay Kelly," she said, offering her hand.

"Very funny."

"It wasn't meant to be. That's my name."

"That was what she said her name was." The woman pulled a rumpled sheet of paper from the console and thrust it in Lindsay's direction. It was a copy of the flyer that Lindsay had posted around town.

Lindsay looked down at Hope's smiling face in the photo, afraid of what she was about to learn from this stranger.

"Her name is Hope. Hope Miller. And you are . . ."

"Jocelyn Hodge."

"You met her?" Lindsay asked, gesturing to the photo.

"I cut her hair. I work at the Lock Box." Lindsay recognized the name of a supermodern, minimalist-looking salon on the main road through Bridgehampton. "She was a walk-in. Most new clients, they're on their phone scrolling through Insta or Twitter, answering their emails, whatever. Or they let me fill the silence, asking if they're out here visiting, their plans for the weekend, typical small talk. But your friend? I couldn't shut her up. Is it true that she had just moved here from New Jersey?"

Lindsay nodded. "A town called Hopewell."

"Hope from Hopewell." The woman gave her a skeptical look. "You sure she's not lying about her name to you, too?"

"When did you give her a cut?" Lindsay asked.

"Two weeks ago? Maybe three." It lined up with Hope's diary entry about the man watching her as she left the salon. "She was super nosy.

It started out with her saying she was new in town. How she was having a hard time meeting people. Like the way the long-term actual human beings who live here don't need to make any new friends. Or it was a bunch of city assholes she had nothing in common with. I mean, she wasn't wrong. You need to move here full time and make your bones if you really want to have a life."

"When you called me, you said you thought she was stalking your boyfriend."

Jocelyn blew her bangs from her eyes. "Stalking? Okay, maybe I exaggerated. But once she was in my chair, she kind of moved the conversation over to whether I was single or not. I told her I had a boyfriend, and she asked how we met. Seemed like girl talk at first. But once we were on the subject, she just kept grilling me. Whether he had grown up here or was new to town. Where he had moved from. How he was settling in as a newcomer. Whether I thought he'd stay for the long haul. If I had met his family. It was . . . a lot."

"I'm sorry for your loss, by the way," Lindsay said. Reminding herself that Jocelyn did not yet appear to know about the police announcement, she quickly added, "You told me on the phone that Alex passed away. When was the last time you saw him?"

"Two weeks ago, a few days before I filed the police report. I found his truck last week in the lot in Montauk. I had a moment of hope thinking I'd find him, too . . ." She choked back a sob.

"What makes you think there's a connection between my friend and Alex? Because she was asking about your relationship?"

"Nope. Because when the cops told me he was shot in the head, they showed me this exact picture." Lindsay flinched as Jocelyn flicked the back of the flyer with her middle finger. "They asked me if she looked familiar. I knew immediately who she was, but they wouldn't tell me why they asked. Was he sleeping with her or something? I mean, I guess it would be better if I just knew the truth, because right now? I'm not sure whether to hate your friend or be worried for her. Maybe whoever killed Alex also—" She let the thought hang in the silence.

"As far as I know, Hope didn't know your Alex. Did he ever mention her to you?"

She shook her head. "He's literally the only guy I've ever dated who never gave me any reason to doubt him. I never caught him hiding his phone or checking out another woman in the corner of his eye. He was just . . . good. Solid. The only thing I can possibly think of is that we had a little too much wine one night and he seemed sort of distracted. He started rambling about how someone he used to know had booked a tour. It was messing with his head for some reason. I tried to press him, but he got really mad and eventually passed out. In the morning, he said he didn't know what I was talking about. His company's a tour outfit called Reel Deal Fishing. Any chance your friend went out on the water?"

Lindsay had already given this information to Carter Decker, so she figured she might recycle it to gain Jocelyn's trust. "A couple of months ago, I think. Do you know where Alex grew up?"

"Arizona. And then he lived in Alaska before moving here."

"Not Wichita, Kansas?"

"Not that he ever mentioned. The police asked me the same thing. Is that where your friend is from?"

Was it? Lindsay didn't answer. Instead, she said, "Sorry, I still don't understand why you said Hope was a stalker."

"Look, it's all in retrospect. When she came into the salon, another stylist was free, but she specifically asked for me, saying it was because we had the 'same style of hair.' Not exactly unique." She pulled at her long dark-blond waves with perfectly manicured fingertips. "And now I've learned she gave me a fake name. Not cool. As much as I loved Alex, his past was a mystery to me. Maybe your friend can cast some light on it. If you find her," she added.

Alex had shared little more with this woman about his history than Hope knew of her own. Had they been running from the same danger? "You said Hope's chitchat only seemed odd to you in hindsight. That was after the police talked to you?"

"Yeah. After they showed me your friend's picture."

"So you told them everything you just said to me?" Lindsay asked.

"Yep, but did they tell me anything in return? Nope. They treated me like some bimbo."

"Do you remember who you talked to? Was it a Detective Carter Decker?"

"Yup. That's definitely the guy. Not exactly sensitive. Alex? Alex was sensitive. I really loved him. And he had such a strong sense of justice, a firm line between right and wrong. When that superfamous movie director got Me Too'd for making passes at teenage girls, and tried to say the times had changed since back then? It was like Alex wanted to stab him through the TV screen. Even though the guy made two of Alex's favorite movies, Alex swore he'd never watch them again."

The comment reminded Lindsay of Katy Barnes's Facebook post. "This is a weird question, but did he ever mention a sports camp to you? Maybe one where kids were getting abused?"

Jocelyn shook her head. "If he had been abused, I really think he would have told me. Why?"

"Just trying to tie some things together."

"So . . . you seem like a good person. Your friend . . . if she's okay, will she help? Or—you know—should I just blame her for all of this?" She hiccupped and then let out an embarrassed laugh.

"Hope didn't know your boyfriend, and she definitely wasn't stalking him." Lindsay realized that she sounded like she was trying to convince herself as much as anyone.

"I mean . . . maybe he was seeing her on the side or something? The police said they found a woman's necklace on his boat. I want to think it was for me, but—"

Lindsay needed to get out of this car and back to Hope. "She's a good person," she said, fumbling with the passenger door. "Again, I'm sorry for your loss."

"Wait. Will you call me if you find her? I need to know what happened."

Lindsay retrieved a business card from the inside of her cell phone case and dropped it on the passenger seat. "My number's there."

Jocelyn inspected the card. "A criminal defense attorney? Are you kidding me?"

"Do you have someone who can drive you home?"

Jocelyn looked at her through narrowed eyes. "Don't judge me. I have a hundred people I can call. I know everyone. I have friends and family who love me. I won't be alone."

Lindsay nodded and left the woman alone with her grief.

LINDSAY TOOK A MOMENT IN the cottage driveway to check her phone for new messages. A text message from Scott: We're knocking this deal out faster than I thought. About to sign the closing docs. I can come back out if you want. Are you okay?

And a new message on Facebook from Katy Barnes: Dear Ms. Kelly, I received your unsolicited direct message and will not be responding further. Please do not contact me again regarding Edgemoor Rec or any other subject matter.

Lindsay used the dictation function to draft a quick response. I respect the right of any woman to speak—or not to speak—her truths, but please hear me out. You could be in a position to help another woman who desperately needs it right now.

She hit the send key and received an error message. You can't reply to this conversation. Katy had blocked her.

How had Katy gone from publicly posting allegations on social media to what sounded like a lawyerly refusal to discuss the subject? Pulling up the Facebook page where she had originally spotted the post about abuse at the camp, Lindsay confirmed that Katy had since deleted the comment.

If Lindsay had to bet, someone had either threatened or paid the woman to keep silent, but she couldn't focus on that now. She needed to talk to Hope.

28

Tuesday, June 22, 4:31 p.m.

S orry, I hope you don't mind." Lindsay's computer was open on
Hope's lap. "I was looking for any updates about the police announcement. Is something wrong? You look upset."

Lindsay's relief that Hope hadn't left the cottage quickly gave way
to impatience. "Tell me again why you told me to stop looking for you."

"Because I thought that guy Alex was after me, and for all I knew,
he had friends in the police department. I was trying to come up with a
plan."

"Did you borrow money from Evan? He says you asked for a cash
advance, but why wouldn't you just ask me?"

"I was really embarrassed. You made it pretty clear that you didn't
think I could swing it out here on my own, and I wasn't ready to admit
I was struggling."

"Evan said you took a rug to the Stansfields', but it wasn't there
when he arrived for the open house."

"What is going on? You're, like, cross-examining me." Hope set the
laptop on the coffee table.

"This is kid gloves compared to what the police will do." Lindsay
crossed her arms in front of her. "What happened to the rug?"

"I went back to the Stansfields' the next morning—like, really early in the morning. Five a.m. I knew Evan had the open house, and I didn't want him to walk in and see a bunch of blood."

"Or a dead body?"

"God, no, Lindsay. You have to believe me. Alex Lopez was definitely alive when I left. When I got back the next morning, I drove around the neighborhood looking for his pickup before I parked. The lights at the house were still on, and the front door was unlocked. I saw the bloodstain on the rug, so I rolled it up, tossed it in my trunk, and got the hell out of there. I dropped it at the dump as soon as it opened and went straight back to the rental house."

"Why didn't you tell me any of this before?"

"Because you started talking about me turning myself in, and then ran off the second you got that phone call. What's up with all this grilling? Did you find that woman who called? What did she say?"

"It was the woman who cut your hair at the Lock Box."

Hope tilted her head. "Why would she call you?"

"She saw the flyers I posted."

"She did my hair a couple of weeks ago. It makes sense she'd recognize me."

"No, it's more than that. You gave her my name?"

Hope scoffed. "No, I didn't. I told her my name was Linda."

"Why? Why would you do that?"

"My whole reason for coming here was to blend in for once. Not to be the town weirdo. When I was talking to the stylist, she seemed pretty fun, and I thought maybe I could make a new friend. Then when she asked me my name, I just sort of froze. I already told her I moved here from Hopewell. If you google Hope Miller and Hopewell, it turns up those early stories from when we were still trying to find someone who might know me. So I reached for a name, and out popped Linda."

"She said you were asking her a million questions, especially about her boyfriend."

Hope pressed her palms against her cheeks. "This is just cringewor-thy, hearing about myself through someone else's eyes. Look, I was ob-viously trying too hard. A little thirsty to make a new friend, okay? I really missed you."

Lindsay felt heat in her chest, knowing that she should have listened to her instincts and driven to Long Island when she first thought some-thing was wrong. "Then why did you keep icing me out?"

"Because I was telling myself I needed to do this on my own. To be less dependent on you—and everyone I know. In Hopewell, it's like everyone still treats me like I'm the town's little sister. What are you not telling me? Obviously, something that hairdresser said has you rattled."

"Did you talk to her about her boyfriend?"

She shrugged. "I guess so. We were shooting the shit. I think I asked how they met because it seems like everyone meets online now, and the whole idea of it freaks me out."

Lindsay decided to rip off the Band-Aid. "The hairdresser's boy-friend was Alex Lopez. And she told the police that you sought her out, gave her a fake name, and then spent the whole appointment asking about him. She also told them that Alex recently mentioned that some-one from his past had shown up on a boat trip. That he seemed upset, but then he wouldn't give her any details."

Hope's shoulders slumped as she processed the implications. "And they know I was the one who made the fishing plans."

Thanks to me, Lindsay thought. She was afraid of driving Hope back into hiding, but it was essential that she understand the gravity of her situation. It was becoming clear why they would suspect her of killing Lopez.

But Lindsay's job was to differentiate a suspicion from actual proof. The police would need physical evidence. They'd need a concrete the-ory. Where did Hope get a gun? Where was the gun now? Where did the murder take place? How did she move the body? Lindsay saw rea-sonable doubt everywhere she looked.

"The keychain you used to defend yourself," Lindsay said. "Do you still have it?"

Hope nodded, reached into her purse, and produced a key ring, the purple cat-shaped self-defense device. "I should probably dump it, huh?"

Hope had clearly washed it, but trace DNA evidence was still a possibility. And even without blood evidence, any physical cuts or bruises left behind on Lopez's body could be matched to the shape of the two "ears" that Hope had wielded as a weapon against him.

As of now, Hope was only a potential witness, not yet subject to a subpoena or search warrant. And to Lindsay's knowledge, no grand jury had been convened. As a result, Hope's keychain did not officially qualify as formal "evidence," which meant Hope could still dispose of it without facing criminal charges.

On the other hand, as a member of the bar, Lindsay was in dangerous ethical territory if she explicitly advised Hope to destroy tangible personal property that was obviously relevant to a homicide investigation.

She was in the process of explaining the law—knowing that Hope would read between the lines and get rid of the little piece of metal that could directly connect her to Lopez's physical injuries—when they both froze at the sound of a car pulling into the driveway, followed by the slamming of car doors.

Lindsay recognized Detective Carter Decker as one of four men approaching the front door. "It's police," she whispered, even as she whisked Hope's keychain from the coffee table. She did not mention the sheet of paper that Decker had clutched in his right hand. Ninety percent odds it was a warrant.

Her Audi was in the driveway, and any number of people could have seen her walk into the house only minutes earlier. If she didn't answer the door, it would look incriminating. Lindsay quickly scanned the room and gestured for Hope to move to an armchair in the far corner of the living room, out of sight of the front porch. If she was wrong about the warrant, she could buy them time.

"No matter what happens, you say nothing, okay?" She slid Hope's key ring onto her own and dropped it into her purse, along with Alex Lopez's phone, then slipped her own cell into her back pocket. "Answer no questions. Offer no explanations. The only English you speak is that you're not talking without the consent of your lawyer. You got it?"

Hope nodded, her eyes filled with fear. Ninety percent odds it was a warrant, which meant only ten percent odds of the encounter ending without an arrest. "No matter what," she said once again. "Even if they bring you in."

Hope blinked rapidly, but nodded again. If anything, the warning seemed to calm her. She now knew what she was facing.

Lindsay managed to get to the front door before the police knocked. She opened it a customary distance. "Detective Decker," she said.

"Ms. Kelly." He held up the sheet of paper in his hands. "We have a warrant to search these premises."

She took it from him and did a quick scan: i's dotted, t's crossed. As she expected.

"That's fine. You should know that my client, Hope Miller, is seated in a chair directly to my right. She is unarmed and ready to—"

"What the fuck, Lindsay—" Carter shook his head.

"She came here seeking legal advice after seeing that publicity stunt you pulled. She had every intention of contacting you but wanted to make sure she had a lawyer with her, since you have obviously jumped to some very mistaken conclusions. I'm going to ask her to slowly rise and walk toward us—"

"Save it for a courtroom," he said. He pushed the door open and stepped inside, and his three fellow officers—all in uniform—followed. Two of them drew their weapons. Hope cowered, raising her hands in the air on instinct.

"Completely unnecessary," Lindsay said firmly. "I told you she was ready to walk outside."

Carter waved for them to lower their guns as he slipped a pair of handcuffs from his belt and reached for Hope's arm to pull her into a standing position. "You're Hope Miller, to be clear?"

Hope looked to Lindsay for guidance. She nodded. Lindsay was confident it was the only question she would be answering.

Carter cuffed Hope's wrists in front of her and signaled that she could resume her position in the armchair. "I want to be clear you're not under formal arrest, but the law gives me the authority to restrain you under the circumstances while we execute a search warrant of this property pursuant to judicial authorization. You want to back me up on that, Ms. Kelly?"

"Actually, you have the right to keep her from leaving, but the right to use handcuffs isn't automatic."

"As I'm aware, Counselor. It's based on the individual facts of the case, which is why your client is cuffed quite comfortably with wrists in front and sitting in a nice cozy chair instead of the back of a patrol car. Any other accommodations we can make?"

"The law gives you the right to keep me from leaving as well, but are you going to handcuff me too?" She knew it wasn't even a close call. She wouldn't be cuffed, but that wasn't her real concern.

He told the other officers to begin searching. "I also have the authority to tell you to leave the premises while we search, which I'm officially using."

It was the decision she was hoping for, but she wasn't going to let him know that. "I'm her lawyer."

"Which she has a right to during custodial interrogation, but she's not in custody, and I'm not questioning her. There's no right to counsel during the execution of a search warrant—as I'm sure you know."

She grabbed her laptop and reached for her purse on the sofa as she started to leave, but he held up a hand.

"I'm going to need to search the purse before you take it."

"Your warrant is for the premises. That doesn't allow you to search me."

"Not your person. But as to any container on the property? For all we know, that belongs to her." He gestured toward Hope.

Carter was more knowledgeable of the constitutional rules than she would have expected. "To represent my client, I need my phone. My driver's license too, unless you're detaining me. And I have notes in there as well, which are covered by attorney work product privilege."

"And you're welcome to take all of it with you once I give a quick look. You'll consent to that?"

"I'm not giving you consent to search my bag apart from the authority you claim to have under your search warrant. Do what you're going to do."

He took a cursory glance into her purse, as she'd thought he would, and handed it to her. "Peace be with you."

He wasn't quite as clever as he thought. "This will likely take a while," she said to Hope. "I'm going to get you something to eat at least." She turned to Decker. "Officers, can I bring you anything?"

They ignored the request.

She made sure that Decker didn't have anyone follow her from the house before parking on Newtown Lane, removing Hope's cat keychain from her key ring, and dropping it in a trash can beneath a rumpled takeout bag. After a quick pop in to Carissa's Bakery, she slipped to the opposite side of the street and dumped Alex Lopez's cell phone.

No turning back now.

She heard Hope's voice in her head. *Don't ask me why, but when you said Wichita, I immediately thought, Doo Dah.* There was only one explanation: like Alex Lopez, Hope had grown up in Wichita.

She opened the Facebook app on her phone and pulled up the summer camp alumni page where she'd found Katy Barnes's post. She scrolled until she spotted a user named Holly Gunther, and then looked up the camp's phone number. She got back into her car to make the call.

The woman who picked up sounded like she had started smoking straight out of the womb. "Edgemoor Rec."

"Oh, hi, my name is Holly Gunther, and I went to camp there when I was a kid." She hoped the woman wouldn't recognize the name. "My old fifth-grade teacher is retiring, and her family is trying to collect messages from all the students she had such an impact on over the years. She's the best teacher I ever had."

"Oh my gosh, that's so sweet!"

"I'm trying to find a kid from my class named Alex Lopez. I know he went to COP camp, too."

She heard keys tapping on the other end of the line. "A few years ago, I did my best to digitize all the alumni info and such, but it's catch as catch can. Yep, he's in here. Enrolled for three summers. But there's no contact information. I mean, that was a long time ago."

"I think he had siblings?" She was spitballing now. "Any other Lo-pezes in those same years?"

"Yep, here we go: Emilia. Enrolled for the same years. We do our best to record their age and grade. It looks like she was one year older than Alex. But we only have her name. Could be two different families, for all I know."

"That's still helpful. Thanks." Emilia was a less common name than Alex. If they were siblings, maybe Lindsay could find the sister, and maybe she'd recognize an old photograph of Hope. A lot of ifs and maybes, but it was better than nothing. "I've got an even trickier request. There's a girl I went to high school with who was super close to Mrs. Jones, but no one can remember her name, and we don't want to ruin the surprise by asking Mrs. Jones directly. Her children found a photograph of her—that's how close they are—and a bunch of us are just trying to place a name to the face. Any chance I can send the picture to you to see if any of the long-term staff remembers her?"

"From back then? Oh, bless your heart, no. I've been here . . . ten, eleven years? And I'm the old-timer of the staff. Some of the cops volunteer year after year, but they'd all be long retired by now."

Lindsay had known it was a long shot that someone from the camp might recognize Hope. "So, wow, you've worked there a while though. Nothing to do with Mrs. Jones, but I heard some pretty dark rumors a few years ago about bad stuff that may have happened to some of the kids at the camp. Abuse, from what I heard. But I never saw even a hint of that, to be clear. The cops were such great role models, and we had so much fun. Sometimes I wonder if people just make stuff up years later to get attention. Did you ever hear whispers about anything like that?"

There was a pause at the other end of the line, and when Smoky Voice spoke again, she sounded less friendly: "What did you say your name was again?"

"Sorry, I didn't mean to keep you so long. Thanks for your help!"

The first hit for Emilia Lopez in Wichita, Kansas, was a LinkedIn profile for a paralegal at the Immigrant Community Legal Office. According to her resume, she'd earned a BA from Wichita State University only four years earlier, but graduated from Southeast High fifteen years before that, making her roughly thirty-seven years old. Lindsay thought she could see a resemblance to Alex Lopez through the eyes and forehead.

When she called the number listed on the profile, it went straight to voice mail. "You've reached Emilia Lopez with the Immigrant Community Legal Office. Today is Tuesday, June 22. I will be meeting with clients for the rest of the afternoon. Leave a message at the tone, or if this is an urgent matter, press zero for a receptionist. If—and only if—you are an existing client and are facing the threat of imminent detention by immigration authorities, press three to be connected to my cell phone." Lindsay was tempted to press three, but she knew it would immediately put her on a bad footing with the woman she was desperate to talk to.

After the beep, she left her name and number, explaining that she was a lawyer in New York City. Before disconnecting, she added, "It's about your brother, Alex."

WHEN SHE RETURNED TO THE cottage, she rapped her knuckles gently on the door, doing her best to pretend that she had not just disposed of two critical pieces of evidence in a murder investigation.

When Decker opened the door, she handed him the box of muffins she had bought at Carissa's. "Have you finished up yet? My client is happy to answer any fair questions as long as she has counsel to represent her."

Lindsay, of course, would be the one to determine which questions were fair.

"Is she? That's good to hear." He turned his head and spoke in Hope's direction. "Let's start with, What do you know about the death of Richard Mullaney?"

"Don't answer that," Lindsay called out, pushing past Carter so she could see Hope, still seated in the corner chair, her cuffed hands on her lap. She searched Hope's face for any sign of recognition. A flicker of light in her eyes, followed by a blink. Had Lindsay imagined it? Or maybe it was a blink of confusion. "And what kind of ambush is this? First you don't look for her after she got attacked by a stranger, then you turn it around and hold a press conference where you basically accuse her of murder. Now you pull some other name out of a hat?"

"It was a simple enough question. If the name means nothing to her, that's all she needs to say."

"On my advice, my client is invoking all her Fifth Amendment rights."

"Yep, that's pretty much what I thought," Decker said. "Hope Miller, you are under arrest." He moved quickly toward Hope's chair and pulled her to her feet. She began screaming. "No. Please. Stop!"

In case there was any doubt that her custodial status had changed, he unlocked her handcuffs only to resecure them more tightly behind her back. Hope winced as he wrenched her shoulders together.

As calmly as Hope had followed Lindsay's instructions not to answer questions, she clearly had not processed the reality that this moment might come. Her expression was panicked, and when her gaze finally met Lindsay's, she looked desperate for a solution that couldn't be offered. "Help me. Lindsay, I don't have anyone else but you."

They loaded Hope into the back of a marked police car in front of the cottage. She looked like a dog being taken away to a shelter as the car pulled out from the curb. Lindsay wiped her eyes with the back of her hands before waving for Detective Decker's attention in the front yard.

"I need to get back inside that house. Your rash and unnecessary decision to take her into custody makes it imperative that I be able to do my work."

"Not here, you won't. The warrant authorizes a search for trace evidence, which means I've got a team in there pulling latent prints—well, you know the drill. We might be done in time for you to sleep there tonight, but I'm not making any promises."

"You're disrupting my ability to provide effective assistance of counsel."

He opened the door to his black Charger and climbed in. "Guess them's the breaks when you set up shop in a murder suspect's residence. Oh, but if you want your muffins back . . ."

She stepped closer to his open door and leaned one arm against it. "So who's Richard Mullaney?"

Decker gazed up at her and shook his head. "Damn, she's really got you fooled."

29

Tuesday, June 22, 6:10 p.m.

Based on Lindsay's experience defending clients before in Suffolk County, she knew that Hope was being transported to the East Hampton town police station, where she'd be placed in an interrogation room. Contrary to the criminal procedural rules of one-hour network dramas, Hope would not have the right to bring Lindsay into the room with her. Her only protection under *Miranda* was to have a lawyer present if the police actually interrogated her. Because Hope had already invoked her right to counsel, police, instead of questioning her, would leave her alone in silence. They'd let her imagine spending an entire night in a jail cell. They'd let her wonder what evidence they might have against her. Maybe she'd "happen to overhear" them speaking to each other about the strength of their case. In short, they'd wait for her to crack.

If she did—if the suspect herself initiated the conversation—then all bets were off. They could try once again to get her to waive her *Miranda* rights. But one thing they definitely would not be doing was calling Lindsay to the police station.

Lindsay was confident that Hope wouldn't break. She'd sit in silence.

If they even asked her if she was hungry, she'd say "lawyer." If Lindsay had to guess, the police might wait three hours, four tops, before pulling the plug. They'd either cut her loose when she didn't incriminate herself or initiate the full booking process—in which case Hope would be photographed, fingerprinted, and held overnight. Lindsay would not see her again until shortly before her first court appearance the following day at the East Hampton Town Justice Court, where they'd learn whether the district attorney planned to pursue charges. If so, she would likely be remanded to the Suffolk County jail in Riverhead, where she'd be strip-searched by a female guard and given a set of dark-blue scrubs to wear.

That meant that Lindsay had three hours, four tops, to find some exculpatory evidence. She didn't need to solve Alex Lopez's murder or prove Hope's innocence to a certainty. She just needed to rattle Decker's cage hard enough to keep him from booking Hope. If that failed, and they kept her overnight, she'd take a second bite at the apple in the morning to persuade the district attorney's office not to file charges.

She hopped into her car and started the engine to get the air conditioner running. The cottage's Wi-Fi signal was fine from here. If the Lincoln Lawyer could run an entire law practice from the back seat of a town car, she could manage this for a few hours.

There was so much she didn't know. She started with a Google search of Richard Mullaney.

The results were still loading when her phone rang. It was Scott.

"Hey," she said.

"Did you get my text? The closing's all done. I'm already in an Uber. I'll be there in ninety minutes."

It would be a $400 car ride, if she had to guess. "You didn't need to do that."

"Of course, I did. I want to be there for you. To help you, even if it's just—to be there."

"They arrested her."

"Who? You mean Hope? They found her?"

"She came to the cottage right after we talked, after the police press conference. We were getting ready for her to turn herself in when the police came. They had a warrant, and I couldn't stop it. She looked so damn scared. I don't know what to do." The words were tumbling out of her faster than she could control them.

"Just breathe, babe. Breathe." She forced herself to do as he suggested and felt the panic begin to settle. "You're a badass lawyer, and don't you forget it. Hope could not be in better hands. So breathe. And focus. And rely on those killer legal instincts and kick some butt like you would for any other client, okay? And when I get there, I can drive you around or knock on doors or make photocopies at the Staples store. Anything you need. I'm yours."

She swallowed and tried to shake the noise from her head. He was right. She could do this. And she did need his help. Jocelyn Hodge had located Lopez's pickup in downtown Montauk. If Lindsay could find just one person willing to say they'd seen him after he was at the Stansfields' house that Saturday night, she'd be able to work with that. "Okay. Let me know when you're close."

"Of course. I'm always going to be there for you." She could tell that he appreciated the feeling of being needed. "I love you, Lindsay."

"You too. I'll see you soon."

When she hung up, the search results for Richard Mullaney had finished loading. First on the screen was a Wikipedia entry.

Richard Mullaney

Richard "Hitch" Mullaney III was a noted attorney and philanthropist. A native of Detroit, Michigan, he earned a BA from the University of Michigan and a JD from Harvard Law School. He was shot to death in the driveway outside his home in Wichita, Kansas, leaving behind a wife, Melanie Locke, and ten-year-old daughter.

She didn't need to click the hyperlink beneath Melanie Locke's name. Even if she hadn't read the woman's book, the coverage of her Senate campaign was inescapable. Lindsay did not like where this was going. One of Alex Lopez's last cell phone calls had been to Locke-Home's headquarters. There was only one reason why Decker would have asked Hope about Richard Mullaney.

She scrolled down for the details of Mullaney's murder. Mullaney, his wife, and their daughter had driven to their horse ranch in the Flint Hills for a long weekend. Richard realized that in the shuffle to pack for the trip, he had left his briefcase at the family home in Wichita. According to Melanie, he made the seventy-minute drive back to town alone. A neighbor called police when she heard what sounded like firecrackers, but possibly gunshots, outside. Responding officers found Richard dead in his driveway in front of the family Range Rover. The sliding back door to the house was open. The single bullet that hit Richard in the stomach was from a .357, the same caliber as the gun that Richard typically kept in his home office and for which he had a lawful carrying permit. The weapon was never found, and no arrest was ever made.

Lindsay clicked out of Wikipedia and found a longer article about the still-unsolved murder, aimed at true crime junkies. The article detailed a crowdsourced online theory that Melanie Locke was behind the killing. Some of the amateur sleuths opined that she could have easily left their young daughter asleep at the ranch, followed her husband back to town, committed the murder, and then returned to Flint Hills in time to be interviewed by police. The problem with that theory was that police had called her within twenty minutes of discovering Richard's body, using a cell phone number they obtained from the next-door neighbor. Cell phone tower data placed Melanie in Flint Hills at the time she answered that call. Based on those records and the daughter's statement that her mother never left the house that night, police had publicly cleared Melanie of suspicion in an effort to encourage potential witnesses to come forward with any relevant information they might have. The most likely explanation, they announced, was that Richard had interrupted an attempt to burglarize the family home while they were away for the weekend.

Despite law enforcement's insistence that Richard's wife was not a suspect, speculation persisted. The more nuanced gloss of the Melanie-did-it theory posited that she intentionally left his briefcase behind, knowing that he had an important federal appellate brief due the following week and would need to return to the house to retrieve it. A woman with her resources, intellect, and ambitions, critics maintained, would have no problem finding a skillful contract killer to do her dirty work while she had an ironclad alibi.

As for motive, the armchair, online detectives had no shortage of ideas there, either. Melanie had married Richard at a young age. The couple met at Harvard—she was an undergrad, he was in law school. At the time, Melanie had no intention of working for her father's company, let alone becoming the corporate heir apparent. The couple's initial plans were to live and work in Washington, DC, Richard as an elite appellate litigator at one of the capital's largest law firms, and Melanie as a congressional aide with ambitions to become a behind-the-scenes power broker, perhaps as a lobbyist or campaign manager.

But when her father told her he might have to shutter all his stores and file bankruptcy unless he found a way to go toe-to-toe with the competition, Melanie hit the books, eventually identifying an inconsistency between the consumers of do-it-yourself TV programs (women) and the targeted audience for home improvement marketing (men). After convincing her father that women were the most important and underserved segment of the market, they decided that she should oversee the corporate transformation personally. Richard gave up his partnership at his white-shoe law firm and moved to Wichita, where he was lucky to argue two federal appeals a year, while Melanie went from behind-the-scenes politico to the public face and eventual CEO of one of the largest retailers in the country.

According to a gossipy former friend, it wasn't only their job titles that changed with the move. Whereas Richard used to pull in more than 80 percent of the household income, his earnings became a mere afterthought given the family largesse. He resented his wife's success, and she resented the resentment. The same gossipy friend told reporters that Melanie had once mentioned matter-of-factly that it had been years since the couple had sex, leaving the friend to wonder whether Richard had other arrangements. The couple reportedly had no prenuptial agreement, meaning that Richard would own half of everything, including LockeHome, in the event of a divorce—no matter which of them was to blame.

The article went on to outline a conspiracy theory that Melanie not only had her husband killed, but also bribed the police to clear her publicly—a theory seemingly backed by the fact that the lead detective in charge of Richard's murder investigation was later named chief security officer for LockeHome's headquarters.

One point that both law enforcement and Melanie's critics agreed on was that the only thing missing from the house was a silver necklace. After an initial walk-through of the property with police, Melanie concluded that nothing had been stolen. It was the couple's daughter who corrected the record. She had been snooping around her father's office in anticipation of her upcoming birthday when she found a small blue gift box in his desk drawer. After her father died, she returned to his desk to claim the necklace he had chosen for her, but it was gone.

The prevailing law enforcement theory was that the burglar or burglars started in Richard's downstairs office. They would have found both his gun and the jewelry box. When they heard Richard's car, they ran out the back door, shot Richard in the driveway, and then fled.

Those who were convinced that Melanie was behind the murder saw the necklace as yet another piece of evidence supporting their theory of the crime. They opined that Melanie did in fact know about the necklace in her husband's desk drawer, because she had found it herself and had concluded that Richard was cheating on her.

Lindsay's thoughts drifted to an image of Jocelyn Hodge, well past drunk, behind the wheel of her Bronco. *The police said they found a woman's necklace on his boat. I want to think it was for me, but—*

Lindsay pulled up Jocelyn's number on her phone, hit call, and then typed a new search into her laptop: "Richard Mullaney stolen necklace description."

"Hello?" Jocelyn sounded like she had been sleeping.

Lindsay identified herself. "We spoke earlier at the beach," she said as a reminder.

"That wasn't cool, what you did. You knew the police were after your friend, didn't you?"

"I'm sorry, I can't talk with you about that. But I just have one question—"

"You're unbelievable."

"Please, it's one small thing." She clicked on the top search result on-screen. "You said the police found a necklace on Alex's boat. Did they show it to you? What did it look like?"

"Why does that even matter?"

The blue bar at the top of her browser slowed and then froze. She knew Jocelyn was seconds away from hanging up. The search results finally loaded, and she gave the screen a quick scan: *silver chain with a pendant of two hearts.* "Was it a heart necklace?" she blurted.

Jocelyn's voice cracked when she spoke again. "Two. Two little hearts. The two of us. He never had a chance to give it to me."

30

Tuesday, June 22, 8:05 p.m.

Like most visitors to the southern fork of Long Island, Lindsay had a tendency to clump the entire East End into "the Hamptons." But to the extent that the Hamptons had become synonymous with glossy magazine images of high-end boutiques, glitzy lawn parties, and celebrity-soaked restaurants, it was defined by pockets of South and East Hampton. With Scott behind the wheel of her car, they were now long past Amagansett, past Napeague Bay, past Hither Hills State Park and the preserves. Though not immune from the onslaught of summer visitors, Montauk had managed to preserve the low-key vibe of an old fishing and surf town.

It had taken Lindsay most of the drive to summarize everything she had learned so far about Alex Lopez and Richard Mullaney. She was impressed at how quickly Scott absorbed the information.

"But isn't the necklace on Lopez's boat actually a good thing?" he asked, slowing as he eyed a spot at the curb on the main strip. As usual, he nailed the parallel parking job on the first try. "It makes it look like he killed Mullaney. Not exactly a sympathetic character. Who knows what else he could have been wrapped up in."

"Except the police obviously think Hope was involved, too. But

New York prosecutors aren't going to charge Hope with anything that may have happened in Kansas fifteen years ago. My guess is the Wichita cops are just beginning to reinvestigate that case in light of whatever Decker found this week. We just need something to get the district attorney's office here to tap the brakes on bringing charges tomorrow."

She had already told Scott the goal for the evening: find someone—anyone—willing to confirm that they'd seen Alex Lopez or his truck in the last ten days. Hope's confrontation with Alex had occurred two Saturdays before. She'd tossed the rug at the dump on Sunday morning, which Lindsay had to assume the police knew. By the time the Stansfields returned to their house on Monday, there was no sign of Hope, Alex, or either of their vehicles, and Jocelyn Hodge had found Alex's truck later the next day. To convict Hope of killing Lopez, the police would need a timeline that accommodated all those facts, which meant Lindsay needed witnesses who might turn their clock upside down.

After two hours of touring Montauk with photos of Hope and Alex, she thought they might finally have a lead when a clerk at the Montauk Corner Store said she remembered Alex showing up a few minutes before the shop opened on a Sunday. He'd tapped on the glass to see if he could come in early to buy a few swimming noodles for his boat. It quickly became clear, however, that the clerk was referring to the Sunday before Alex and Hope both went missing.

Another hour later, they were leaving yet another restaurant empty-handed when Lindsay's cell phone rang. She felt a rise of resentment at the sight of Carter Decker's name on the screen. "Did you finally realize what a mistake you made?" If only she had the evidence to back up her bluster. "When can I see my client?"

"Tomorrow morning. Just letting you know that she's been booked and will be held overnight. We didn't interrogate her."

"Maybe not," she said, heading back toward the car, "but you surely left her alone in a holding room for hours, hoping she'd open the door to you questioning her without a lawyer." Pushing away images of Hope being shuffled toward a jail cell, she signaled to Scott to pop the locks and got into the passenger seat.

"I assure you we followed all the rules, Counselor. I didn't even owe you this phone call, as you know."

"Can I get into the cottage now?" She and Scott had already rented a room at Gurney's for the night, but she wanted to see how intrusive the police search had been.

"Techs were still pulling some latent prints, last I heard."

"What about tomorrow morning?" She hadn't packed a suit before coming out from the city, but she thought she could find something appropriate in Hope's closet.

"You'll be good to enter by then."

Scott had started the engine by the time she hung up. "That didn't sound good."

"It's not." She had missed the chance to end this nightmare tonight. She leaned back against the headrest, a growl of frustration escaping from her throat. "I need to get back to the hotel and prepare for court tomorrow. Maybe I can at least patch together a half-decent bail motion." She had wanted to prevent charges altogether, but now she was lowering the bar to getting Hope released from custody.

When they reached the hotel, Scott bypassed the parking lot and pulled directly in front of the lobby's entrance. "You do what you need to do."

"Where are you going?"

"I'll head back to Montauk and keep trying."

"You've already done so much. You must be exhausted."

"Nah, I'm in full investigator mode now. Besides, you'll work better if I'm not here."

Two hours later, she jerked awake at the sudden sensation of motion next to the bed.

"Just me," Scott whispered.

The hotel room was pitch-black except for the red glow of the nightstand clock. It was nearly one in the morning. "I didn't even hear the door open. Is everything okay?"

She squinted as he clicked on the bedside lamp.

"Oh, it's better than okay. Remember that dive bar at the marina? The one that was locked up?"

A simple Closed sign had hung on a heavy black door on a brick building under a red awning. It could have been a hardware store or a tackle shop except for the one other sign to the left of the door: Beer and Booze.

"It was open when I went back. It's called Pier Bar, by the way, but apparently everyone calls it B&B because of the Beer and Booze sign. Anyway, I showed the bartender the photos, and he immediately asked if I was a cop. Let's just say he didn't seem like he was real interested in talking to cops."

Lindsay sat up in bed and leaned against the padded headboard. The bar he was talking about was directly across from the parking lot where Alex's pickup truck had been found.

"I could tell he knew something, so I told him I was working for a defense lawyer and threw in two hundred dollars to sweeten the deal. He said he recognized Alex from having been at the bar a few times. Said he was easy, low-key, whatever. But the Saturday night we're talking about, Alex came in late with this big gash on his temple. The blood was still kind of crusting over. He asked for a Four Roses, downed it, then asked for another one and an ice bag. When Alex was on his third drink, he said he'd lost his cell phone and asked the bartender if he could make a call."

"Please tell me this bartender has a name?" She realized she had not even given Scott instructions about what information to collect if he did happen upon a helpful witness.

"He does indeed. Kevin Mitchell. Anyway, Kevin figures any guy with a gash in his head at eleven o'clock might just need a break, so he hands over his cell phone, and Lopez steps outside. Twenty-five minutes later, he's thinking Lopez dashed on his bill, stealing the phone while he was at it, but then he comes back in and apologizes, saying Kevin might want to recharge because the battery's low. Then he asks for one more drink and a pen and paper. Kevin finds him a notepad, and Alex starts scribbling away like it's some kind of contest. When he was done, he asked if the bar kept envelopes and stamps around. Kevin finally told Alex that he wasn't running an office supply store and handed him his check. He offered to call him a cab, but Alex said he was going to walk home to clear his head."

"Oh my god. Scott, you did it. We have Alex alive and well on Saturday night—just like Hope said."

Scott reached into the front pocket of his shirt and pulled out a slip of paper. "From Kevin's phone. The two calls Lopez made." The first phone number had a 316 area code and was followed by the number 19 after a dash. The second was an 873 number, followed by dash-3.

Lindsay reached for her own phone on the nightstand to confirm her suspicions. The first call, which lasted nineteen minutes, had been to Emilia Lopez's work number. Lindsay grabbed her briefcase from the floor beside the bed and found the list of numbers that Hope had jotted down from Lopez's cell phone. The second call Lopez made from the bar—three minutes long—was a match to the now-disconnected Chicago number that Lopez had contacted three times in the weeks before he died.

"Oh, and one more thing—" Scott handed her his phone as he hit the play button on the screen. Scott's voice rose above the background din of a noisy bar, followed by a low voice Lindsay didn't recognize. He had recorded his entire conversation with Kevin the bartender. His face broke out into that perfect Scott smile. "Who do you love?"

"SP! For the win." She jumped out of bed, threw her arms around his neck, and then held his face in her hands, planting an exaggerated kiss on his lips before AirDropping the voice recording from Scott's phone to hers. "This is perfect. It's exactly what we need."

Scott stood motionless as she took a seat at the desk in the corner of the hotel room and opened her laptop. The celebration was over.

"I'm sorry, babe," she said, opening a new document. "I've got to make this perfect for tomorrow."

"No, I totally get it. Do what you need to do. Pretend I'm not here."

When she crawled between the sheets two hours later, Scott pulled her into a tight spoon position, wrapping his top arm around her waist.

He'd done it. He had come through for her, just as he promised he always would. And she felt nothing but guilt.

31

Wednesday, June 23, 9:32 a.m.

The Fourth Amendment of the United States Constitution requires all searches and seizures to be reasonable. It mentions warrants and probable cause. But it says nothing about the police needing to be tidy about it.

Lindsay had seen more damage in the aftermath of a search warrant's execution, but it was going to take a few hours to get the cottage back to its previous state. The police had not yet filed a return with the court, which would itemize the evidence they seized, but the bottom two shelves of the bedroom bookcase were empty. She envisioned the motion to suppress she would file, arguing that fifteen years of journals were beyond the scope of the warrant, but then reminded herself that if everything went according to plan, there would be no criminal trial at all.

Police had left behind smudges of gray powder from the dusting technique used to lift latent fingerprints. Hope's, Lindsay's, probably the landlady's. Alex Lopez's prints would be a worst-case scenario, but she had to be prepared. If he'd followed Hope to the Stansfield house, it was also possible he had broken into the cottage.

Most of the contents of Hope's bedroom closet had been tossed onto the bed. Lindsay carried a few articles of clothing at a time back to their proper place until she spotted what she was looking for—the royal-blue St. John suit that she had given Hope last year. Lindsay thought she'd won the lottery when she found it 70 percent off on a Saks clearance rack. The skirt was a few pounds away from fitting, but Lindsay bought it anyway, convinced it would be an incentive to make healthy choices. Two years later, she found it at the back of her closet, tags still on. She gave up and passed it on to Hope. To Lindsay's knowledge, Hope had never worn it either. She was relieved when the skirt zipped into place effortlessly. All that worrying had taken a toll.

Her phone buzzed as she looped the top button of the jacket. A text from Scott: Making sure everything is okay.

He was waiting in the driveway, taking care of emails. All good. Be right out.

As she hit the send button, an incoming call appeared on the screen. Area code 316. Wichita, Kansas. She picked up immediately.

"May I please speak with Lindsay Kelly?" The voice itself was smooth and appealing, like a public radio host's, but the caller seemed rushed. Nervous.

"This is Lindsay."

"You left a message for me yesterday—Emilia Lopez? You said it was about my brother? Are you his lawyer? I told him he needed to get one."

Clearly the police had not yet located Alex's sister or notified her about his death. Lindsay needed to be careful about how much she disclosed, and in what order. "Your brother's name came up on another matter I'm handling, and it dates back a number of years. I actually got your name from a summer camp the two of you attended as children— the COP camp at Edgemoor Park—"

"Wait, you're defending that camp?"

Lindsay wanted to start the conversation over again. This would be an entirely different exchange if they could meet in person. "No,

I definitely don't represent the camp." Why had Emilia jumped to the conclusion that someone was suing the camp? Lindsay took a guess. "I have been looking into allegations that kids may have been abused there in the past."

There was a long pause. Then: "What does my brother have to do with this?"

"The Wichita Police Department got a cold hit from a DNA database. Alex's blood was found at the house of a woman named Janice Beale."

"She was the nicest lady. She made us sandwiches and Kool-Aid and taught me how to hem a skirt with Elmer's glue and an iron."

"Do you know why your brother's blood would have been on her sofa? Did he hurt himself? Or did someone hurt him?" The thought came to Lindsay for the first time as she was thinking out loud. Had Alex been abused at the camp?

"Wow, this whole time, I guess we had at least some kind of proof about what happened."

"About the abuse, you mean." Lindsay tried again to sound as if she already knew the answer.

"I still can't believe Alex did that for me. Trying to take on a grown man."

"He was defending you," she said, making up for the gaps. Emilia was the one who had been victimized.

"Janice was out at the softball field, coaching one of the teams. I went inside to use the bathroom. It was so hot out. I decided to take my time and enjoy some more of her air-conditioning. He came in, saying he was just checking on me, but I could tell the way he was looking at me what he wanted to do."

Emilia wasn't talking about her brother. She was talking about her abuser. Lindsay said nothing, waiting for Emilia to fill the silence.

"Alex must have had a bad feeling because he showed up right when . . . well, in time to stop it from actually happening. I had never seen him like that before. He charged right at us and pushed him to the ground and was just throwing punches as fast as he could, but there's only so much a thirteen-year-old can do. I felt bad for not doing more to help him."

"How badly was he hurt?"

"Just a black eye and a cut on his cheek, from the guy's wedding ring." Her voice didn't disguise her disgust at the mention of a ring. "He told us if we said anything, no one would believe us and we'd get in trouble for lying, but my parents could see that Alex was injured."

"So you told them," Lindsay said.

"Not at first. I wanted Alex to say he got hit by a softball, but he didn't want to lie. He told them what he saw when he walked into that house. I still remember the way they looked at me. I felt so guilty."

"You were the victim. You were just a kid."

"I didn't feel like one. I was fourteen, and I looked even older than that. At least that's what he told me. Look, I've read a lot about this since then, so I understand now that he was grooming me. But at the time? I felt complicit. He would tell me a joke, and if I laughed, he'd say I understood his sense of humor better than his wife did. He gave me a copy of his favorite book. He'd practice the high school Spanish he remembered, but it was always something like 'Eres tan bonita' or 'Me allegro de que somos amigos'—You're so pretty, I'm so glad we're friends. I liked the attention. We had kissed a few times before that, and I have to be honest—it was thrilling in the moment."

"You were *fourteen*, at a summer camp," Lindsay said. "And you said this person was a grown man. He had a wife and a wedding ring." Lindsay noticed that Emilia still had not spoken her abuser's name.

"Of course. But I was just old enough that I was willing to take on some of the responsibility. To see myself as participating in it. I realize in retrospect that's exactly what he wanted. He manipulated the mixed emotions any girl that age is starting to feel about love and sexuality. But he was supposed to be there to guide us and help us, and instead . . . well, he followed me inside and tried to take my virginity."

"But Alex stopped him, and then told your parents."

"He wanted to call the police and file a report, but my mother and father—we couldn't risk it."

"Because of their immigration status," Lindsay said, completing the thought.

Another call was coming through on her phone. She glanced at the screen. Scott, pressing her to get to the courthouse, but she wasn't about to cut short her conversation with Emilia. Even if she managed Hope's release, police in both Long Island and Wichita would continue to probe her possible connections to Alex Lopez.

"Alex had a mentor at the camp and told him everything. He said he couldn't promise that our immigration status wouldn't be a problem if we filed charges. According to him, the volunteer I was accusing was very powerful and could use his influence against our family, so he offered to investigate quietly on his own. If he found any other victims in a pattern, perhaps the other girls could be the ones to testify and I wouldn't need to be involved. But then he came back and said he was squeaky clean, and that really sealed the deal for my parents. It was clear they thought I had done something to encourage his attention."

"I'm sorry. That must have been awful."

"Well, thanks to a whole lot of therapy, I understand now it was cognitive dissonance. They didn't want to feel like they were giving their own daughter's victimizer a free pass in order to protect their own security, so it was easier to place the responsibility on me. The whole thing sort of split our family apart. The same way my parents subconsciously blamed me, I think I resented Alex for telling them in the first place. The whole situation was always simmering beneath the surface, even though we literally never spoke of that man ever again. I didn't even realize until after he was killed that he was such a big deal. I can see why they were afraid to have me go on record against him."

After he was killed. The camp. The rumors. A powerful man who volunteered. Why hadn't Lindsay seen the connection earlier? "Richard Mullaney," she said, hoping Emilia would confirm her theory.

"We just knew him as Hitch," she said. "We had no idea he was married to such an important person. Alex left town a few days after we saw the news that he died. I think seeing that man's face again— even on TV—brought back all of the pain of how we were treated as disposable. And that we were forced into this decision where we let him get away with it. Alex was always so sweet and protective, but he had this underlying anger—a low boil—about having to make adjustments every single day because of our legal status. I really hope he has found a better life now. I was able to go to college, and now I'm starting law school in the fall. No one's ever going to silence me that way again."

Lindsay's phone was beeping again. She needed to go, but she didn't feel right keeping the death of this woman's brother from her. "Emilia, I'm so very sorry, but Alex passed away last week. The police here are investigating it as a homicide."

She winced as she heard the sharp intake of breath on the other end of the line. "Oh god no, that can't . . . No, I just—" Emilia caught herself and fell silent.

"You just reconnected with him," Lindsay said. "He called you two Saturdays ago, late at night. You spoke for quite some time."

"How do you know that?"

"It's part of another case I'm working. I'm sorry not to give you more time to grieve, but I think the key to helping my client is to figure out who shot your brother."

"So that's how he died? Someone shot him?"

Lindsay apologized once again for pushing on with her questions. "Had you been in regular contact with him over the years?"

"Not at all. He left and never came back. Like I said, I thought he wanted a clean break from our whole family."

"But then he called you that Saturday night. What did he say, Emilia? I think it was the reason he was murdered."

"It's like you said. He called . . . late. He sounded a little drunk and said he was going to jail. I thought maybe he was asking me for legal help or something, and I was like, After all these years, you come to me for help? But then he told me—"

She stopped herself again mid-sentence, leaving Lindsay to guess again. "He told you that he shot Richard Mullaney," she said. "He's gone now, Emilia. This has to be the reason he was killed. Please trust me. I want to help."

"I was in total shock. He said he and some friends were partying in some fancy house while the family was out of town. He saw some pictures and realized the dad was the guy from the camp—Hitch. Alex freaked out and started throwing things and breaking stuff. He was leaving when Hitch pulled into the driveway, got out with a gun, and told him to freeze. Alex charged at him, and the gun went off. He could tell that Hitch was dead, and there was nothing he could do, so he just ran. The next day, he went back to that cop he knew when we were kids. The cop told Alex that it wouldn't matter if the shooting was an accident, or even if we could prove what Hitch had done to me. It was felony murder, no matter what. So that's why Alex left town."

"To start over," Lindsay said. "From all appearances, he was never a suspect in Richard Mullaney's murder. So why did he call you and say he was going to jail?"

"Because he was turning himself in. He said that something happened recently that made him realize he was still living in limbo, and he had forced others to do so as well."

"What others?"

"I asked him the same thing. All he said was that he had to make it right. I kept pressing him to see if he was sure, and he finally said he was, and that he was going to hang up before he changed his mind. Then he was gone. Days went by with no news, so I thought maybe he came to his senses."

The other line was beeping again, coupled now by a knock on the front door. "Linds, we really need to go if you're going to make the court hearing. Is everything okay?"

On the phone, Emilia was asking if Lindsay needed to take the incoming call. Lindsay repeated how sorry she was for Emilia's loss, but she knew the words sounded hollow. "Would it give you any comfort to know that you weren't the only girl that Mullaney targeted?"

"I mean, I don't want anyone else to have gone through what I did, but I guess I'd at least feel validated."

"There's a woman named Katy Barnes." Lindsay told her about Katy's deleted Facebook posts alluding to other children being abused at the Edgemoor Park camp. "She won't talk to me, but she might open up to you. I'm pretty sure she got paid off with a nondisclosure clause, probably by LockeHome."

"And whoever covered up for Hitch's abuse might not have wanted my brother coming forward, given everything he knew. Especially if she was about to launch a Senate bid."

Neither of them mentioned Melanie Locke's name aloud, but they were clearly on the same page. The exposure of her husband's crimes would overshadow her entire life's work. "Do you think you could look into that?"

"I told you: I'm gonna be a lawyer. I got this."

32

Wednesday, June 23, 10:15 a.m.

The East Hampton Town Justice Court, tucked behind City Hall, one turn before the bagel shop, looked more like a suburban post office than a courthouse. Lindsay jumped out of the car at the curb and rushed past two news teams with camera crews.

On the door to the main courtroom hung a piece of paper listing the docket for the morning. It was a single case: *People v. Tara King*, with a Judge Catherine Harper presiding. Lindsay could hear voices inside. She cracked the door open.

A man stood in the front row behind the courtroom bar, addressing the court. "That's correct, Judge. I personally notified Ms. King's lawyer last night as to the time and location of the hearing this morning."

Lindsay recognized the lawyer at the prosecution table as Mike Nunzio. She had tried a felony assault case against him two years earlier, when he was still considered an up-and-comer. Now he was Suffolk County's go-to ADA for major trials. She was about to let the door close when the man who had been speaking turned his head slightly. She recognized him as Carter Decker. Her eyes moved to the defense table.

Sitting there alone was a woman in dark blue scrubs, her hair pulled into a knot. It was Hope.

"I'm here, Your Honor," she said, rushing to the front of the courtroom. "Lindsay Kelly on behalf of the defendant, who's known as Hope Miller. We do not stipulate that she has ever used the name Tara King."

"We called this case fifteen minutes ago, Counselor. Your client, whatever name she is using, was in discernible distress at the lack of representation."

Lindsay had never appeared before this judge, and she knew she was making a terrible first impression. "I was working to lock down the details of important evidence that I hope you'll be open to hearing this morning, Your Honor. This entire situation has been a rush to judgment on the part of law enforcement."

Judge Harper's expression made it clear that she was unimpressed. Nunzio was on his feet before Lindsay could speak again. "That actually brings us back to the threshold issue we opened with, Your Honor, which you were reluctant to take up prior to Ms. Kelly's belated arrival. As stated previously, the People move to disqualify Ms. Kelly as defense counsel in light of a conflict of interest that we believe could jeopardize any conviction we might obtain against Tara King, aka Hope Miller, were she to proceed with Ms. Kelly as her representation."

"There's no conflict of interest, Your Honor. This is a blatant attempt to interfere with my client's Sixth Amendment right to counsel, which the police already violated yesterday by refusing to permit me access to my client while she was in their custody."

"Despite the fact that Ms. Kelly knew that police were actively searching for the defendant as a material witness, police happened to locate the defendant in the very same room as Ms. Kelly when they were in the process of executing a search warrant."

"My client sought me out for legal advice as soon as she learned that police were interested in contacting her. That does not create a conflict of interest. In fact, it evidences the existence of a meaningful attorney-client relationship, which the state is actively attempting to undermine."

Nunzio shook his head and asked the judge for permission to approach the bench, which she granted. In one hand, he held a thin notebook with a dark-green cover. In the other, he held two sheets of paper, which he handed to Lindsay before stepping toward Judge Harper.

The photocopy of the journal entry confirmed Lindsay's suspicions. She objected immediately. "Your Honor, this is outrageous. The police removed years of my client's diaries from her home—private journal entries that have absolutely nothing to do with the crimes police were supposedly investigating. A search warrant is not blanket permission for a fishing expedition. The law requires that the evidentiary nature of property must be 'readily apparent' for it to be seizable."

Nunzio was prepared for the argument. "Your Honor, the search warrant expressly authorized police to search for and seize any evidence, including documents and writings, that pertained to the defendant's true identity or to any prior contact between her and Alex Lopez. Journals authored by the defendant would be an obvious place to look in light of the unusual circumstances of this case. It was only in the course of scanning those journals for evidence that we came upon this."

Once Judge Harper opened the journal to a page that Nunzio had marked with a neon-yellow Post-it, her gaze lowered as she silently read the words Lindsay had confronted at the cottage herself only a day ago. *She kissed me. Or maybe I kissed her. But she definitely kissed me back. Finally, after all these years, it happened. And it was good. Really, really good. Gentle at first . . .*

The judge was suddenly looking directly at her. "Is this true, Counselor? You had a romantic encounter with this client within the last year?"

Lindsay's face grew hot. In her periphery, she saw Carter Decker cover his eyes with one hand. Even he was disgusted with the prosecutor's argument.

"This is completely improper, Your Honor. If Mr. Nunzio had concerns about my ability to provide representation in this case—or my client's wishes with respect to her choice of counsel—he could have asked for a conference in chambers instead of dropping these salacious accusations in open court in front of the press. He's doing this to demonize my client, deprive her of the right to counsel, and distract from the fact that he has absolutely no evidence upon which to charge Hope Miller of any crime whatsoever."

"Your Honor, we can place the defendant inside a home where Alex Lopez's blood was found. Hours after she left that home, she was seen on camera disposing of a rug from that same home that also contained traces of the victim's blood. We are filing a prosecutorial information charging her with one count of felony assault today, but we anticipate additional, more serious charges once we go before a grand jury for indictment. We are also aware that she is being investigated for involvement in another homicide in a different state that we believe formed her motive to move to Suffolk County for the sole purpose of finding Alex Lopez and harming him. We are seeking to detain her pending indictment and trial because she is an extreme flight risk. She has lived for fifteen years under an alias and then disappeared for nearly two weeks since the events that gave rise to the probable cause for her arrest. She has no ties to the jurisdiction or even to New York."

Lindsay needed to steal the momentum from Nunzio, and she saw her opening. "So the prosecutor wants to file assault charges but detain my client as if she were accused of murder. Presumably the prosecution's theory is that Alex Lopez was killed at the house in question during this supposed assault, so why isn't he charging my client with homicide? The answer, Your Honor, is that he knows he doesn't have probable cause—either for assault or for murder—but thinks he can cover up this failure by proceeding with the lesser charge." From her briefcase, she pulled the affidavit she had Scott sign late last night, sum-marizing his discussion with Kevin Mitchell, the bartender at the Pier Bar. "This is the evidence I was in a rush to prepare for the court. May I approach?"

Lindsay felt a brief but satisfying moment of schadenfreude as she dropped a copy of the affidavit on the prosecution table for Nunzio on her way to the bench to hand the judge the original, but as she returned to her seat, she spotted Scott in the back row of the courtroom. From his facial expression, she had an idea how long he'd been there.

Seconds felt like hours as the judge processed the information in the affidavit. Lindsay couldn't bring herself to look at Scott again, and she didn't want Scott to see her look at Hope. She forced herself to stare straight ahead.

"And you have a recording of the entire conversation described here?" Judge Harper finally asked.

"Yes, Your Honor. I can play it now if the court desires." In truth, she was hoping not to share the full recording. In the affidavit, she had spelled out only the evidence that Alex Lopez had been at the bar drink-ing, requesting an ice pack for a visible cut on his temple. She had omit-ted the details about Alex borrowing the bartender's phone, hoping that for once she was actually a step ahead of the police.

The judge let out an exasperated sigh. "Mr. Nunzio, are you aware of this witness?"

Nunzio was already conferring with Carter Decker, who had flipped to the second page of the affidavit and was shaking his head.

"Mr. Nunzio?"

"No, Your Honor. This is the first I've heard of him."

"Is it fair to say that it would drastically alter your theory of the case if there is in fact a witness who saw your victim alive but visibly injured at the date and time described here?"

"It is still our position that the defendant was responsible for that injury, Your Honor, and that is the basis for our assault charge today."

"That's not a satisfying answer, Mr. Nunzio. Does it change the theory of your case or not?"

"It would be premature to answer that before I've had a chance to talk to the witness myself."

"Then I'd say it's also premature for me to hold this defendant over for trial."

"But—"

"No buts. The state clearly has more work to do, Mr. Nunzio. I suggest you get on it. In the meantime, Ms. King, or Ms. Miller, if you prefer, you're free to go. But I would strongly advise—and your lawyer, I assume, will back me up on this—that you remain within the jurisdiction. Were you to hide, or flee, or otherwise go missing, a judge would be likely to view that quite negatively at a detention hearing were you to be charged in the future with a crime. Similarly, a jury would be entitled to see the same facts as evidence of your guilt. Do you understand?"

"I do, Your Honor." Hope seemed so small in her oversize scrubs as she looked up toward the bench. "I won't go anywhere, I promise."

"As for the prosecution's other motion, there's no need for me to rule in light of my decision not to hold the defendant over for trial."

With the crack of the judge's gavel, Hope jumped from her seat and wrapped her arms around Lindsay. "Oh my god, thank you. You did it."

Lindsay turned to see Scott walking out of the courtroom. "Sorry, Hope, just a second." She quickly made her way through the courtroom doors, down the hall, and out to the parking lot. He was already walking away from the Audi, heading in the direction of the main road.

"Your keys are in the front seat," he said.

"Where are you going?"

"I'll get an Uber to the train station."

"Stop it, Scott. Let me at least explain."

He shook his head and looked down at the asphalt. "How many times?"

"It was only once. I swear. And it was just a stupid kiss, and we were totally drunk. It was dumb."

"No, that's not my question, Lindsay. How many times did you accuse me of not giving you enough room, saying I didn't understand the importance of female friendships? How many times did you tell me I acted controlling when it came to her? How many times did you fucking gaslight me into thinking I was the one who was crazy, wondering if you cared more about her than you ever would about me?"

"Scott—please." At last they were having the conversation they'd found a million ways to avoid. "Can we just talk?"

"It's over, Lindsay. We're done."

"Will you stop?" she asked, reaching for his hand. "We can't just be—"

"Do not. I mean it. It's the least that you owe me."

She waited until she could no longer make out his figure in the distance before walking back to the courthouse.

33

Wednesday, June 23, 12:45 p.m.

H ope lifted the V-neck of her white T-shirt to her nose. "I still stink like that jail cell."

Her hair was still damp from the long shower she'd taken as soon as she got home, but Lindsay had seen the toll that a night in custody inflicted on first-timers. Whatever smell Hope thought she detected was likely etched in her mind forever.

The last hour had been arduous, both physically and mentally. They had managed to get the cottage back into order. As they worked, they also talked through next steps to protect Hope from whatever the DA's office was planning for the future.

But Lindsay knew she was preoccupied. When she heard the whistle of the Long Island Railroad in the distance, she pictured Scott on the train. She had sent him one text since he walked away from her at the courthouse. I'm not pushing you, but please let me know when you're ready to talk.

He had not replied.

Hope must have sensed where her mind had wandered, because she offered yet again to call Scott and explain that the prosecutor's office had completely overblown one journal entry about one drunken evening.

Lindsay shook her head. "You have other things to worry about right now. He'll come around." Even though Lindsay didn't buy her own assurances, she also knew that Hope was the last person Scott would want to hear from. "Let's go back to what Alex said to you that night. He said 'What kind of game are you playing?'"

"Yeah, I think those exact words. My best guess is that when I showed up on his boat, he must have recognized me. But when I didn't acknowledge any recognition of him, maybe it set him off."

"Except in a normal situation like that, a person would say, like, 'Hey, don't I know you?' He must have had a reason for not asking you directly. And it probably comes back to Richard Mullaney. You're sure you don't remember anything about him?"

Hope shook her head. "But going back to Alex, he must have seen me again once I moved here and thought I was messing with him somehow. So that's why he followed me and finally asked me what game I was playing. I can't even remember everything I said, I was so frantic. But I tried to explain I had amnesia."

Lindsay shut her eyes against a wave of her own memories. Hope, unresponsive on the side of the road as Lindsay waited next to her in the downpour, and then reaching for her hand from the gurney. Scott, a confident grin on his face, when he asked her to move in four months ago. Hope, dragged away in handcuffs, her eyes pleading with Lindsay to help. Scott's back as he walked away from the courthouse.

Blinking her eyes open, she willed herself to focus. "Alex told his sister he realized that his decisions fifteen years ago had forced other people to live their lives in limbo. He must have been talking about you. Whatever happened back in Wichita, you must have left town together and then gotten in that car accident. The car was stolen, and so he just bailed."

"I was the one he left behind to pay the price," Hope said. "Being in a constant state of limbo is the perfect description."

"When you showed up on his boat, and then ended up moving to town, he must have thought you were running some kind of con.

Maybe he thought you were going to blackmail him. Or sell whatever he thought you knew about him and Mullaney to Melanie Locke. But once you were in the house together, and you tried to explain the memory loss, he could have realized the truth about the long-term repercussions of whatever happened back in Wichita. He called his sister and said he was going to turn himself in."

"But now he's dead," Hope said.

"He couldn't admit to killing Richard Mullaney without explaining his motive. It would have exposed Melanie Locke as the wife of a sex offender and a pedophile." Lindsay recounted the online conspiracy theories speculating that Melanie had the Wichita police on her payroll.

"So is it possible Melanie somehow found out that Alex was planning to confess?"

"It's even possible that she was the person he tried to call at Locke-Home's offices—maybe to apologize or tell her he was planning to come clean. She could have been talking to him directly after that with a burner phone. If so, she might have preferred to shut him down rather than have the truth about her husband's death come out."

"Especially now that she's running for office," Hope added.

"I wonder if the police are even considering the possibility."

Lindsay opened the browser on her laptop and searched for "Richard Mullaney murder lead detective" and found a *Wichita Eagle* article that mentioned a Detective Steve Thompson. It was too generic a name to be memorable, but now she wondered if she had seen it before. Was it possible?

She searched for "College Hill Strangler detective suicide partner." The very first hit was the newspaper article she was thinking of. Same guy.

It made sense. Lindsay's father would play a role in any major crime that went down in Hopewell. Wichita was bigger than her hometown, but small enough not to have many longtime, go-to homicide detectives.

"Earth to Lindsay. What exactly are you looking at?"

Lindsay pulled up Ellie Hatcher's number.

34

Wednesday, June 23, 1:05 p.m.

Ellie Hatcher heard a crack as she rose from the floor of her brother's apartment and arched her back.

Jess apparently heard it, too. "You're getting old, little sister. Welcome to the club."

"I'm not old. I'm broken from being hunched over that satanic piece of torture furniture for the last two hours." When he mentioned he had bought a wall unit online, she'd volunteered to help assemble it, declaring that it sounded *fun*. Now, staring at what seemed like another 2,700 pieces to go, with no written instructions, she was ready to throw the entire project out the window. She made her way to the kitchen and opened the cabinet where she still expected to find her water glasses.

"Other side of the sink," Jess called out. It had been nearly two years since Ellie formally turned the apartment's lease over to her brother, but this rent-subsidized Murray Hill one-bedroom with paper-thin walls and aquamarine bathroom tile was always going to feel like her home.

She had slammed one glass of water and was refilling from the sink when her cell rang in her back pocket. Thanks to her weird memory for numbers, she was pretty sure she recognized the digits on the screen. She answered anyway.

Yep, it was Lindsay Kelly. "I'm sorry to bother you again," she said. *But are you?* "I'm calling because Hope's case has taken an unexpected turn. The state believes her actual name is Tara King, and that she's from Wichita, Kansas."

If Ellie had to guess, the police had probably found a connection between this Tara King person and Alex Lopez—a connection that might establish a motive for murder. She kept this suspicion to herself. "Doesn't ring a bell, but it's not that small of a city."

"Oh, that's not why I'm calling. It's a long story, but the police asked her if she knew anything about the death of a man named Richard Mullaney."

That name, Ellie recognized. Melanie Locke's husband. Still, she kept quiet.

"The lead detective on the case was also on the College Hill Strangler task force. I thought it was possible you might have met him through your father. His name is Steve Thompson?"

Ellie could tell the first time she spoke to Lindsay that she was a good lawyer. She had no doubt that Lindsay already knew the connection between Steve and the Hatcher family. "I know him well," she said. "He's the one I called when you first reached out to me." *Which you also probably knew.*

"Oh, wow, great."

Good lawyer, bad actress.

"So here's the thing," Lindsay said. "I'm working on this theory that might implicate Melanie Locke, which is a hard enough hill to climb, but it doesn't help that the detective on her husband's case is now the head of security at her company."

Jess was still hunched on the floor, rotating a wood panel edge over edge over edge, trying to figure out where it fit in the larger puzzle. Catching Ellie's eye, he whispered for her to hurry up.

"It's not like that," Ellie said. "Steve was the go-to guy on the WPD. It's no coincidence that he would have gotten assigned to such a high-profile murder case, and he'd also be an obvious contender for the job he has at LockeHome."

"Don't take this the wrong way," Lindsay said, "but that's a pretty major job for a retired detective from a midsize police force, no matter how heavy of a hitter he was at home."

"No, it's really not," Ellie assured her. "They've got retired FBI and military intelligence to do the really high-speed stuff. Most of that's cybersecurity anyway, and Steve would be completely out of his element. He oversees the physical security at the Wichita office complex. Look, if you want me to call him and see if he's willing to talk to you and your friend about the case, I can."

"Thanks for the offer, but please don't do that yet. I need to learn more about whatever wild-goose chase the police here are on before I can develop a strategy for my client."

Ellie knew that would be her response. No defense attorney would allow a client to talk to a homicide detective, even one who was retired. She found herself wondering how Hope—or Tara King—might be connected to the Richard Mullaney case. Even without the lawyer's permission, she might have to give Steve a ring.

By the time she hung up, Jess had given up on the wall unit. "What was that about?"

"It was that lawyer who called me about the missing friend and the DNA match."

"You told me you dropped that."

"I did, but now it's pretty clear the friend's also a suspect in a murder case. Didn't you see on the news that the police were looking for her?"

Jess flashed a *really?* expression. Her brother definitely did not keep up with the local news. She gave him a quick summary of the little she knew about Alex Lopez's death and Hope Miller's arrest.

Jess still looked confused. "So why was the lawyer asking about Steve?"

"Because the police think this woman Hope is actually named Tara King. And they asked her what she knew about Richard Mullaney's murder, which was one of Steve's cases."

Jess suddenly fell quiet and began chewing the inside of his cheek, the way he did when he was nervous, which was almost never. "Do you have a picture of her?"

Lindsay pulled up a *Newsday* article and handed her phone to him. "That's from this year. Wait, do you actually think you know her?"

She watched as his gaze shifted to the screen. He pressed his lips together as he studied it. When he stood from the floor, he returned her phone but avoided looking at her, seemingly focused on something in the distance.

"Jesus. I think I'm going to puke." He walked to the kitchen, turned on the faucet, and splashed water on his face.

"Okay, you're scaring me right now." She grabbed his arm and led him to the sofa, where he took a seat. "Jess, talk to me. What's going on?"

He pressed his face into his hands. "Why do you have to be a fucking cop? Fuck!"

"Stop it. I'm your sister first and foremost. If I have to hand in my badge and go back to beauty pageants to pay the bills, I will. Tell me what's happening here."

He lifted his face and, for the first time since he'd seen Hope Miller's picture, made eye contact with her. "You're thirty-four. That's some pageant."

His grin brought a moment of relief, but she flipped him off with both fingers anyway. "Fuck you twice. Now are you going to tell me what's going on, or do I need to get my handcuffs and beat it out of you?"

He made his way to the refrigerator for a bottle of Rolling Rock, taking a long draw before returning to the sofa.

"You've got to promise me I can trust you."

"Say that again, and I'm going to——"

"I can't, Ellie. It's not fair. You've got everything going right now. I don't want to pull you into my shit."

"It's about to be our shit, okay? What is happening?"

"I was at Richard Mullaney's house the night he died."

"DO YOU REMEMBER TC ATKINSON?" Jess asked, handing her two shot glasses. After slamming the rest of his beer, he had retrieved a bottle of Four Roses bourbon from the top of the refrigerator.

Ellie was about to say no but then paused. "Is that the girl I called Woodstock?"

"Oh wow, I totally forgot about that."

"She reeked of pot and patchouli oil and thought she was Stevie Nicks. What were you thinking?"

"I was twenty-two, and she was a wild woman. What do you think I was thinking?"

"So what were you doing at that house, Jess?"

"TC and I were chilling, and then she told me that this girl she worked with was a babysitter and that the family was out of town for the weekend, so we had a place to hang out for the night. You know . . . to party."

"And it was Melanie Locke's house?"

"I didn't know whose house it was, and I wouldn't have been able to pick Melanie Locke from a lineup back then if my life depended on it. It was just some rich people gone for the weekend—that's all. It's not like it was a big rager or anything. Just me, TC, her friend, and the friend's boyfriend. We got there and were drinking, smoking some pot, being pretty mellow. But then it becomes obvious that TC's on something else. She's totally out of it, giggling like an idiot, and she tells me she and her friend ate some mushrooms. I was pissed because if I'd known that was the plan, I wouldn't have gone."

Once Ellie joined the police force, she'd been careful to avoid the details of Jess's recreational activities. Though she wanted to believe those days were over, it was no secret that he had enjoyed more than his fair share of illegal drugs over the years. She was more surprised about his disapproval of someone else's illicit drug use.

"Sorry, but I would have assumed you'd join the party."

"Hallucinogens? Hours of living in an altered reality where, let's say hypothetically, you think murderous clowns are tickling you? That's a hard pass. I was trying to talk TC down, but then her friend's dude started freaking out and was breaking shit. Like total batshit crazy town. Pulling crap off the walls, smashing glass everywhere. I was like, What the fuck, man? And the other girl's totally out of it. I was worried she was going to pass out or something. And then TC starts tripping even worse, and her happy giggles are now a raging paranoia. So I'm trying to get TC to sober up, and get angry dude to stop breaking shit. And then the zoned-out girl goes wandering out the front door, and the boyfriend runs after her. It was a clusterfuck, and I just wanted to bail, but I didn't feel right leaving TC there."

He paused, and when he spoke again, his voice was monotone. "I caught what looked like headlights through the front window. Some-one was pulling into the driveway. I knew it was too good to be true, some rich family letting the babysitter hang out in their house while they were out of town."

He shook his head and poured himself another shot.

"It was Richard Mullaney coming home?" she prodded.

"I had no idea, not at the time. I literally picked TC up over my shoulder and ran out the back door. We were halfway into the yard when I heard a gunshot. The shock of it seemed to sober her up enough to get her moving. We jumped the back fence and ran like hell."

It was the summer after Ellie's high school graduation. It was also the summer when her older brother declared that he was moving to New York City to try to live his dream of being a rock star. She couldn't remember the exact dates—summer was summer back then—but she had her suspicions.

"Is that why you left?"

"Steve found me the next day. He got the callout after the responding officers realized who the victim was. He told me he knew I was partying at the house and that the owner had come home and been shot in the driveway and died."

"So how did he know?"

"I'm not sure, but I've always assumed the house had cameras or something, and that he covered up for me. I can't even tell you how fucking scared I was. I explained everything. Told him I'd go to the station and take a lie detector test, because no way did I shoot anyone. It had to be that lunatic who was having his rage attack. But Steve said that even if everyone believed me, we were there without permission, and a bunch of stuff was broken, so they'd argue it was a residential burglary, plus someone had died as a result. Everyone at the house was guilty of murder. Lights out, we'd be done."

The legal analysis wasn't wrong. The felony murder doctrine was the biggest shortcut in the world for prosecutors, allowing them to convict every single person involved in a felony, regardless of who pulled the trigger or whether the shooting was even intentional.

"I can't believe you and Steve didn't tell me any of this. What am I, Mom?"

"Oh my god. Ellie, please, don't do that. You wanted to be a cop like Dad. I wasn't going to screw that up for you. That's why I left. Don't you get it? I was banishing myself. I realized how messed up it was that I was even in that situation to begin with. And forcing Steve into a corner like that? I needed to get out of Dodge."

"So do you recognize her picture?" Ellie asked, gesturing to her phone.

"Not really, and I honestly don't remember the girl's name, but it's got to be her, right?"

"Is there a way to reach TC and ask?"

He shook his head. "About ten years ago, I saw on Facebook that she died of an oxy overdose. I mean, maybe she would have ended up down that road anyway, but Jesus, I know what kind of guilt I've carried around all these years. When she found out what happened, she said it was all her fault for bringing the mushrooms in the first place."

"What about this guy?" She pulled up a photograph of Alex Lopez.

He tilted his head, studying the picture. "Yeah, that could be the boyfriend."

"This all happened in the summer, right? Do you remember when?"

He recited the exact date, fifteen summers ago, without hesitation.

Ellie texted Lindsay Kelly. When was Hope's car accident?

Three days after Richard Mullaney was shot in his driveway.

Ellie sent another text. We should meet in person. There's someone Hope needs to talk to.

35

Wednesday, June 23, 4:12 p.m.

The address to which Ellie Hatcher had summoned them belonged to a five-story red-brick apartment complex on a tree-lined street in Murray Hill. As Lindsay reached for the building's buzzer, Hope grabbed her hand. She looked almost as terrified as she had when the police arrested her.

"What if this is some kind of trick? She's a cop. She could be helping Decker."

"She's NYPD. She doesn't even have jurisdiction over anything you're remotely suspected of doing. And you didn't hear her voice when she called. She was definitely worried—like she needs help as much as we do."

Hope took a deep breath and then hit the buzzer herself. They were in.

THE APARTMENT WAS CLEAN BUT modest. The countertop in the small kitchen beside the entry was clear except for two shot glasses next to the sink. The floors were unfinished parquet, and the walls sorely needed a paint job. The apartment's tenant, however, was considerably easier on the eyes. Tall and lanky with dark shaggy hair, he had the look of a retired rock star. Ellie Hatcher had introduced him as her brother, Jess, before they all got settled around the steamer trunk that doubled as the living room coffee table.

"So Hope . . . ," Ellie said. "Should I call you Hope?" Hope nodded. "Lindsay told me the police think you used to live in Wichita, Kansas, where Jess and I were raised. I don't suppose either of us looks familiar to you?" She apologized for her "giant hair" as she handed Hope her phone. The photo was of a younger Jess and Ellie, side by side on a lawn in front of a ranch house. Jess had his arm draped around his sister's shoulder, but his extended middle finger had made it into the shot.

Next to Lindsay on the sofa, Hope shook her head.

"What about the name Jess Hatcher? Or TC Atkinson?"

"No, I'm sorry."

Lindsay was scrolling through her own photos. "Let me show you an older picture of Hope. Maybe—"

Ellie's brother spoke for the first time. "I don't need the picture. Now that I see you in person, I definitely remember you. You worked with my friend TC—short for Tricia, which was short for Patricia, but everyone called her TC. You guys worked together at the mall—at Hot Dog on a Stick."

Lindsay grabbed Hope's arm. "Oh my god. Your lemonade." She shifted her gaze to the Hatchers. "She makes the best lemonade anyone has ever had in their lives, but she had no idea where she learned how to make it."

"TC used to talk about how much she hated pumping those lemons. All the horny little boys used to watch from the mall benches because of all of the bouncing up and down."

"So you and I were friends?" Hope asked, her eyes bright with curiosity. In all the years they had known each other, Lindsay had never seen Hope this trusting around strangers.

Jess Hatcher shook his head. "No. I only met you once. TC told me you had a house for us to party at for the night. We met you there. You were with a guy. I had the impression he was your boyfriend—not casual like me and TC, but actually tight. It was a big, fancy house, and you knew how to get in because you were their babysitter. The family was gone for the weekend. I pretty much assumed we didn't have permission to be there, but it seemed harmless enough."

Lindsay wanted to ask whose house it was, but allowed him to continue uninterrupted. For the next twenty minutes, he spoke as if no one else was in the room. Lindsay could picture every moment of the night. She imagined this young woman TC, full of the kind of effortless but frenetic energy that would have pulled a young Hope—a young Tara King—into her orbit. *Come on*, she'd probably said, *it'll be fun. You and me. Just a little taste.* The boys—not boys, because they were all adults by then—two men of that age, alone in a house with their girls, would have had plans for them that didn't include tripping on hallucinogens.

Jess's voice rose as he described Alex coming out of the master bedroom. "It seemed like a switch had flipped. He seemed so chill when we first got there. I read him as a bit of a pushover, actually, but after you guys disappeared into one of the bedrooms, we heard this male voice yelling. I thought maybe he was pissed that you were tripping, so I went to check on you. He stormed out of the room, ranting and raving like a lunatic—just screaming and cussing. Breaking vases. Pulling picture frames off the shelves. Punching the walls. Absolutely crazy. Then you came walking out and were completely out of it. I was trying to get the guy to calm down, but it was like he didn't even know I was there. Then you wandered out the front door, and he went after you. When I saw a car pull into the driveway, I was out of there and dragged TC with me. I found out the next day about the shooting."

"You weren't there when it happened?" Lindsay asked.

He shook his head.

"You didn't even hear the shot?"

He shook his head again, but Lindsay noticed the accompanying glance in his sister's direction. She knew at least some of this was bullshit but saw no reason at this point to confront him.

"We went out the back door and jumped the fence," he said, turning toward Hope. "You really don't remember any of this?"

"Nothing at all. Did I have a car there? When Lindsay first found me after my car accident, I was in a stolen car, but the plates were from Indiana."

"No, I don't think any of us were the kinds of kids who could afford cars. You know how Wichita is."

Lindsay reminded him again that Hope didn't really know anything.

"They've got Uber and Lyft whatever now. But back then? We all had the bus routes down cold, or we hitched rides with friends. TC and I bummed a ride from a guy who was leaving the mall the same time we were. We didn't want him tagging along, so we told him we were going to Denny's. Once he was gone, we hoofed the rest of the way to the house."

"I must have left town with Alex," Hope volunteered. "Maybe we hitchhiked to Indiana and then managed to steal a car there. My accident was three days later."

"The same day I decided to live my dream of moving to New York City."

"So did we all talk about it afterward and agree to leave?" Hope asked.

"No, I never saw you or your boyfriend again," he said. "I went to TC the day before I took the train for New York to make sure she understood the situation. No matter who pulled the trigger that night, we'd all be guilty of felony murder."

Ellie touched her brother's wrist at the mention of felony murder.

"How exactly did you know that?" Lindsay asked.

He shrugged. "Our dad was a cop. You pick stuff up, whether you want to or not. It had to be your boyfriend who shot Mullaney, though, right?" he said to Hope. "That's what I've always assumed, at least."

Hope had one hand over her mouth. "I can't believe this. I basically got that man killed—and then skipped town with the guy who shot him?"

Lindsay wrapped an arm around Hope's shoulder and gave her a quick hug. "Stop it. You have no way of knowing what Alex told you at the time about that night. Jess just said you were in a complete daze."

Jess nodded. "For what it's worth, TC was totally blacked out about most of the night. She vaguely recalled having to jump the fence, but not the reason why. It's possible you left town without even knowing what went wrong at the house."

"So what do we do now?" Hope asked. "Call the police? Give ourselves up?"

The Hatchers spoke over each other, Jess saying he knew this was a mistake as Ellie blurted, "You can't be that stupid."

Hope rose to her feet. "Are you fucking kidding me—"

Lindsay held her hands up in a T. "Stop. Everyone stop. No one's going to the police. Hope, please, sit down. They're right. You'd be giving yourself up for nothing and could face felony murder charges. What about this woman, TC? Do we need to worry about her?"

"She passed away several years ago," Jess said.

"I'm sorry to hear that," she mustered. "But that means you're really the only one alive who can definitively place yourself, Hope, and Alex at that house the night of the shooting."

"And I assure you I have absolutely no plans to do that." Jess Hatcher's tone was softer than his sister's. "I came to terms with what happened a long time ago. I still feel guilty sometimes that the case never got solved, but we were practically kids at the time. A life sentence for being in the wrong place at the wrong time? What kind of system is that?"

Hope turned to Lindsay. "I think we should tell them," she said softly.

"Tell us what?" Ellie insisted. "I thought we were on the same page here. My brother did not have to help you. We're either all in, or I'm going to find a way to make life very difficult for both of you."

Lindsay had no doubt the detective would be true to her word. It was a good thing they were on the same side now. "I located Alex Lopez's older sister," she said. "Her name's Emilia. She told me Richard Mullaney assaulted her when she was fourteen years old—at that camp we talked about. Alex recognized Mullaney's pictures at the house. That's why he flew into a rage."

"Oh shit." Jess Hatcher gave her an anguished look. "If I had known, I might have joined in."

"So if Lopez was the one who killed Mullaney," Ellie said, "his sister's abuse would be a powerful motive."

Lindsay felt Hope's eyes on her again. She nodded for her to pick up the narrative.

"It's not a matter of *if*," Hope said. "Alex admitted to his sister that he was the one who pulled the trigger—an accident, he said, after the two of them got into a struggle in the driveway. He called her two weeks ago, saying he had decided to confess. No one saw him again until they pulled his body from the water."

"And *that*"—Lindsay held up an index finger for emphasis—"is another reason why neither of you should tell anyone what you know about that night. Someone obviously doesn't want the truth about Mullaney's murder to come out."

Jess looked up at the ceiling until the full impact of Lindsay's statement seemed to dawn on him. "Oh Jesus. Melanie Locke?" He lowered his voice, even though it was only the four of them in the room. "Is that seriously what we're talking about here?"

Ellie rose from her seat and began pacing the path between the living room and kitchen. "I knew a girl in school who said her sister had something happen to her at that camp, but her name wasn't Lopez. So there could be other victims—not just Emilia."

"We're working on that," Lindsay said. "I think it's possible Melanie Locke has been paying them to keep quiet."

"But if Alex had come forward—," Ellie said.

"No more Senate campaign. No more book tours. Maybe even no more LockeHome."

Jess looked up at his sister. "What if we call—"

Ellie shut down the idea with a stern shake of her head.

"We can't pull anyone else into this yet," Lindsay said. "I do have one idea, though. Melanie Locke is speaking at Wharton Business School tonight. It's open to the public." She had found the information on Melanie's campaign website.

"What time?" Ellie asked.

"Six thirty," she said, "but it's scheduled to last an hour." Philadelphia was two hours away. "My car's out front."

36

Wednesday, June 23, 7:24 p.m.

So if you were president—" The questioner had to have been in her late eighties, wearing an oversize black linen sundress and hot-pink Crocs. She looked tiny in the well of the lecture hall, taking her turn at the mic. "Would you do for all workers what you've done at LockeHome—equal pay for equal work? Because we sure as hell have waited long enough!"

When the audience broke out in cheers, the woman turned to face her new admirers and pumped her fists in the air as she returned to her third-row seat.

Lindsay turned her head to see Ellie Hatcher smiling. They had slipped into the back of the room ten minutes earlier during the applause that followed Melanie Locke's speech, blending into the standing-room-only crowd.

Melanie Locke was as effortlessly put-together as she always appeared on television. Her hair, dark-brown with just the right number of highlights, swooped perfectly into place at the neckline of a purple sheath dress that showed off tanned, toned arms.

"Well, first of all, thank you very much for that question and for your absolutely infectious enthusiasm. Can I take you on the campaign trail with me?"

The older woman raised one hand in the air from her seat while she let out a wolf whistle with the other.

"But my only campaign, to be clear, is for a seat in the US Senate to represent my home state of Kansas, where I'm proud to have been born and raised and to be runnin' one of the largest family-owned retailers in the country." Melanie was already droppin' her g's like every politician tryin' to be folksy, Lindsay noticed. "But, yes, absolutely, if elected, I would sponsor and support legislation aimed at true gender equity. And though it would be a nice starting point, it is not enough to pay men and women the same wages for the same jobs—not if we continue to denigrate and devalue work that has traditionally been performed by women." Lindsay found herself nodding along as Melanie ticked off a list of underpaid professions on her fingers: nurses, teachers, secretaries . . . "Ask yourself—why do janitors make more than housekeepers? Or radiologists more than pediatricians? Because we systematically undervalue women's work. I know we can do better, because I've been doin' it at my company for years."

A man who looked unmistakably like a university professor in his cardigan sweater and plaid bow tie rose from the front row, asked the audience to give a final round of applause for their distinguished speaker, and invited those guests who were registered for the ticketed reception to proceed to the plaza.

Despite instructions, a handful of audience members pressed to the well of the lecture hall as everyone else proceeded to the exits at the rear. Lindsay noticed that the bow-tied professor remained at Melanie's side. As the host of the lecture, he'd be the one to escort her to the next location.

She and Ellie slipped from the room as the crowd thinned, but lingered in the atrium, keeping their eyes on the doors. When Melanie and her guide finally emerged, they followed a few feet behind.

The professor gestured toward a door marked with a piece of paper that read "Reserved," and Lindsay saw her chance as Melanie moved toward it. "Oh, thank god. Is that a ladies' room? I feel like a rat in a maze in this building."

The professor stepped forward with one arm raised. "I'm so sorry, ma'am. There's a restroom open to the public. Uh, I think it's the end of this hall, then take a right, and then the next left?"

Ellie didn't miss a beat. "But I can see the stick-lady sign under that piece of paper. TMI, sorry, but my friend really needs to go."

"Um—"

Melanie was already holding the door open. Lindsay was certain that Carter Decker would have contacted Melanie by now about her husband's murder, but if she recognized Lindsay from her connection to Hope's case, she wasn't letting on. "Oh, there's plenty of space in here. I don't need a room all to myself," she assured the professor. "Come on in, ladies."

LINDSAY WAITED UNTIL MELANIE WAS drying her hands to introduce herself. "Ms. Locke. My name is Lindsay Kelly. I'm a defense attorney in Manhattan." Ellie had remained in the hallway outside, prepared to distract the professor in the event he decided to check on his guest speaker.

Melanie gave Lindsay's business card only a casual glance before she returned the handshake and thanked her for attending the event.

"I enjoyed your comments very much," Lindsay said, "but that's not why I'm here. I represent a client with information about your husband—information that would be damaging to his reputation. She is interested in reaching a financial settlement—with an NDA, of course."

Melanie folded Lindsay's card neatly in half and then dropped it in the trash can. "Well, first of all, that sounds like blackmail. And second, you can drop the act, Ms. Kelly. The second I saw your name, I recognized it. You know my husband is deceased because you represent Tara King."

"But in the course of that representation, I have met one of your husband's victims—"

"I have absolutely no idea what you're talking about, and this conversation is over."

"I can also tell you who killed Richard."

Melanie's forced smile was filled with disdain. "You should have your ticket pulled by the bar, do you know that? Are you seriously offering to sell out your own client for a payoff? Because as much as I'd like my husband's murderer brought to justice—"

"That's not what I'm talking about."

"Because I finally know who killed my husband—Tara King. And if you knew anything about my husband, you'd know that no one who actually knew him called him Richard. He started going by Hitch in the sixth grade to have a different name from his father. What exactly are you trying to achieve here?"

"Is that really what the police think?" Lindsay asked. "That Hope did it?"

"*Hope?*" the older woman scoffed. "You're buying that bullshit? It's pretty obvious, isn't it? She's been hiding out under a fake name, claiming to have amnesia. And when her old boyfriend recognized her in New York, she killed him and then planted evidence to try to frame him for Hitch's murder."

Lindsay had hoped to lure Melanie with a potential nondisclosure agreement with Emilia Lopez, which she could then use to prove her motive to have murdered Alex. Now, however, she found herself focusing on her defense of Hope.

"That's absurd," she said. "What motive would she have to kill your husband?"

"You really don't know anything, do you?"

"I know she was your babysitter."

"Emphasis on the *was*. Hitch caught her taking cash out of his wallet one day and had to let her go."

When Evan Hunter believed Hope had ripped him off after asking for an advance, Lindsay had sworn that Hope wasn't the type of person who would ever steal. She opened her mouth to defend Hope again, but found herself speechless.

"It was a shame, too," Melanie continued. "Sophie adored her, and she'd been through so much."

"Sophie? Or Tara?"

"Tara. That's how we met her. Tara's mother was in prison for child abuse, and she spent her high school years in a group home. She had gotten counseling through a child advocacy nonprofit that we supported and then became a volunteer there. We thought we might be able to help her out, and then she went and stole from us. I even pressed Hitch to see if it might be a misunderstanding, but he was adamant that she had to go. All these years, it never even dawned on me that she'd do something violent."

Lindsay felt a lump in her throat at the thought of Hope being physically abused by her own mother. She knew from her legal work how bad it had to be for prison to be involved. If Hope had slipped a few bucks from some rich guy's wallet, it would only be because she desperately needed it.

"I've got to hand it to you, Melanie. You're a really good liar. You honestly sound like a woman who believes every word of the bullshit you're spewing. There's only one problem: Alex told someone that he killed your husband, and, more importantly, *why*. And we have his phone records. We know he called you. You didn't want him to confess."

The minute the words were out of her mouth, she wanted to hit rewind and start over again. She had said too much. Melanie was going to walk out of this bathroom, and she'd never get a second chance.

But Melanie stayed put, looking down at her designer heels, her shoulders slumped. When her gaze returned to Lindsay, the color had drained from her face. "Is this some stunt you have planned for trial, or do you have actual proof that that man was the one who killed Hitch?"

"He told everything to his sister—one of your husband's victims."

"Victim? What are you even talking about? And you think this man also confessed to me? I would have gone straight to the police."

Lindsay heard a low male voice on the other side of the door, followed by Ellie Hatcher's. As the door slowly cracked open, she made out the end of Ellie's sentence: "At least let me."

"Is everything all right, Ms. Locke?" the professor called out over Ellie's shoulder. "The reception has begun."

"Be right out," Melanie said brightly. Tidying up her already perfect mascara with one fingertip, she said quietly to Lindsay, "This wasn't the time or place, but it's clear to me that you have more information than the police do about my husband's murder and yet have drawn some very misplaced conclusions about me. I'll be in touch."

"I REALLY DON'T THINK SHE knew." Lindsay could barely keep up with Ellie Hatcher's march across the campus parking lot.

"I told you, you should have recorded it," the detective said, shaking her head.

"Which I already told *you* is illegal in the state of Pennsylvania, which means we could never use it as evidence."

Ellie flashed a thumbs-down sign. The irony of a defense attorney respecting the law more than a cop was not lost on Lindsay.

"She seemed completely shocked when I said Alex admitted to the shooting. I think Decker convinced her that Hope killed both her husband and Alex."

"Trust me. I've seen Oscar-worthy renditions of 'Who? Li'l ol' me?'" Ellie flashed wide eyes and clutched at imaginary pearls as Lindsay pulled onto I-95. "My dad used to tell me, 'Find the motive, and the motive will lead you to the man.'"

"So how does that play out here?"

"Well, Carter Decker apparently thinks all roads lead to Hope, because he doesn't know that Alex was about to confess."

"But if you know that," Lindsay said, thinking aloud, "who has an incentive to keep that from happening?"

"Hope, to be honest. If Alex had come forward, she could have been dragged into it. Felony murder for everyone."

"Except Hope couldn't remember any of it. And if Hope has a motive, so does Jess."

"But Jess didn't even know Alex Lopez's name, let alone what he was planning to do."

Switching into the left lane to pass a U-Haul, Lindsay said, "So that leaves Melanie Locke."

"Exactly."

"Unless someone else had a reason to want Richard Mullaney's crimes to remain hidden."

Lindsay's subconscious was on the verge of forming the next sentence when her phone rang. Seeing the 316 area code on her screen, she recalled what Emilia Lopez had told her. *He went back to that cop he knew when we were kids. The cop told Alex that it wouldn't matter that the shooting was an accident, or even if we could prove what Hitch had done to me. It was felony murder, no matter what. So that's why Alex left town.*

Lindsay fumbled her phone with one hand, eager to accept the call before it dropped to voice mail. "This is Lindsay."

"Hey, is this a good time to talk?"

It wasn't, but Lindsay wanted confirmation. "Sure. What's up?"

Ellie glared at her, clearly frustrated with the interruption. Lindsay mouthed that the call was from Alex's sister.

"I got hold of Katy Barnes," Emilia said, "and you were right. She also was one of Hitch's quote 'chosen favorites.' He told her she was brilliant and glamorous and special, all the things he used to whisper to me. She made that Facebook comment you found but didn't pursue an actual complaint until the Me Too movement had her thinking again about how Hitch got away with everything he did. She found three other victims, and they all came forward together. At the end of the day, they decided to take a settlement offer in exchange for keeping quiet."

"The city didn't require her to delete that Facebook post as part of the settlement?" Lindsay asked.

"She didn't even bother going to the city. The money came from LockeHome, and they probably didn't know anything about that old Facebook comment. Katy had forgotten about it until you messaged her."

"So it *was* Melanie Locke." Next to her, Ellie was pointing to the phone, asking her to put the call on speaker. Lindsay shook her head.

"No. Katy said she figured out that one of the cops she used to see buddying around with Hitch went on to work at LockeHome. She went straight to him. I was so sure it was going to be Melanie Locke who paid her off, but Katy said it was that guy who worked for Hitch who did all the dirty work."

"That cop Alex went to at the summer camp—the one who said he couldn't find any other girls to back up your complaint—was his name Steve Thompson?"

Emilia didn't hesitate. "How did you know that?"

Lindsay spotted a sign for the Holland Tunnel exit. "It's a long story, and I'm driving right now. Can I call you later to fill you in? And again, thank you so much for doing this when you're still processing the news about your brother."

"It's actually nice to have something to work on. I'm going to stay in touch with Katy. We were talking about starting a support group for Hitch's other victims once the news gets out."

"I have a feeling that might be right around the corner."

When Lindsay hung up, Ellie didn't miss a beat. "Steve . . . knew? About Emilia and Mullaney?"

Lindsay nodded. "I'm so sorry. I know you're close. Back at your brother's apartment—I noticed you touched his wrist when he mentioned the felony murder rule. It seemed like pretty technical knowledge, even for the son of a cop. Did he also go to Thompson after the shooting?"

Ellie shook her head. "No. Steve came to him. He was assigned to the case and already knew Jess was there. He told him he should get out of town, so he did."

A truck honked at Lindsay as she maneuvered into the exit lane. "So Steve must have found out from Alex."

"But Jess couldn't even remember Alex's name. Would Alex know Jess's?"

"Yeah, because girls talk. Hope probably knew all about Jess from her friend TC."

Ellie's next question took Lindsay by surprise. "Tell me what you think about Carter Decker. We're going to need his help."

37

Friday, June 25, 7:17 p.m.

Lindsay could not get over the flatness that was Wichita, Kansas. She had expected it to look a bit like Pittsburgh, but she saw nothing resembling Steel Tower or the Mellon Center or any of the other skyscrapers that converged over downtown Pittsburgh. If she had to guess, the tallest building in Wichita was twenty floors at best. Flat, flat, flatness, as far as the eye could see.

Lindsay had broken down and called Scott before the flight. He didn't pick up, but she left a message that she was taking a short trip and was sorry for everything. His only response was a text message: I wish you all the best, Linds.

From the passenger seat of the rental car, Ellie had finished pecking on the screen of her cell phone. "Decker's all done in Boston, and he confirmed the timeline," she said. She slid her phone into the side pocket of a backpack on her lap as she gestured toward the high-end strip mall ahead of them. "It's coming up here on the right."

The place in question was a restaurant called the Rimrock Grill, where Ellie had arranged for them to meet Steve Thompson, supposedly for Lindsay to pick the retired detective's brain about the Richard Mullaney case on behalf of her client, Hope Miller, aka Tara King.

The sun was still high, and a hot gust of wind washed over Lindsay when she stepped out of the rental car. She immediately felt sweat bead above the collar of her silk blouse. "I don't know if it's my nerves or this heat," she said, futilely trying to fan herself with one hand.

"One of the great mysteries of my childhood—how the wind some-how makes it worse. It's like standing in front of gigantic blow-dryer on full blast." Ellie led the way to the restaurant entrance and paused before reaching for the door. "You ready?"

"Just a second." Lindsay slipped her phone from her purse and sent a quick text. Heading in now. I love you. No legal ID meant no airplanes, not to mention the assurances they had given to the court about Hope not leaving New York.

A series of dots, followed by a brief reply. PLEASE be careful. Love you too.

She hit the voice memo app on the phone, pressed record, and returned the device to her bag. Kansas was a one-party state, meaning that she could lawfully record any conversations as long as at least one participant consented.

"Let's do it."

THE AIR CONDITIONER WAS CRANKING inside the dimly lit restaurant. Lindsay felt a sour taste in her throat when she spotted Steve Thompson, halfway through a stein of beer. Alone at a booth table in the back corner, he was older and thinner than in the photos she'd been studying for the last two days.

She watched as Ellie Hatcher accepted a hug from the man they believed had enabled a sexual predator for years and then killed Alex Lopez to prevent others from discovering his complicity. She marveled at the detective's ability to appear completely and utterly thrilled to see her father's former partner.

By comparison, it should have been easy for Lindsay to simply introduce herself, but she was certain that her facial expression would reveal her suspicions. "Thank you so much, Detective Thompson," she said, trying her best to sound dispassionate. "I know it's unusual for a defense lawyer to try to involve a detective, but I at least had to give my best pitch. I know who killed Richard Mullaney, but I need to trust that the police here won't try to pull my client into it."

"Well, first of all, I'm off the job for nearly a decade, so call me Steve. And I hope Ellie didn't get your hopes up. I'll hear you out and see what I can do, but I can't make any promises. To be honest, I wasn't going to turn down the chance to see my favorite NYPD detective—especially when it's on some defense lawyer's dime. No offense."

"None taken."

Thompson flagged down a passing waiter and asked him to bring two more of what he was having as he looked to Ellie, who flashed a thumbs-up. "How about for you, Counselor?"

"Just a Diet Coke to start," Lindsay said. "Flying makes me woozy."

Lindsay slid into the booth first. She didn't like the idea of being trapped in place across the table from Thompson, but she knew that Ellie should be the one to jump up if it became necessary. She had brought a gun from New York in her checked luggage. Lindsay placed her purse on a ledge abutting the table, then began by saying that she represented a woman named Hope Miller. Though police had not yet charged Hope, she explained, they clearly suspected her of involvement in the murders of both Alex Lopez and Richard Mullaney. They also claimed to have determined that Tara King was her true name.

Across the table, Thompson was already shaking his head, arms crossed in front of him. She even detected a chuckle. "Ellie told me the amnesia part. That's one hell of a long con. People actually fell for that?"

He had to have googled her, so he would know that Lindsay was the one who found Hope after the accident—or at least that she was the local police chief's daughter. The fact that he was pretending to be unaware of that confirmed their suspicions.

She and Ellie had spent the last two days nailing down the evidence, with Carter Decker digging in as well. They both felt more than a little anxious being here in Wichita without telling Decker what they were up to after all of his cooperation, but they were far outside the lines of a typical criminal case. To Decker, Alex Lopez was just another case, and Steve Thompson was just another suspect. She and Ellie were fighting for the people they loved.

Lindsay forced a polite smile. "Granted, cases of retrograde amnesia spanning that many years are rare. But so too would be the case of someone managing to fake it successfully for that long."

Thompson held up his hands in mock surrender.

"So does the name Tara King mean anything to you?" Lindsay already knew that Decker had reached out to Thompson after connecting the necklace he found on Alex Lopez's boat to the shooting of Richard Mullaney.

Thompson shook his head. "Never heard it until I got a call from a Long Island detective on, let's see, it must have been Tuesday. A guy named Decker? My understanding now is that Tara babysat for the family a few times. They met her through their charitable work."

"I'm surprised a babysitter wasn't on your radar," Lindsay said. "I would have assumed you'd look into every person who might have access to the house."

"Well, you'd assume right. We got a complete list of the house staff from Mrs. Locke. Also a list of anyone who might possibly have a key. No Tara King."

"So why wasn't Tara on the list?" she asked.

He shrugged. "You'd need to ask someone else. I worked with the list I had."

According to Decker, Melanie had said they never entrusted spare keys to part-time babysitters, but according to Jess, Hope had been able to let herself into the house.

By the time the waiter brought their orders, Lindsay was telling Thompson about the secret Facebook group she had found of women who claimed to have been groomed and sexually assaulted by Richard Mullaney.

"I've never heard anything about any kind of group like that," he said.

The group didn't actually exist, so his response wasn't surprising. "But what about the underlying allegations themselves?" she asked. "Nothing like that came up when you were investigating Mullaney's murder?"

"Not once." He sounded appropriately shocked.

"But what about since then? It's been fifteen years. The Me Too movement. Women are coming forward in ways they never have before."

"Well, if they have with respect to Richard Mullaney, I can't speak to that."

He was good. She had to give him that.

Ellie interrupted to provide another nudge. "I have no idea if it was Mullaney or not, but when I was little, a girl was telling everyone after lunch at recess on the first day of school that her older sister got a, quote, 'pervert' vibe from a volunteer at the COP camp. I even told Dad about it, but I can't remember exactly what summer that would have been."

In fact, Ellie had told Lindsay she was certain she'd spoken to her father only a few weeks before he died. That's why she was here.

He shook his head. "Sorry, he never mentioned it to me."

As planned, Ellie was the one to shift the conversation to the phone call Alex Lopez had made to LockeHome in April.

"That Decker fella mentioned that to me, too," Thompson said. "Unfortunately, we've got no way of knowing who in the building he might have been connected to."

"Unless it was you," Ellie said.

His eyebrows shot up in exaggerated amusement. "Me? Yeah, that's funny."

"He called you because Tara King showed up on his fishing boat." A kid carting a pitcher of ice water approached their table, but scurried away when he read their body language. "He remembered her, but she acted like she'd never seen him before. It spooked him. He started wondering if she had figured out that he was the one who killed Richard Mullaney, so he turned to you for help, just like he did after he shot

Mullaney. Just like he did eight years before that, when he found Mullaney climbing on top of his sister."

"Ellie, I don't know what this lawyer has convinced you of, but this is crazy. Let's me and you talk alone, and I'll answer whatever—"

"He was a rapist, Steve." Her voice was low but seething. "Emilia Lopez was only fourteen years old, and she trusted you—her whole family trusted you—because you let them think you cared about them." She slapped the table for emphasis. "What did you do instead? Shake down Mullaney for money?"

Thompson wiped his upper lip with his hand. "Do you know the good that family has done? The Locke Foundation educates girls all over the world who would otherwise be banned from reading. And Wichita wouldn't be the same without the Locke fortune. This is a completely different place from when you grew up."

"And that justifies letting him get away with rape? How many other girls did he abuse before he was killed?"

Thompson looked to Lindsay, searching for someone to intervene, but she held his gaze, her jaw set.

"You two are from a different generation," he said. "Times were different back then."

Ellie laughed mockingly. "Give me a break, Steve. That's just disgusting."

"Things were less black and white than they are now. It was complicated."

"Fourteen is fourteen. Do you know how old fourteen is? That's how old I was when my father died. I was just a child. Would you have let Mullaney fuck me, too, if he had wanted me?" She spit out the words contemptuously.

Lindsay was silent. It was Ellie's right to call the shots at this point. Hope would get her life back, but Ellie needed this, too, and Lindsay and Hope had decided they were going to trust that her plan would work, as dangerous as it was.

"Trust me, Emilia Lopez was nothing like you."

"Because her dad was undocumented, and mine was a cop?"

"No, because there's fourteen and then there's fourteen. You know, even now, the age of consent in this state is sixteen. And we're talking about twenty-plus years ago."

"So you admit you knew Mullaney was a predator."

"You're putting words in my mouth."

"Learned the job from the very best, Uncle Steve. You admit you know Emilia Lopez, which means you were the cop who looked after her little brother. He called you after Hope showed up on that boat." Ellie's finger was in the older man's face now. "His cell phone records show it was a short call. A message on your office voice mail is my guess. 'Sorry for calling after all these years. I know I promised I never would . . .' Something like that? The next day, a new number appears in Lopez's phone records. An incoming call from a Chicago-based number. You used a burner. You probably gave him a hundred reasons not to worry about Hope—maybe she wasn't really Tara King, or she simply hadn't recognized him. You talked him down and thought he'd go away. But then he called the burner again, a month later, after that same woman moved to town."

Thompson started to reach for his beer mug but took a sip of water instead.

"You tried to calm him down again," Ellie continued. "Maybe you even looked up her name and found out about the amnesia. Did you offer him money to stop asking questions? Because one thing you definitely could not allow was for his story to come out, or everyone would know that you aided and abetted a serial rapist and then covered up the motivation for his murder. Hell, you even got a new job out of it. Bravo, by the way."

"Jerry would be ashamed to hear you talk to me this way."

Ellie flinched as his words hit their target. Lindsay couldn't hold her tongue any longer.

"Keep her father's name out of your mouth. We know everything.

You tried to keep Alex quiet, but his mind was made up. He confronted Hope. She was terrified. She had no idea what he was talking about. She thought he was trying to kill her. He realized then that she wasn't faking. She had lost fifteen years of her life because of what he did. He called his sister to say he was turning himself in. And then he called you. You couldn't allow that to happen. You killed him the next day."

"You can't possibly believe this." Thompson reached for Ellie's hand on the table, but she pulled it away.

Instead, she reached her purse for a set of printouts, unfolded them, and slid the papers across the table. "We have the flight records, Steve. You flew to Boston Sunday morning—just hours after Alex told you he'd made his decision to confess." She flipped to a second page. "You rented a car at the airport. The mileage was just about right for you to have taken the ferry over to Long Island." Carter Decker had shared the documents after they told him what to ask for.

"You mean this happened while I was in Boston? I went to see my brother. I go there every few months. You know that, Ellie. And I have no idea how many miles I put on the car, but I drove out to the Cape to see the ocean. Not exactly beach scenery around here, as you know."

Lindsay could see that Thompson was getting nervous. She stacked yet another brick in the walls they were building around him. "Carter Decker just left your brother's house."

"Mark only hung tough for twenty minutes before he broke," Ellie added. "Your trip wasn't planned. You called him Sunday morning and told him you had vacation time you needed to use or lose and to expect you late that night. The reality is that you were already in Boston when you called. The early direct flight from KC landed at eleven a.m. You didn't show up to your brother's until nearly ten at night."

Thompson forced himself to smile as if he were laughing off a ridiculous conversation, but the effect was unsettling. Lindsay was convinced that she was looking into the face of a sociopath.

"You're too good of a cop for this, Els Bells. It's a nice theory, but it's not proof."

"Well, I'm apparently a better cop than you are," she replied. "It was a stupid move to plant that necklace on Lopez's boat. It was the only thing that tied him to Mullaney's murder, which eventually brought us here—to you."

The smile shifted again. Amusement. Like he knew more than they did. Lindsay assumed he wanted to say something to make him feel smarter than them but didn't want to implicate himself. She decided to wipe the smirk from his face with another brick.

"We've met with Melanie Locke," Lindsay said. Melanie had kept her promise to contact her after their initial conversation at Wharton and was also cooperating fully with Carter Decker. "She says she never heard one word about these women being paid off. Whether that's true or not, you know people will believe her. She's laying every little bit of this at your feet. She's the victim here, hoodwinked all these years by her husband's wingman. Your job is gone."

"The WPD will go after your pension, too," Ellie added. "You saw how they fought my family after my father died."

"Well, unlike my old partner, I've saved plenty of money."

"When I told my father about that girl at school—what she said about her sister and the camp—he said he'd look into it."

"And I told you he never mentioned it to me," he said firmly.

"It took me a long time to come to terms with this, but my father was not a good father. He cared more about the job than he cared about us. Shit, he cared about *you* more than us. He didn't even pretend to be the kind of guy who was going to show up to my school concerts or soccer games. But when he told us he would do something for us, he did it. And I remember the look on his face when I went to him about the camp. He was so disturbed. He got angry and told me that something so terrible should not be gossip on a school playground. That it was the worst kind of harm an adult could perpetuate against a child. So I know he looked into it."

"And I told you that if he did, he never said a word about it to me."

"You were his best friend on the force. And, unlike him, you were still helping out at the camp. He was way too far down the William Summer rabbit hole by then to have time for anything else."

Thompson jabbed an index finger across the table. "Don't you dare," he hissed.

"You killed him to protect Richard Mullaney and seal your place at his side. I already told the department. They're pulling up everything they can about where you were the night my father supposedly committed suicide. Even if they can't make it stick, everyone will know. By the time you try to fall asleep tonight, this will be the only thing every single cop you ever knew is talking about. You're the guy who murdered his partner on the side of a deserted road and then let his family believe he ate his own gun."

The color drained from Thompson's face as he blinked in silence. Ellie stared back, emotionless.

"I need a second."

He rose from the table and, after an initial stumble, moved swiftly toward the restrooms at the opposite corner of the restaurant. They watched as the men's room door closed behind him. A moment later, a man in a trucker-style cap emerged. He was still wiping his damp palms on the thighs of his jeans when they heard the crack of a gunshot.

A woman screamed as Trucker Cap dove for the floor, crawling beneath the nearest table. A waiter dropped a tray of dinner plates that had been carefully balanced on one shoulder and ran through a back exit door, setting off an emergency alarm. A male voice yelled out, "Active shooter! Run! Everyone, run!"

As customers pushed past one another in search of a safe place to hide from an expected onslaught of bullets, two women remained still, side by side in the back corner booth. They knew there would be no more gunfire.

Ellie downed the rest of her beer but said nothing. Lindsay reached into her purse and tapped the record button on her phone. "You called it," she said.

Ellie dabbed at her eyes with her dinner napkin before placing it on the table. "It's done now."

38

Tuesday, June 29, 11:49 a.m.

According to the Dodge Charger's dashboard, it was nearly noon, but objective concepts of time had stopped meaning anything to Carter Decker about fourteen hours earlier. He had pulled his first all-nighter in the last four years, and the second longest shift in his entire police career. He was ready to inhale the breakfast burrito he had picked up from Rosie's and then crawl into bed and pass out.

He had almost forgotten what it was like to do his job the right way, but he was feeling pretty good about sealing up the Alex Lopez case tight, even though the perpetrator had taken his own life. There was no doubt that Steve Thompson was the guy. It had taken Decker days, but he finally found the cabdriver who had picked Thompson up from the Cross Sound ferry and dropped him off near the piers at Montauk. The news had not yet gone public, but Wichita police were probably a day or two away from naming Alex Lopez as the person who had killed Richard Mullaney—and divulging the circumstances surrounding the shooting. If Carter had to guess, the news would encourage other women Mullaney had abused to come forward. This morning, Melanie Locke had announced a "pause" in her Senate campaign events for "personal family reasons," but he had a feeling she'd find some way to spin to her favor the coming revelations about her deceased husband. He had no idea whether the WPD would be looking at felony murder charges against Tara King, but that wasn't his call to make.

When he pulled onto his street, Mrs. Stansfield threw him a cheerful wave from her front path. He stopped at the curb and rolled down his window. "You're back. I was wondering if I was ever going to see you again." The couple had come home from Hawaii only to leave again for Palm Beach three days later. When Carter saw a Sold banner added to the For Sale sign outside their house, he realized how much he was going to miss his neighbors.

"You're not quite rid of us yet, but, boy, it's going to be hard to say goodbye to this house. And to you, young man." She pulled a stack of mail from her mailbox and began flipping through it. "Junk, junk, catalogue, junk." She paused on a white letter-sized envelope and then held it up in his direction. It was addressed by hand to *Homeowner.* "Probably someone trying to buy the house and cut out the realtor. You wouldn't believe how shady people are out here with the real estate."

She split the envelope open with her thumb and pulled out another envelope, folded in half and tagged with a Post-it note. "Well, this is weird," she said.

The Post-it note read, "Please give this to Hope Miller. She works for your realtor and doesn't have a mailbox."

39

Tuesday, June 29, 1:10 p.m.

Lindsay heard the sizzle of melting butter. "I can't believe you're making me a tuna melt."

Hope looked up from the stovetop, one hand on her hip, the other holding a spatula. "You said you were craving one."

"I meant from the deli."

"This will be way better." Hope had disappeared to the grocery store on the corner and returned with a can of fancy Italian tuna fish, kewpie mayonnaise, extra-sharp cheddar cheese, celery, onion, and tarragon.

Lindsay rotated her laptop on the kitchen island. "The application's all done. Are you absolutely sure?"

"Of course."

"You could be Tara King again, you know. Or pick any name you want," she quickly added. Carter Decker had explained to them how he discovered Hope's true identity after connecting the necklace he found on Lopez's boat to Richard Mullaney's murder. When shown photographs of Hope and Alex, Melanie Locke did not recognize either of them. It was Sophie, now twenty-five years old and a vice president of marketing at LockeHome, who remembered her former babysitter.

Once Hope learned more about her background, she had wanted to know where her mother was. Decker informed her that Laura King had been released from prison three years after Hope left Wichita, but died of a drug overdose five years later. It was a lot of new information at once, and Hope seemed open to the suggestion of resuming therapy to help process it. Lindsay had offered to track down the police reports for the criminal case against Hope's mother, but Hope said she wasn't ready to learn the details of her childhood quite yet. It was no surprise that she didn't want to revert to her given name.

"How about Beyoncé?" Lindsay suggested. "You'd never have problems making a dinner reservation again."

"Sacrilege. There's only one Queen B. Besides, I picked the name I wanted fifteen years ago. I'm Hope Miller, and I have no desire to be anyone else."

On Lindsay's screen was the electronic form to petition for a legal name change. Now that Hope had a birth certificate for Tara King, she was taking all the steps to establish a legal identity. Once the name change was complete, Hope Miller—no middle name—would get a driver's license and insurance. Hope reached over and hit the enter key. "Done! And so are these," she said, sliding their sandwiches onto two plates.

Lindsay took a bite and nodded. "Okay, that's good."

"See?" Hope was mid-bite when her cell phone rang on the kitchen counter. She answered on speaker. "You should be calling my lawyer, Detective Decker."

She flashed a smile in Lindsay's direction. God, she was beautiful.

"I just wanted to make sure you were by your phone," Decker said. "I'm sending you something right now on email. I think it's going to make you very happy."

Attached to the message that landed in Hope's inbox was a copy of a handwritten letter. Lindsay read over Hope's shoulder.

PLEASE READ.

Dear Hope,

Let me start by saying, I swear on my life, I thought you were dead after the car flipped. I was heartbroken and guilt-stricken, but also terrified. I didn't know what to do. I saw head-lights coming and ran into the woods. Then police cars and an ambulance. They took you away, and I was out there alone in the rain. I was a coward, and so I hiked out through the woods and hitched a ride down the road rather than get arrested with a stolen car.

I was checking the internet after for news about the accident and saw that you survived but couldn't remember anything. I told myself that maybe that was for the best. I wished I could be the one to forget what happened that night. I wish I hadn't lived for fifteen years knowing that I could go to jail for the rest of my life. I let myself believe that you were going to be okay.

Then one day, you show up on my boat, and I had to face the reality of the choices I made. I chose to believe you were better off, but how could that possibly be? Maybe your amnesia is be-cause your subconscious has been burying the truth—or at least the truth as I allowed you to believe it.

After that boat ride, I struggled with whether to tell the truth. I even made some calls to someone from my past, even though I had promised never to make contact again.

But then you came back to East Hampton. I saw you walk-ing out of Rowdy Hall and followed you home. It was clear you were living here now. I was shocked. It seemed too impossible to be a coincidence. And then I saw you through the salon win-dow, talking to my girlfriend. I convinced myself you were fak-ing your amnesia, but I couldn't figure out why you'd do that. I thought maybe you remembered the truth about what happened that night and were going to find a way to punish me—God knows I wouldn't blame you. So after another night of following you, I finally said, Fuck it, let's find out.

Your reaction at that house. You were so afraid. It became clear to me you were telling the truth about your amnesia. And so now I owe *you* the truth.

Your name is Tara King. Fifteen years ago, after a rich family (Melanie Locke and Richard Mullaney) fired you as their babysitter, you decided we should have a party at their house while they were out of town. You and the other couple at the house that night had left by the time Richard pulled into the driveway. I stayed behind to keep trashing his things to get back at him for what he did to my sister. When I left, he was pulling into the driveway. He got out with a gun and told me to stay put. All those feelings from when I was a kid came flooding back. I pictured him going after my sister, and I just charged at him and knocked him down. We were wrestling for the gun when it went off.

I told all this to someone I trusted, who said there were no mitigating circumstances. Because the killing happened during a felony, I'd get a mandatory life sentence. I needed to leave town, but I was terrified to go alone. I was begging you to come with me, but you didn't understand why we needed to leave. You couldn't remember anything at all from that night. I finally blurted out that you were the one who shot him, but I only told you that to convince you to come with me. We hitched a ride to Indianapolis from that truck stop by the airport, and then I stole a Toyota from a gas station when the guy went inside. We were heading for Montreal. Once we were settled there, I was going to tell you the truth, I swear. I just didn't want to leave on my own. The next thing I know, we're flipping over in the car. I thought you died still believing that you had killed a man.

But now you know the truth. I am the one who shot Richard

Mullaney. I alone am responsible. I hope this gives you freedom, Hope. I hope it gives you peace. You can live your life now.

HOPE SAT IN SILENCE FOR a few seconds when they were done reading, scrolling through the document again, as if to make sure it was real.

"Oh my god. He didn't just confess. He totally cleared me."

An announcement in Mullaney's case was imminent. Lindsay had been trying to persuade the Wichita police to declare Alex Lopez the sole suspect in the killing, but she'd been given no assurances. This letter changed all that.

"He most certainly did," Lindsay said. "Alex didn't deserve to die for what he did, Hope, but he did owe this to you. He took away the last fifteen years of your life, but now it's really over. You've got your entire future in front of you."

Hope pulled her hair over one shoulder, twisting it as she spoke. "It's weird, but in a way, I don't regret it—what happened, I mean. It sounds like I left behind a pretty shitty life. If I hadn't left with Alex, if there had been no car accident—who knows where I would have ended up? I could have ended up like that girl TC, or my mother."

Lindsay placed a hand on Hope's wrist. "You would have been fine. You're a survivor." She remembered Scott saying the same thing about Hope when she first disappeared. He had been absolutely right.

Hope's gaze returned to Alex's letter. "We should send this to Jess, too."

"But Jess said he and TC actually *were* at the house when Mullaney pulled into the driveway. They heard the gunshot."

"Why don't we just let Alex's words speak for themselves? It's obviously what he wanted."

40

Tuesday, June 29, 1:28 p.m.

It had been only five days since she flew to Wichita, but Ellie realized it was the longest she had gone without seeing Max since they'd gotten together four years before. She usually preferred texting, but they'd been on the phone for twenty minutes and damn if she didn't miss him. As if reading her mind, he said, "I know you needed this time with your family, but I can't wait for tomorrow."

Depending on the flight gods, she'd be back to their apartment by the time Max got home from work. "Me too. It's been a rough few days."

"You guys did the right thing sticking around for a while. Are you going to be okay today?"

"Yeah. It'll be good for the three of us to do this together."

"Okay. Gotta run to court, but call if you need me. Love you."

"Love you too."

She decided to wash the dishes from lunch while she was still in the kitchen. Five days was also the longest amount of time she and Jess had spent with their mother in years, and she was enjoying being alone for a few minutes. Roberta Hatcher was . . . a lot.

Ellie and Jess had not told their mother the actual reason for their sudden visit until late Friday night—after Ellie and Lindsay were finished answering the police's questions. They didn't want to upset her with only a theory. Steve's final act in that restaurant bathroom had provided an ending to the story. They left out the part about Jess being at Richard Mullaney's house the night of the shooting, but their mother now understood that her husband had been murdered by his closest friend because he had gotten too close to the truth about Mullaney's predation.

Their mother drank what seemed like half a liter of vodka before going to bed, and emptied the bottle the next day. But on this afternoon, as Ellie dried her hands and walked into the living room, she thought Roberta actually looked better than she had for years. Clear-eyed. Focused. And there had been none of the morose reminiscing and self-pity that Ellie always dreaded.

"I wish you didn't have to leave tomorrow," her mother said. "Maybe you can stay long enough for Max to fly down so I can finally meet him."

At least she wasn't referring to Max as "that man" anymore. "He's in trial, Mom. And Jess and I need to get back to our jobs."

"I know, I know." Her mother waved a hand. "I just like having my kids here. Maybe I'll move to New York so I can see you more."

Jess didn't even hesitate before replying. "Mom, it's so expensive. You would hate living in a shoe box."

"Well, I could move in with Ellie and Max. You have a second bedroom, don't you?"

Jess looked to Ellie with a self-satisfied grin.

For the first time Ellie could recall in years, their mom broke out into the staccato belly laugh their father used to call her machine-gun chuckle. She pointed a finger toward both of them. "I got you, didn't I?"

She had, indeed. "Maybe come for a visit though, okay?" Ellie was surprised to realize that she actually meant it.

Her phone buzzed with a new text. Lindsay Kelly. I don't have your brother's contact information, but you'll both want to see this.

Ellie forwarded the PDF that followed to Jess as soon as she finished reading. Alex Lopez hadn't just cleared Hope in Mullaney's murder; he'd guaranteed that no one else could be implicated. Only their small circle would ever know that Jess had been at the house that night.

"The two of you, constantly on your screens like a couple of those TikTok kids."

Jess met Ellie's eyes and nodded as he slipped his phone into his back pocket. "You guys ready?" he asked, grabbing their mother's key ring from a cat-shaped hook by the front door.

"You drive like a bank robber," she said, snatching the keys from Jess.

"And *you* stop on greens."

If their mother was behind the wheel, the trip to the cemetery would take twice as long as it should. Ellie extended her palm, a solution that seemed to satisfy everyone.

As Ellie slid back the seat of her mother's CR-V, she recalled the last time she had made this drive, four years earlier, to sit at the foot of her father's grave while she tried to force herself to finally accept the likely truth that he had chosen to take his own life. Today, she would apologize for ever doubting him.

41

Thursday, July 22, 1:07 p.m.

"So, it's official. How does it feel?"

Hope could tell from Melissa's expectant smile that the therapist already knew the answer.

"Fucking amazing. On the way here, I even did seventy-five on the LIE with the rest of the hooligans. Part of me almost *wants* to get pulled over so I can go, *bam*, that's my face right there." In addition to having a legal name, date of birth, and social security number, Hope no-middle-name Miller was now the proud carrier of an actual, legit New York State driver's license. "Sometimes I wake up, and it all seems too good to be true. It's like I'm finally one integrated person with a past, present, and future."

"So, you were on the LIE. Does that mean you were in the city?"

"Just for a couple of days."

Hope and Lindsay were keeping the cottage for now, so she had chosen a therapist in East Hampton for her twice-a-week sessions. Once the owner came back to town, maybe she would move to the city, or she and Lindsay could be like the fancy people who "split time" between two "homes."

"You mentioned during Monday's session that Lindsay was going to pack up Scott's things from her apartment."

"That happened yesterday."

"Is that why you went into the city? To be there?" An arched brow signaled that Melissa, once again, assumed she knew the answer.

"It's not like that. I go into the city a lot. I have to. Lindsay works there, and I'm with Lindsay." With each passing day, Lindsay seemed more comfortable about the idea of them being together and had finally (thank God) stopped trying to label it.

"Okay, but you did mention on Monday that you weren't totally convinced Scott was going to remain out of the picture."

Hope avoided her therapist's intense gaze. "I just thought she might be upset when he picked up his stuff, so it was a good idea for me to be on standby. He was there for all of two minutes. They didn't even hug to say goodbye or anything. I'm pretty sure he's gone for good. Frankly, if I had to guess, he'll be engaged in a year to some woman willing to let him prove to himself he can be a good husband and father." It had been so obvious to Hope all along that Scott cared less about Lindsay as a person than about his desire to have a marital do-over. "The irony is that she would have married him a year ago if he hadn't told her the truth about cheating on his first wife."

"But then their relationship would be built on a lie."

Hope shrugged. "Not a lie so much as an omission. And she never would have known, and it wouldn't have mattered as long as he didn't screw around on her, too. That saying, 'Ignorance is bliss'? It exists for a reason."

How many times had Hope steeled herself to tell Lindsay the truth? But she always found a reason to wait until another day. And after weeks and months and then years passed, she convinced herself that leaving Lindsay in the dark was the only way to spare her from having to protect Hope's secret.

"I hear a slight edge in your voice when you talk about Lindsay and

Scott. To suggest someone might be 'blissfully ignorant' is not exactly a compliment."

Melissa might be too insightful a therapist for her intended role, as it turned out. After all, Hope wasn't here for true introspection. Maybe a man would have been a better pick—someone who would have hung on every word, eager to help the beautiful amnesiac with the tragic past regain her memory.

"Look, I don't fault Lindsay. It's just that she treats me like I'm so naive and in need of protection, but she's actually the one who's too trusting. If anything, I'm kind of envious. I was never given that luxury. I believe her when she says losing her mother scarred her, but she had Jimmy. And Miriam. And an entire town who thinks she walks on water. I had . . . well, Tara King's life." A screwed-up childhood, a screwed-up mother, and a sorta screwed-up boyfriend who accidentally killed a man and then let Hope think she did it. No ignorance, no bliss.

"Well, and that was the biggest breakthrough on Monday. You said you're starting to remember things from Tara's past. *Your* past. Has that continued?"

Hope put on her most enthusiastic smile. "Yes, it's the strangest feeling. I can't describe it, but it's like there's a dam or a wall of some kind in my mind, and these little cracks are starting to form. Does that make sense? I was chopping an onion last night and had this sudden image of my mother getting so mad, she threw a knife down on the counter and it ricocheted and sliced open my ankle. That one flash of a moment opened up all these other details. I remember her pressing the wound with this filthy dish towel—it was yellow with little pink elephants on it—cradling me on the ground, rocking me like a baby, saying she didn't mean to do it. And all I could think was, But you do it all the time. You hurt me . . . all . . . of . . . the time."

"That's a very specific recollection."

"Yeah, but I've probably read as much about memory as you have, and fabricated memories can be extremely rich in detail. It doesn't make them real." Hope had told Melissa during their last session that even though she was beginning to recall moments from her childhood, she wasn't certain the events had actually taken place. But the knife incident? Oh, it had definitely been real, all the way down to the dish towel that Hope had bought for her elephant-loving mother, only to watch it grow dirtier and dirtier, until it was stiff and stank of mildew.

Melissa crossed her arms. "Of course, you know there's one way you might be able to confirm the accuracy of these flashbacks."

Her mother's court file. The trial transcript. The photographs of Hope's injuries. It remained to be seen if the stenographer captured the continual interruptions in the victim's testimony as she repeatedly broke down in tears, but Hope remembered every excruciating moment of her three hours on the stand, knowing that she was sealing her mother's fate, but also knowing it was the only hope she had of surviving.

"I'm just not ready for that. Not yet." A few more weeks of therapy would do it, though. More cracks would appear in the metaphorical dam in her mind until the whole barrier collapsed. It would be her breakthrough moment. She'd fly to Wichita, finally prepared to scour the court files that would confirm the authenticity of her "recovered" memories. She would be, as she said, one integrated person with a past, present, and future. By the time she started classes at Stonybrook in the fall, the lying—most of it, anyway—could stop. She'd no longer be the girl without a memory.

At least she wasn't a total liar. Hope really did suffer from amnesia: actual, blackout, zero-memory amnesia from the moment she ate those stupid mushrooms with TC until she woke up the next morning.

Her wrist. That was how all of this started—when Lindsay's father took them to the shooting range last winter. The doctors in Hopewell naturally assumed that the lingering weakness in her left wrist was from the injuries sustained in the accident, but Hope had one of her mother's many arm-yanks to thank for that. The gun Jimmy handed to her at the range was only a nine-millimeter. He said he picked it because her hands were too small for most of the other options.

So, what are the bigger guns that might not be right for me? It was an innocent enough question—the idle curiosity of a gun novice—but Hope's interest had been anything but casual. As he rattled off a quick list of larger weapons, it was the .357 that leaped out at her. Then she pulled the trigger of the much-smaller weapon. After all that free physical therapy no one had ever offered her until Hopewell, she thought her wrist strength was almost normal, but nope. Then how in fuck's sake, she wondered, had she managed fifteen years before, wasted on a bucket of vodka Red Bulls with some mushrooms on top, to not only fire a .357 but land a clean shot into Hitch's stomach? She obviously hadn't, and yet Alex had sworn it was so.

She'd googled him over the years, more so in the beginning, but the name was too common to be of much use. But after that trip to the shooting range, Hope had treated it like a full-time job. It was an article that popped up in January from the *East Hampton Star* that alerted her to his job at the fishing guide operation.

Before she had decided what to do with that information, the pieces began to fall into place by themselves. Lindsay said she was going to check out a summer rental. They'd make a weekend out of it, and Hope floated the idea of a fishing trip for a little adventure.

As they approached the docks, Hope had tried to anticipate Alex's reaction. Would he hug her, thrilled to discover she was still alive? Ask what she'd been up to all these years? Pull her aside and beg for forgiveness for lying to her about the shooting? But he did nothing. He *said* nothing. He treated her like a complete stranger. So she moved to East Hampton, intent on proving that he was the one who killed Hitch, blamed her for it, and then left her for dead at the side of the road.

Melissa was asking if she had any memories yet of the night Hitch died.

She shook her head. "Still a total blank." *Pretty close to the truth.*

"What about Alex?"

"When I look at a picture of him, I think I sort of remember being with him, but, again, maybe it's just because I've gotten used to the idea by now." Not at all true.

She remembered so much about Alex. The way he smiled at her when he tore her ticket to see *Pirates of the Caribbean* at the Old Town movie theater and then found her during the previews to bring her a pack of Twizzlers because the red matched her lipstick. Lying next to him for hours on the merry-go-round at College Hill Park, dreaming of ways for two poor kids—one in a group home, one without papers—to get rich. And she remembered the look in his eyes as he begged her to leave Wichita with him. She was dead set against it until Alex told the lie that spiraled into all the lies that would follow—that she had shot that man at the house.

"Why?" she had asked. "Why would I do something like that?"

Much of what Alex told her back then lined up with what she now believed was the truth. He recognized Hitch in the family photographs as the man who had tried to rape Emilia when they were kids. When Hitch stepped out of the car with a gun, Alex charged at him, and the two struggled for control of the weapon. But in the version Alex spun to convince her to leave with him, she was the one who grabbed the gun after it slid across the driveway pavement. She killed Hitch with one shot.

And Hope believed every word of it. Of course she believed him. If you just found out that the man you thought you loved was a child molester, you might shoot him too.

Before she agreed to leave with Alex, she pressed him to explain exactly what Hitch had done to his sister. "He spent months telling her how special she was," he said. "That she was too good for any boys her own age. He practiced his Spanish with her and gave her a copy of his favorite book. That's what's so sick about it. When he finally decided to rape her, he made her feel as if she'd agreed to it."

His words forced her to replay the entire relationship with Hitch in her head. For Hope—for Tara—it was true, romantic love. Hitch told her *she* was special. That her "life adversity" had matured her. That she understood him better than his wife ever had, and that all Melanie cared about was her father's company anyway. He always said she was too good for Alex, and that once his marriage was over, he'd give her the life she deserved. He even gave her a key to the house. And a copy of *The Scarlet Letter*, his favorite book.

It was exactly what he had done to Alex's sister. He picked Hope not because she was wise beyond her years, but because she was a girl from a group home whose mother had abused her so badly that her left wrist barely worked. She was vulnerable, and he was the kind of man who could smell vulnerability—and needed it. At least Emilia Lopez had enough self-esteem to recognize she had been taken advantage of. In Hope's case, Hitch was the one to break off their "relationship," giving her a silver necklace from Tiffany "to remember us by." Even after knowing what Hitch had done, she couldn't bring herself to throw it away, hiding it in the tampon case in her purse before leaving Wichita.

Melissa was droning on about Alex. "You told me during our first session you didn't think you'd ever be able to forgive him, even though he ultimately told the truth at the end and lost his life because of it. Do you still feel that way?"

Alex hadn't deserved to die for what he did, but, no, Hope wasn't ready to forgive him—not yet, at least. "It's complicated. I know the letter was meant to give me a fresh start, but it was still self-serving. He said that after the accident, he saw headlights coming and ran for the woods—*heartbroken, guilt-stricken, terrified*—leaving only after I was in the ambulance?" She could recite Alex's letter from memory—that's how many times she had read it. "Well, there was no wallet in my purse. No identification. No money. He must have taken it, right? That doesn't sound very heartbroken. It sounds like someone willing to sacrifice me so he can go on with his life."

But if Alex's letter had portrayed him more sympathetically than he deserved, it had done the same for Hope. *I convinced myself you were faking . . . Your reaction at that house. You were so afraid. It became clear to me you were telling the truth about your amnesia.*

When he showed up at the Stansfields', Hope was anything but afraid. She had flown into a rage, unleashing fifteen years of a life spent in limbo because of him. She told him she knew he was the one who killed Hitch. *You ruined my fucking life, and now I'm going to ruin yours, too.*

And yet, still, he chose to cover for her in that letter. So . . . could Hope forgive him? Like she said, it was complicated.

If Alex hadn't decided to confess, would her plan have worked? When Jocelyn cut her hair, she mentioned that her dad suspected Alex of being a drug dealer, so Hope called in a detailed tip to the police, claiming to be a ripped-off customer. By the time Alex confronted her at the Stansfields', she had already hidden the necklace on his boat. She was hiding at that vacant rental house until the cops got around to doing their jobs—but then Alex decided to turn himself in and made the mistake of telling Steve Thompson.

Melissa took a sip of coffee from a mug that read I TOLD MY THERA-PIST ABOUT YOU, which struck Hope as both slightly unprofessional and completely hilarious. "And have you been looking at photographs of Wichita—your childhood home, the group home, your former schools, the places we discussed?"

Hope nodded dutifully. "Yeah, and I definitely think it's helping. It seems like every day I remember a little bit more. All those years, I assumed the amnesia was from my head injury, but maybe it was trauma after all. Maybe I just needed to know that I wasn't a killer to allow my mind to go back to my past."

"And what about the Locke family? Do you remember them at all?"

Hope had trained herself over the years not to think too much about

Hitch or the wife and daughter he left behind. "Not in the least," she said.

Sometimes she did wonder what would have become of Alex and her if not for the car accident. By the time they were settled down in Canada and he came clean with the truth—*if* he had come clean—she would have needed him or loved him enough to have forgiven him. It might have all worked out. She might be running Reel Deal Fishing with him. They could have been happy together.

So maybe someday, she would tell all of it to Lindsay, when the time was right, when she was sure Lindsay would understand.

Or maybe not. Lindsay said so many times she wished she didn't know the truth about Scott. Lindsay trusted Hope. She never doubted her, not even once. And why would Hope want to take that away from her?

Melissa glanced down at her watch. "Our time is up, but see you again Monday?"

"Definitely."

"And keep up the good work. I can see how committed you are to this process."

Maybe she had chosen the right therapist after all.

Acknowledgments

"Where do you get your ideas?" It's the question authors are asked more than any other. For me, the response is different for every book, and for *Find Me*, I have two different answers, each of which dates back more than a decade.

First, there's Hope. About thirteen years ago, I was riveted by a series of newspaper articles about a missing woman who was eventually found but who had lost any recollection of the previous weeks to a rare type of amnesia called dissociative fugue. Dubious of the explanation (sorry, I'm a crime fiction writer) and with a longtime interest in the human memory, I learned about other cases in which people suffered a complete inability to remember their own identities. Though the amnesia is typically short-lived, in some cases, the memories never return, and yet the person must go on. What is it like to move forward without a sense of the past?, I wondered. And what if someone finally got comfortable in their new identity only to disappear once again? I kept playing with that concept over the years, but wasn't ready to commit until I could fully nail down the character—who she was today, who she had been before, and who she would eventually become once she knew the truth about her past.

Then there's the second answer: Ellie Hatcher. *Find Me* might have been your first encounter with the NYPD detective, but some of you already knew her well from five of my previous novels. I have known from the moment I began writing *Dead Connection*, the first book in the Hatcher series, what Ellie would eventually learn about her own past. I did not, however, know when she would learn it—or how.

And somehow—because brains are magic—these two ideas eventually came together into a single story. If I've done my job well, this novel reads like a stand-alone and yet provides a satisfying resolution to an important part of Ellie Hatcher's journey for those loyal readers who have been following it.

So as I transition to the part of this note where I thank everyone who made this book possible, I'll start by thanking you—the reader. Whether you're part of the original "kitchen cabinet" and have been waiting for years to see Ellie on the page again, or you took a shot on an author who was totally new to you, or anywhere in between, I am so grateful to you for making it possible for me to earn a living as a storyteller. It really is a dream come true.

It's also a dream that wouldn't be possible without the support and skill of others. My editor, Jennifer Barth, and I have been working together long enough to have raised a high school graduate by now. No one pushes me harder, and the books are always better for it. I'm extraordinarily lucky to have such a talented champion on my side. Plus she's awesome.

I am also thankful to Philip Spitzer, Anne-Lise Spitzer, Lukas Ortiz, and Kim Lombardini at the Spitzer Agency; Jody Hotchkiss at Hotchkiss & Associates; Jonathan Burnham, Heather Drucker, Doug Jones, Katie O'Callaghan, Sarah Ried, Leah Wasielewski, and Lydia Weaver at Harper, as well as Jimmy Iacobelli and Miranda Ottewell; Angus Cargill, Lauren Nicoll, and Sophie Portas at Faber & Faber; Caspian Dennis at Abner Stein Ltd.; and Giulia De Biase at Edizioni Piemme. I am grateful to Jonathan Hayes, senior medical examiner in the Office of the Chief Medical Examiner of the City of New York, and to Harvey

O'Brien, Michael Koryta, David Newman, and Andi Daniel for generously sharing their expertise.

I would not have gotten through what was a terribly difficult year-plus for all of us without a whole crew of incredibly kind and caring friends and family, especially my rock, Sean Simpson. Everything, always.

About the Author

ALAFAIR BURKE is the *New York Times* bestselling author of fourteen novels, including *The Better Sister*, *The Wife*, and *The Ex*, which was nominated for the Edgar Award for best novel. She also coauthored the bestselling Under Suspicion series with the late Mary Higgins Clark. A former prosecutor, she continues to teach criminal law and lives in Manhattan and East Hampton.